In the MONTH of the MIDNIGHT SUN

CECILIA EKBÄCK

HODDER

First published in Great Britain in 2016 by Hodder & Stoughton
An Hachette UK company

First published in paperback in 2017

A CIP catalogue record for this title is available from the British Library

Paperback ISBN 978 1 444 78997 3
eBook ISBN 978 1 444 78995 9

Typeset in Plantin Light by Palimpsest Book Production Limited,
Falkirk, Stirlingshire

Printed and bound by Clays Ltd, St Ives plc

Hodder & Stoughton policy is to use papers that are natural, renewable
and recyclable products and made from wood grown in sustainable forests.
The logging and manufacturing processes are expected to conform to the
environmental regulations of the country of origin.

Hodder & Stoughton Ltd
Carmelite House
50 Victoria Embankment
London EC4Y 0DZ

www.hodder.co.uk

HUN

...the Month of the Midnight Sun

'...ing is atmospheric, vivid and compelling.'

Choice Magazine

'Masterfully thrilling.'

The Bookbag

'With *In the Month of the Midnight Sun*, we're given more ambitious, literate Nordic Noir . . . an elusive poetic feel not common in the genre.'

Independent

Wolf Winter

'Visually acute, skilfully written; it won't easily erase its tracks in the reader's mind.'   Hilary Mantel, author of *Wolf Hall*

'Fans of *The Miniaturist* will love flashing back to the dark bleakness of 1717 Lapland in Cecilia Ekback's debut.' *Grazia*

'*Wolf Winter* repays reading for the beauty of its prose, its strange compelling atmosphere and its tremendous evocation of the stark, dangerous, threatening place, which exists in the far north and in the hearts of all of us.'

Guardian

About the Author

Cecilia Ekbäck was born in the north of Sweden; her parents come from Lapland. During her teens, she worked as a journalist and after university specialised in marketing. Over twenty years her work for a multinational took her to Russia, Germany, France, Portugal, the Middle East and the UK.

In 2010, she finished a Masters in Creative Writing at Royal Holloway. She now lives in Calgary with her husband and twin daughters, 'returning home' to the landscape and the characters of her childhood in her writing. Her first novel, *Wolf Winter*, was published to great acclaim. You can find out more about Cecilia via her website www.ceciliaekback.com and you can follow her @CeciliaEkbäck on Twitter.

To Sam Bennett and Oonah McFarlane Wells – then practically strangers to me – who wouldn't let me fail at a difficult time, but showed immense love and compassion by teaching me how to draw myself a new map in life.

IN STOCKHOLM

Magnus Stille	Administrator at *Bergskollegium*, Swedish Board of Mines.
Isabella Stille	Magnus's wife. Daughter of State Minister of Justice.
Ellen, Harriet, Peter	Their children.
Karl Rosenblad	State Minister of Justice.
Ingeborg Rosenblad	His wife.
Lovisa Rosenblad	His daughter, Isabella's sister.
Gabriel Mårtensson	Works for Magnus at *Bergskollegium*.

ABOARD STEAMER

Hans Rexius	Priest, journeying to Norwegian border.
Fredrik Wetterlund	Priest, journeying to Norwegian border.
Lars (last name unknown)	Warden of the county prison in Luleå.

IN LULEÅ

Gunnar Cronstedt   County Governor.

Frans Svensson   *Bergskollegium*'s regional master of the mountain.

AT TANA RAPIDS

Ove and Anna-Maria Edgren   Farmers at Tana Rapids.

IN TOWN

Axel Bring   Priest.

BLACKÅSEN VILLAGE

Jacob Palm (Merchant)   Born in Stockholm. Arrived to Blackåsen in 1845.

Helena Palm   Jacob's wife.

Ulf Liljeblad (Priest)   Born on Blackåsen. Educated in Uppsala. Deceased: one of the victims.

Frida Liljeblad (Priest's Wife)   Originally from Uppsala. Arrived in Blackåsen in 1835.

Jan-Erik Persson (Constable)   Born on Blackåsen. Educated in Uppsala. Deceased: one of the victims.

His wife (Constable's Wife)   Born on Blackåsen.

Her father (Blind Man)   Born on Blackåsen.

Lina (Constable's Sister)   Born on Blackåsen. Maid at the vicarage.

Adelaide Gustavsdotter (Holy Woman)	Born on Blackåsen. Leader of a religious sect of separatists (have exited the state church).
Matts Fjellström (Hunter)	Born on Blackåsen. Farmer.
Daniel Fjellström (Long Beard)	Born on Blackåsen. Matts's brother. Farmer.
(Giant)	Born in Stockholm. Farmer.
Rune Dahlbom	Born on Blackåsen. Educated in Uppsala. Teacher at Falu Mining School. Deceased: one of the victims.
Sigrid Rudin (Child of Village)	Born on Blackåsen. Lives with Adelaide Gustavsdotter.
Susanna Rudin (Singing One)	Born on Blackåsen. Deceased in 1840. Self-murderess. Sigrid's mother.
Per Eriksson (Night Man)	Born on Blackåsen. Spent time in prison for murdering his father. Returned and became the night man.
Anders (Lone One)	Born on Blackåsen. Recluse. Lives on the other side of the lake.

SAMI TRIBE

Biijá (Ester)	One of the elderly women in a Sami tribe.

Nila (Nils)	Biijá's deceased husband, former *noiade*/leader of the tribe.
Dávvet	Likely new leader of the tribe.
Livli	Sent away for illicit love affair with Dávvet when young.
Suonjar, Innga, Aili, Beahkká	Tribe members.

GLOSSARY

sita – Sami tribe

kåta – Sami tent

joik – traditional Sami singing style

rievsak – willow ptarmigan

akja – sleigh

noiade – Sami shaman

The Sami nomadic tribe counts eight seasons: EARLY SPRING March–April, SPRING May–June, EARLY SUMMER June, SUMMER July–August, LATE SUMMER August, AUTUMN September–October, LATE AUTUMN November, WINTER December–March (Source: *People of Eight Seasons*, Ernst Manker, Wahlström & Widstrand, 1972).

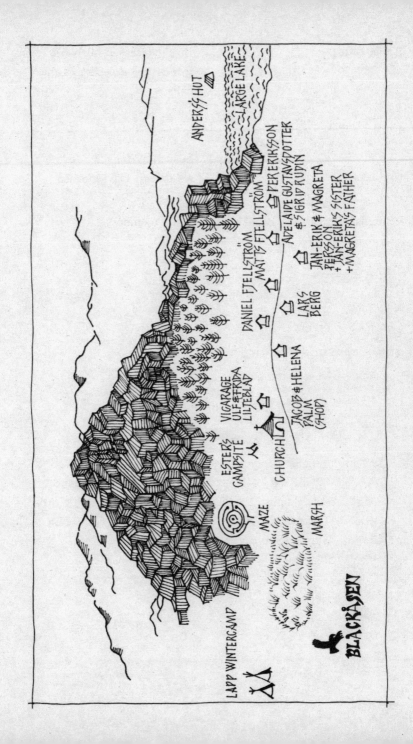

PART ONE

B

Blackåsen, Spring 1856

In death, something departs. Life – yes, yes – but also something physical. Why else would a person's bulk shrink so? Their chest caves in, their arms shrivel, their legs shorten . . . The skin droops and the palate blackens. It is clear that there remains nothing but the dry shell of a nut.

At the Resurrection, Jesus will return to wake the Faithful. What will He do if He finds them incomplete?

This is what I first think when I see Nila's body.

Then I wonder when he became so old.

We give him the ancient burial. None of us suggests we imprison the man who led us under six feet of soil. Not even Suonjar says we ought to take him to the village to be put in Holy Ground. Our fingers work to some forgotten cadence; wrap his body in bark – the dry wood against our hands smooth as water and coarse as rock. We lay him into his sleigh and lift it in a hollow tree trunk on the ground.

Then we stand in silence. At once, my chest pulls together and I can't breathe. I lurch forwards. Hands grasp my elbows, bodies press against mine. I have to bite the inside of my cheek not to scream and push them away. For the members of the *sita* are one and the same. And so I don't struggle. I

3

make no noise. I think myself up, up, and gone, pretend it is not my body being touched.

I sit in my *kåta*. I light a fire though it is hot, and after a while I stink of sour sweat. I stare into the thin flames and wait for grief to find me, but I am as empty as the wooden food bowl by my feet. Outside, the *sita* is quiet, waiting for me to mourn. We ought to leave our spring camp and continue our walk – the snow has disappeared, the reindeer herd has left for the high mountains followed and guarded by a few of ours. Yes, early summer will soon be upon us with midges and gadflies, and here we are, caught in journey land, first because of Nila and now because of me. And inside my *kåta* – inside me – still nothing.

My mother once said the *sita* was a castle. I thought of thick walls, of safety inside. But she didn't look happy when she said it. I guess walls can do many things.

Early morning on the fourth day, before the others wake, I pack my reindeer hide and my kettle. I hesitate and add my china cup. I take some dried reindeer meat, coffee, cheese. In my pouch I have my knife, steel, flint stone, birch-bark, spoon, and comb. The others will hurt when they discover I have gone, but they will settle down. 'Wandering', they will say. 'Biijá has gone wandering.' I step outside, and one of the dogs yelps. I point at the ground with my walking stick and it lies belly down, nose to the dirt, only its eyes trailing me.

My feet take me back down Crowfoot Trail. They follow the river for a while, and then cross it – me wobbling on the wet stones, supporting myself on my stick – and carry me into the valley. The smells of fresh pine and lofty summer wind remind me of the journey we undertook, Nila and I, newly married: the excitement and curiosity about each other;

4

the freedom of a future yet to be revealed. Night comes, light blue, starless. I am not tired and keep walking. When the cuckoo tells me morning has come, I lie down under a spruce tree, sheltered by its branches. I wake again as the sun weakens.

And so I continue: during the night, I walk, during the day, I sleep. I don't eat. I am in a dream, going wherever my feet take me.

Then, one night, my feet turn determined. The feeling of leisure disappears. Now they hasten towards the mountain on the other side of the valley, and now I try to divert them – aim them perhaps towards the round hillocks in the west, or, better, the coast by the eastern sea, but they won't have it.

By the base of Blackåsen Mountain, they stop.

I look up at the ashen mountain. I don't like it. But my limbs refuse to move. This is where grief will come and find me. Here. Perhaps it is appropriate.

I set up camp on the south side, in a glade thick with reindeer moss, close to some juniper shrubs and a stream. From a rock, I have a view over the mountain top. I will sit here and wait until my soul catches up with me. Then I shall pick recent events apart like you clean a fish from its bones, lay them bare and look at them until I understand them and can sort them back into myself again, one by one, in some kind of order.

I build a fire ring. Old age can mellow a being – I put one stone down, then the next – slow them down and soften them. Or it can rouse them, garble their qualities, so what used to please begins to jar and shriek. We didn't expect it to happen to Nila, that's all.

In my mind there is a sudden image of Nila, eyes round, white beard quivering, screaming: 'Listen to me!'

5

I shut it down. Tomorrow. Tomorrow, I will think about all of it.

This night, I lie awake and listen. I know the Blackåsen of winter very well; our usual site is not far, but never before have I been here this late. The high mountains have different sounds. Here, the forest ticks and croaks. The high wind is absent, there is no *gahw* of snowy owls.

I lift myself off the craggy ground and adjust my body, all angles and aches. Old age again. Lately, my past has started cohabiting with my daily life, the one becoming more vivid than the other. As I go about my chores, I think as much about people long gone as I do about those alive. We used to say the dead and the living were two sides of the same coin. Priest would be horrified. Anyway, that was a long time ago.

'Dear Jesus.'

I hear myself mumble this in between consciousness and sleep.

The second morning, Merchant comes. Not to see me – when he notices me on my rock, he flinches.

He has airs, Merchant. Walks with the stiffness that makes a person stumble in the forest, or scrape their side against a tree. Merchant. Jacob Palm. We have names for all of the settlers. There's 'Priest'; 'Constable'; 'Holy Woman' . . .

Nila used the settlers' real names. Even with me, he did. 'Ulf Liljeblad,' he said, or 'Jan-Erik Persson,' lips pointed in a whistle. Behind his back, I laughed. His eagerness to get it right made me think of a child.

The settlers might call me things, too. Though most likely, they just use my other name, the one the priest bestowed upon me and printed into his book with ink: Ester. Said out

6

loud, it sounds like a person who is going and coming at the same time. Es. Ter.

Biijá is my real name. It's what my mother whispered that autumn night when I was born – scent of snow in the air, reindeer rustling outside the *kåta*.

In Nila's mouth, the B softened to a P. 'Piijá,' he said. 'My Piijá.'

'Are you living here now?' Merchant asks.

His eyes have already walked over my bed, my fire, and back. He wipes his forehead with a cloth.

It might anger the villagers that I have come here. Perhaps they will say I should have asked permission, though this is Lapp land and it is they who ought to ask. But Merchant doesn't seem upset. He wants to go, looks up mountain, body tense in an arch.

'Then we'll meet again,' he says, and that's when I say, 'Do you want coffee?' And he says, 'Perhaps another time,' and leaves.

I sit back down on the stone and stick my fingers in its hollows.

Merchant had neither rifle to hunt, nor vessels to gather. Perhaps he was out taking stock. Knowing where to find a specific plant or where to set a trap can be the difference between life and death. Perhaps Merchant is learning.

I put my hands at the back of my knees and raise them up – first one, then the other.

When my mother died, I grieved so much I vomited out my insides, and what remained was raw, newborn, shrieking in sharp light.

Time has come to think it through, I tell myself, but my mind stays blank. I can't remember a thing.

There is only this: I am relieved my husband is dead.

M

The State Minister of Justice is standing with his back towards me, looking out. The light coming from the window might make his shoulders seem hollow, but that's an illusion. He is as tall and broad-shouldered as me.

'The man who came said it was the worst thing he'd ever seen.' He turns to look me in the eyes to make sure I have understood the gravity of what he's just told me. I nod. A massacre in one of the Lapland mountain settlements – a priest, a law enforcement officer, and a local settler – slaughtered by the Lapps. That's what he's telling me now: 'slaughtered', not 'killed'.

The minister sits down and waves to the chair at the other side of his desk. 'This is worrisome. A similar tragedy took place in Norway four years ago.'

'I remember. A local religious movement turned violent. Lapps demanding a ban on the sale of spirits?'

'I need to know what happened. And why. Is this a coincidence, or are we at risk of a Lapp uprising? Of course, I can't afford to be seen interfering with any local process, nor, God forbid, can I be suspected of doubting the capacities of my esteemed colleague in charge of the Lapps.'

8

As he says the last sentence, he scowls. He and the Minister of Public Administration have been warring since they were students. Something about a woman.

He sighs, leans back in his chair, joins his fingertips and gazes at the ceiling. 'My real concern is the King's sale of the *Gällivare-verken* that took place last year. What most people don't know is that the transaction is not yet secure. Already there is some dispute between the Swedes and the Norwegians in the acquiring consortia; the bill of sale is not signed, and nothing has been paid. The King has been trying to sell the estates for several years. If the sale were to fall through, it would be the second time this has happened. How on earth would he then find a purchaser?'

I am not surprised at the news. The King's mines in Lapland, with their accompanying land, iron works, and sawmills that jointly go under the term *Gällivare-verken*, are highly cumbersome administratively and not profitable. Only last week I saw numbers documenting how, at the moment, it is cheaper to mine the iron in central Sweden, bring it north and develop it in the ironworks there, than to transport the Lappish iron found inland the short distances to the smelters at the coast. There aren't any means of passage, the terrain is hopeless, as is the weather. All signs indicate that the war in Crimea, albeit over, has stifled the economy. In fact, I've been certain these men of affairs are after the forest, not the minerals. If they really bought the *Gällivare-verken* for the sake of the iron, I can imagine that after getting a closer look at the estates, they might regret their decision . . .

I look up to find the minister watching me. As always, his eyes have come to rest on my scar. As always, because it's him, I don't mind. 'Shame about the scar,' he has said many times, 'though it does give you a certain draw.'

'The event took place at Blackåsen Mountain. The perpetrator has been taken to Luleå town pending his trial. Justice will run its course. But I was hoping you might find a reason to travel north? In view of the mineral resources of the region, if an administrator at *Bergskollegium* were to ask questions, I don't think it would be perceived as strange. Do you, Magnus? After all, looking after Sweden's mineral deposits is what you do.'

'I'll go,' I say.

The minister studies me. 'I don't want you on Blackåsen. There is no need. People in Luleå will be able to give you answers. The county governor has just taken up residence there. Perhaps you can get access to the perpetrator. Ask him . . .' He shakes his head. 'You know what to ask him. And then I want an account of events to shut this down before it turns into something that could be seen as a valid reason for the sale to be reversed.'

He rises, and I follow suit.

'Shut it down,' he repeats. 'And tell no one the real reason behind your journey.'

I wonder if this includes not telling his daughter, my wife.

'No one at all,' the minister says. 'This city of ours sometimes feels no larger than a village, and I don't want the Minister of Public Administration to hear we are taking an interest.'

As I am walking out, he says: 'Magnus—'

I turn. 'Yes?'

At once, he looks his age; the short wrinkles that run along his eyebrows are deep, the white-yellow hair that coils around his temples, unwashed. He shakes his head. 'Nothing, Magnus. Nothing. Be careful.'

★

The sun has warmed the wooden door to the *Bergskollegium* and it reflects the heat a yard away. It's been hot since the middle of May. I have expected an outbreak of cholera, like last summer, but so far we have escaped. The stone stairway inside lies cool. I take the stairs two at a time.

As I enter my office, Gabriel Mårtensson, my clerk, stands up. 'What did the minister want?'

I throw my hat on my desk. 'To complain about his poor health.'

Gabriel guffaws. Yes, you can't easily imagine the State Minister of Justice, ill. 'I'd like to see the maps of the area around Luleå,' I say to Gabriel. 'Blackåsen Mountain in particular.'

Gabriel disappears. He has been at the Board of Mines much longer than me. I inherited him on my arrival, and he is a good worker, conscientious . . .

I flick through the papers that have gathered on my desk in my absence.

'Shut it down,' the minister said. I am hoping I won't find anything that needs shutting down. The minister is used to opening doors and then closing them by the turn of a hand or a mere signature on a paper. He doesn't want to accept that things might be changing, with the marches, the riots, and the demands for equality. He has taken to shrugging whenever people speak of the dissent – a rapid motion, irritated, as if to say, obviously not everyone can be pleased. Perhaps the nation's unrest has reached the north? Apart from that one time in Norway, I cannot remember ever hearing of any problems with the Lapps. They are a peaceful group. Ignorant, yes. Some say apathetic; without any willingness to better themselves or create proper lives . . .

The doorway is still empty. No Gabriel. I am excited about

the journey ahead. For a mineralogist, Lapland is the most interesting region in Sweden; Blackåsen itself the largest find the nation has. I ought to have travelled there a long time ago. In fact, I don't know why I haven't.

'We can't find it.' Gabriel speaks before he enters the office.

'Find what?'

He has brought just one map roll, which he flattens out on my desk. It is a coloured print. The upper bodies of tiny conjoining angels create a frame at its edges. With a white finger, Gabriel trails the coastline. 'Blackåsen Mountain is on the same latitude as Luleå.' He moves his finger inland.

The mapmaker has drawn forest, lots of forest. There is a river and a lake, forest, forest, forest . . . But no mountain.

'Whose map is this?'

'Hermelin's.'

Some of *Gällivare-verken*'s properties once belonged to Samuel Gustaf Hermelin. His efforts as a cartographer of the region were successful. And his maps are usually accurate.

We lean over the print. What about further north, west, south . . .? No elevation. Blackåsen lies inland of Luleå. Everyone knows this. Am I mistaken? Is it further towards Norway? No.

'And we have nothing else on Blackåsen,' Gabriel says. 'The file is empty.'

He speaks the last words more quietly, as an afterthought, but he looks at me, waiting.

'How is that possible?' I ask.

All the finds have been charted, often many times over. Developed or not, *Bergskollegium* has drawings, maps, accounts of mining claims . . .

'Perhaps the information was needed when the King sold *Gällivare-verken*?' Gabriel sounds hesitant.

'The papers would never have been removed from our building.'

We both look again at the map before us.

Gabriel clears his throat. 'There were rumours about Blackåsen.'

'What kind of rumours?'

'Things happened there . . . Accidents, other mishaps.'

I think about three dead people. Three *slaughtered* people. I shake my head. 'But that makes no sense. Is there then no order in our archives?'

'I don't understand it.'

'Look again. And I need to leave for Lapland as soon as possible. Book me a steamboat ticket to Luleå.'

'I am going away,' I say to my wife, Isabella.

The dining room feels muggy. Supper has been cleared from the table, and my daughters sit there doing their schoolwork. Their foreheads glow and their hair has curled of its own accord. The boy looks as if he's folding paper. Isabella sits in her rocking chair embroidering, her blonde hair parted, wound around her head and pinned up above her neck. From time to time, she pushes with her foot and rocks the chair. It seems to me it's too hot for needlework, but then what do I know? At least plenty of light enters the large windows, so she can see what she is doing. The city has constructed a gasworks by Klara Lake. Soon, street lamps will gleam on Brunkenberg Square – yellow, soft balls in the air – but until that day we must rely on natural light and paraffin. Stockholm is changing. Buildings are going up everywhere, the town metamorphosing into something unknown before my very eyes.

'Yes,' Isabella says.

'Not for long.'

'Are you going on behalf of my father? I heard you went to see him today.'

The minister is right; how small then Stockholm is. When I don't respond, Isabella pushes with her foot again, rocks and focuses on her handiwork. I don't understand why the minister minds her knowing. She and her father are close, and Isabella knows better than most how to keep secrets. Though it's true one doesn't need to tell everyone everything. In general, people talk too much.

I walk out onto the balcony, feel in my pocket and retrieve my pipe. The sun hovers orange-red above the horizon. The angles of house roofs turn the town into a patchwork. Beneath me, the square lies vacant. The perfume from Isabella's orchids imbues the air. She cultivates them in clay pots to press their flowers and make pictures; she pricks the leaves and petals with a needle so the mucus can ooze out and the flower dry. I never knew orchids were full of slime.

At least the scent of the plants covers the stench from the streets. If only it would rain. Even the minister looked worn today, though that was most likely the matter at hand. It's a journey of about five hundred miles to Luleå. Not as arduous as it might sound. The steamboat goes all the way. Four or five days' journey perhaps, depending on the amount of cargo to be unloaded. A few days to meet with people and find out what happened, and then the journey back. The missing information bothers me. My staff has searched in vain for it the whole afternoon. It is clear it was not simply mislaid, and I don't know what that means.

'Slaughtered.' I shake my head. Inside the apartment my father-in-law has been renting for us ever since our marriage, my family sits with their heads bent over their pursuits. Some consider me, too, one of the minister's children. I grew up in his household, lived there before the minister married and had children of his own. Later, much later, I wedded Isabella, and my membership of the family became official.

I feel a rush. Nausea?

My hearing fades. I can't breathe. The orchids . . . the smell. I sway, reach out for the stone wall, and my hand trembles. My pipe falls to the ground. Through the open door, as if in a fog, I see the children rise. Isabella stands behind them, a spirit dressed in white.

'Go and say goodnight to your father,' this spirit says, voice warped. The sentence reaches me through the haze.

It takes a massive effort for me to stand up straight as the children join me.

'Goodnight, Father.' Ellen, my eldest, kisses me on my cheek, a cool peck.

Harriet picks up my pipe, sticks it in my hand, then leans in towards me and squeezes my waist hard. Peter kicks one of the clay pots with his foot.

'Give Father a kiss,' Ellen says, so like her mother.

Peter comes close enough for me to kiss him, but I can't bend down. I lift my hand, which weighs a thousand tons, and put it on my son's head. I want to lean on it for support.

Inside, the white spirit opens the door to the hallway, waits as the children go through, and follows them.

My thought is absurd, but unmistakeable: something has begun, something I ought to have no part in. And it has to do with the events on Blackåsen Mountain.

All night, I sit in my leather chair in the library with the painted wallpaper from England, the outsized crystal chandelier, and the thick carpet. With my eyes, I trace the spirals of the gilded picture frames, I draw the pattern of the wall-paper's velvet medallions. The smell of decay coming from outside is overbearing. I can taste it in my mouth. The hand of the mahogany wall clock moves forward, one step, then another, and the sound is not one of stillness but of threat. I wait for the fever, the runs, the vomiting. Why haven't we talked about what to do if one of us gets cholera? Where to go so as not to infect the others? Do we think we are beyond its reach?

When the sun rises over Brunkenberg Square nothing more has happened. The dizziness must have been due to not taking enough fluids. I feel fine. I'll remember to drink more.

Before leaving, I look in on my children. Harriet sleeps on her back with her hands behind her head, her black hair spread over the pillow. Peter's face appears flushed, his bowed neck and back sweaty. I push his covers away. Ellen lies on her side, knees pulled up, both hands underneath her cheek. She has braided her hair and pinned it up on the crown of her head, like Isabella does before she goes to sleep. I don't enter her room, but stop in the doorway. Ellen is too old now for me to look in on her. It won't be long before she leaves our home to marry. I am losing my children, I think, but know I am not thinking of loss through marriage. The door to the bedroom I share with Isabella is ajar. I try to be quiet as I walk out of the house.

It's a short walk from Brunkenberg Square down to Gustaf Adolf Square. The sunshine floods the cobbled street. The open sewers teem with refuse. I lengthen my steps. In Gustaf Adolf Square, the large buildings of the Hereditary Prince's Palace and the Royal Theatre sit stout and pale, windows like empty eyes, resting between what must have been an eventful night and what will be an equally demanding

16

morning. Across the water lies the yellow building that is the King's Palace. Further away, in Blaiseholm Port, men load the boats, rolling barrels up the wooden walkways, carrying chests and crates.

The line to board the steamer is quiet. People don't speak, but shuffle towards the boat, eyes half closed to the bright light.

A team of horses storms onto the quayside. The coach behind them slithers on the cobbles, and I recognise the black carriage as the minister's horseman jumps down and runs towards the steamer, his eyes searching the queue until I step forward.

'It's the minister,' he calls. 'He needs you.'

'The boat is leaving within the hour.'

The horseman shakes his head and runs back to the carriage. He doesn't open the door, and I climb up beside him on the coachman's seat. He uses his whip to set the animals in motion. People run left and right to avoid the horses' hooves.

The State Minister of Justice's house lies quiet. As the carriage pulls up, the door opens and the maid stands in the doorway. She takes a rapid step aside and glances towards the library. Someone's sick. I knock.

'Enter.' The minister's voice. 'Close the door behind you.'

The minister stands in front of his desk. By the hearth, Ingeborg, his wife, sits on the edge of the sofa, holding a handkerchief to her face. On the other side of the fireplace stands Lovisa, their twenty-year-old daughter, my sister-in-law, eyes closed, dark red flames on her cheeks and neck. Oh, no. What has she done this time?

The minister's breathing sounds laboured. A twitch on the left side of his nose pulls his skin upwards in tiny irregular movements.

'Lovisa will be coming with you,' he says, his polished voice at odds with the scene in front of me.

Long wisps of brown hair lie scattered around Lovisa's feet. A pair of scissors rests on the minister's desk. He's cut her hair.

'Her travel pass and her ticket.' The minister holds out a set of papers. His hand trembles.

'With all due respect, that's impossible.'

The minister stares at me. The vein by his nose pulsates.

'It is not appropriate.' I manage to catch his eye.

'I'll explain the matter to Isabella,' he says, but the air seems to have left his lungs.

'It's Lapland,' I say. 'It's no journey for a woman.'

The girl's mother emits a loud sob, and the minister's gaze hardens.

'She thinks she's a man, then let her live like one,' he says. 'For all I care, you can leave her up north. I don't want to see her again.'

'Karl . . .'

We ought to speak about this without the girl, without the girl's mother.

'Have I ever asked you to do anything important for me?' the minister shouts. His eyes bulge from his head. 'And yet have I not raised you like my own?' He takes a deep breath and lets the air out.

'I am asking you for something now.'

L

Voices, horses' hooves, and the slamming of boxes being loaded come together to press against my eardrums. I try to swallow it away. The boat tilts, and I imagine water moving underneath it, a thick body. I cannot breathe. I put my arms on the railing and lean my forehead on them. On the lower deck, people circulate, prattle: *Oh how lucky we are with the weather now that we are undertaking such a long and dangerous journey* . . . Their laughter resembles the honking of geese. A man in a top hat and a jacket with long tails glances up. Our eyes meet.

I stand, collect my skirts in one hand and with the other I run my fingers along the side of the cabin wall. *Excuse me. Excuse me. Move!*

But people abound on the other side of the boat, too. I grab the warm railing and strain to look past our city, out to sea. There, where water meets sky. I stare at the horizon until my eyes hurt. A whistle sounds. Breathe, I tell myself. Don't think, just breathe.

He cut my hair. My father cut my hair. The blue before me turns to white haze. My ribs cave in on themselves. For a moment, I am certain I will have to fold myself over the pain in my chest and wail it out. He threw me out. Oh God. What will I do?

The engines whir. Another whistle, and black smoke blows

out of the chimney on top of the boat. We can't be leaving already?

I begin to walk, then I run. I collide with someone. My heart thumps. I taste iron.

'Goodbye!' the people around me shout to those on shore. They lean against the railing and wave.

I push, but so does everybody else.

'Goodbye.'

A yank underneath us. Water gushes, churns.

'Wait!' I scream.

But my voice drowns in the third whistle. My heart rips, my eyes well up. We are off.

The steamboat chugs its way up country. Outside Stockholm, there were a thousand islands, as if our nation had smashed into shards. Here, further north, the coastline arches in a solid line, smeared by a giant finger. Forest. Dark green, thick, tall – a barricade of it. On the other side of the boat, water, choppy and inky. I try to make my mind blank, keep it blank, listen to the steam engine. *Chug-chug-chug*.

What did you think? My mind won't leave me be. What did you expect?

My father's face. Never have I seen him look the way he did this morning, as he threw open the door to the library – I rose to escape, though I knew I wouldn't make it. Then he had me by my hair and pulled me. I had to bend sideways and run so as not to fall. From the library, out into the kitchen. I glimpsed the housekeeper with a hand clasped to her mouth, my mother's white face . . . My father groped in the drawer, found the scissors. This time, he'd kill me. He turned and dragged me into his study. His hands shook and the scissor points quaked before my face. Then there were only the thick sounds of blades cutting into hair and my mother's yelps with each lock that fell to the floor.

I shut my eyes. A fluttering image of Eva. What did I expect?

In the afternoon, the wind howls more strongly and white hats top the waves. People have retired into the dining saloon or their cabins, but I remain, chest challenging the gusts. Freeze me. Numb me. If I can relax into it, the wind will take me. A flash of ballooning skirts and I'll be gone. But my body refuses to let go. Soon I shiver so much I can barely stand.

'Here.'

Magnus has appeared beside me. He holds out a coat. The long, dark hair he has combed back from his face and tied at the nape of his neck in a twist hits his shoulders. His scar is unavoidable in the white light: ragged deep, ringing his left eye and emptying down his cheek.

I don't want it. I want to tell him this, and about ballooning skirts. I don't want your coat. I don't want to be warm.

He pushes the coat into my arms.

'There is bread in the pocket,' he says, and leaves.

'I don't want it,' I say.

B

Blackåsen, Spring 1856

I lie on my knees at my campsite, drinking cold water from the rivulet; in the village, a woman screams. Her cry slashes down the settlement dirt road, tumbles onto the forest trail, and hits the mountain side beneath me.

I push off the ground and climb the rock. I stretch, but I can't see.

All turns quiet. Much too quiet.

I pace the glade. Back and forth. Back. Forth. What happened?

The silence endures, and I have no choice but to go there, to the settlement. My chest is heaving. Still, I tell myself, and put my hand on my heart as though to hold it. It was likely nothing.

But that silence . . .

I make my way in amongst the trees, between the trunks of pine, on the dense mat made from their needles. By the village entrance, an owl barks, its warning followed by heavy wings indenting the air. I hesitate, but take the road. I am not coming with evil intentions. I should not hide.

Then the smell of blood engulfs me. Walking this dirt road is like wading the River of Blood. My limbs become heavy. My heartbeats slow down, deepen and press inwards until the sound hurts my ears. I leave the road for the forest and become part of its shadows. The church appears first. Inside, people stand and walk about. They pass before a window and disappear again.

Coming towards me on the road, shoes crunching gravel. I squat down beneath the tough leaves of marsh tea.

It is Holy Woman. She passes so close I could touch her skirt if I stretched out my hand. Cold sweat, the reek of fear. Holy Woman runs towards the church. More steps: Hunter, and his brother. The door opens to let them in.

The muscles in my thighs quiver as I rise. I float amongst the trees – a fog – then between gravestones – a breeze. One of the windows yawns open. I sit down beneath it, back against the wood, the boneyard in front of me, beyond it, the spruce forest. At first, from inside, there is a mass of sounds. Footsteps, voices: 'But that is impossible!' and 'Do something!'

The evening sunlight turns the headstones dark grey. They lean in towards me, towards the building. The light reddens the outer spruce trees of the forest but can't touch the blackness behind. The noises from inside separate into a hushed conversation.

'Who is in there?'

'My husband!'

Another desperate voice: 'Mine, too!'

'They are dead.'

I hear myself gasp.

'We know!' A woman's cry. 'But why won't he leave? He's killed them now, why is he still there?'

'Who is he?'

'I want my husband. Oh God. I want his body!'

Grief. I have to close my eyes.

'A Lapp did this.'

My eyes spring open. The last person speaking was the Holy Woman.

Inside, they have fallen silent.

'I . . . I ran back inside,' Holy Woman says. 'Then Frida came . . . We both saw him.' She falters.

'One of the Lapps has set up camp westwards,' Merchant says. 'Old Nils's wife.'

'She's set up camp? Here? But why?'

'Was Nils with her?'

'No, she was alone.'

'Well, was it Nils who . . .?'

'No, no. That is not him inside.'

'But it can't be a coincidence . . .?'

Then the voices are too many. They shriek like crows and I can no longer follow.

Back at my campsite, I start pacing anew. Three people are dead? Killed by a Lapp who is still with them?

Nila said something would happen on Blackåsen. Impossible. He couldn't have known.

The image of Nila shouting is before me again – 'Listen to me!' I press my hands against my temples.

I have to leave. No. The settlers will come and find me. If I leave now, they'll think I have something to hide. Who knows what that might unleash?

Why is this Lapp with the bodies? What is he doing with them?

Bile rises in my throat. I hurry to the stream, huddle and rinse my mouth with the cold water, again and again, spitting it out. I wish I could use the reindeer brush and scrub my insides.

Why did I come here? To sit on a rock and gawk? What a

stupid old woman I am. I should be walking along with my people towards the blue massifs, seeing the herd move above us, a dark cloud on the mountain's side. Grief would have found me eventually. Now I am trapped here. Oh, what shall I do?

Sleep.

As if Nila has said the word out loud. Not the Nila of late, but the young Nila, the one I trusted to tell me what to do. Yes. I must sleep, so my mind will be clear when the settlers arrive and the words will come out right. I must think away what I have heard and pretend it's new to me.

I lie down with my back against the rock. It's warm after the day's sun and I shuffle closer. Sleep, I tell myself. Sleep, sleep, sleep.

None of ours would commit a crime like this.

I try to evoke a memory of young Nila . . . the short, dark hair, the firm chin and straight nose, the eyes that glowed as though he were made of a different material. But all I can summon in my mind is the white-haired stranger he was towards the end.

That last night, his screaming woke me up. It woke all of us. 'Worship?'

I reached for him even though I already knew, and when his place was empty, shame washed over me. Shame and something stronger, blinding white, hot. Why? I thought. Why was he doing this to me? To himself?

'Worship!'

I grabbed a shawl, folded the opening of our *kåta* aside. Nila stood by the large pine, hands bloodied. The dogs were loping around him, back pelts raised. Nila had carved a face into the tree and smeared it with reindeer's blood. Dear Jesus. I looked around for the carcass.

'Nila.' Dávvet appeared beside me. For once, I felt happy for him trying to take control. 'You've had a bad dream,' Dávvet said.

The whole *sita* was there now, huddling together in the dull night light, rubbing their eyes, nodding with Dávvet. Go back to bed, old man. A dream.

Nila wavered. For a moment, I thought he was coming to his senses. But when Dávvet took a step forward, Nila raised the hand holding the knife. 'Don't come near!' He stabbed in the air around him.

I didn't meet Dávvet's gaze. I didn't dare to try to soothe my husband, couldn't have the others see me fail.

We could do nothing but leave him, but there was no more sleep to be had. This . . . person that used to be my love shrieked and moaned. There was smacking, as if he were hitting himself. I put my hands over my ears; I covered my head. Still, I heard him. Later in the night, it stopped. After a while, the door to the *kåta* was pushed aside. Nila stepped in, his knees buckled and he fell face forward onto the birch twigs and into deep sleep.

Morning came and the *sita* pretended everything was normal. We made as if we didn't see the tree and the face carved into it. But our sentences were short, our manners, harsh. It was supposed to be our day of departure, but it was clear we wouldn't leave. Not that day.

How I hated the carving with its chiselled nose and high forehead. Wherever I went, whatever I was doing, it sat in the corner of my eye, watching me.

I bite the memory off there. Ten days and nights I have been on Blackåsen Mountain seeking grief, begging for the memories to come, all the while remaining cold, unfeeling. Now it comes?

I slap at a mosquito. The insects are wearing. Up in the high mountains, there are none. Once the settlers have been to see me, I will pack up and leave. I grab the corner of my reindeer hide and roll so it covers me.

'I came here because of you,' I say out loud to Nila, but my words sound hollow, my voice flat. My chest constricts and I close my eyes.

Day comes too slowly yet too quickly, both.

The villagers troop through the woodland like clumsy elks. My fear turns to annoyance. Oughtn't they have learned how to behave in the forest by now? Most of them were born here.

Holy Woman, Merchant, and Hunter enter my glade.

'Oh, there you are, Ester.' Merchant pulls out a kerchief and wipes his forehead. 'Here she is,' he says to Holy Woman.

Holy Woman's gaze doesn't waver. But beneath, there is the same fear – I can smell it.

'Yesterday, a man entered our village. A stranger.' Holy Woman's voice sounds strained. 'A Lapp. He killed three of our men. Jacob said he'd met you. We thought it odd that you are here at the same time.'

'I'm here for the reindeer. I'm choosing the location for the winter camp. My husband died. He usually came.'

The lie has flowed out of me too eager, like the rivulet in the glade, when I ought to have seemed shocked. We use the same winter site year after year. But I don't think the settlers pay attention to the Lapp ways.

Merchant wipes his forehead again. He studies my shelter with clear eyes. He doesn't yet understand what's happened. Or . . . is he excited? Behind Holy Woman, Hunter is a block of stone. There for her to lean on, should she need it.

'Nils is dead?' Holy Woman asks.

I nod. Holy Woman's face distorts and she raises her hands to rub at her head, her ears.

She cares that Nila is dead. I hesitate. Or perhaps it is just too much death to manage – her fellow settlers and then Nila.

I have to know. 'What did he look like . . . the Lapp?'

Holy Woman inhales and focuses her eyes. It's not the first time she's forced herself back together like this, I can tell.

'Long black hair.' She makes a gesture towards her own arm to show the length. 'Large hooked nose, elderly.'

It doesn't sound like anyone I know. It could be everyone I know. But Holy Woman saw him.

Holy Woman's blue eyes seem black. 'I walked in on them afterwards.'

I squint. I don't want to share the image she has in her head.

'We thought it strange you were here at the same time,' the woman repeats. She looks at Hunter, as if to say they can go now. I don't understand. They ought to ask whether he could be someone I know, whether I have heard anything. If this is a Lapp, they ought to be more distrustful.

But they nod and gather themselves up.

Holy Woman walks first, the other two follow her. Holy Woman's back is as straight and hard as if she were going to war.

I went to one of Holy Woman's gatherings once – we all did. Priest himself was a follower, and Nila said he wanted to see what it was about.

The assembly was unlike those of the Church. Vibrant, dancing like the beams of the sun on spring water. As they prayed, the participating settlers lifted fisted hands to the sky. My soul soared, strove to join the rejoicing of other souls and burst out into a *joik*. I had to bite my hand to stop myself.

Nila was not impressed.

'To each what they need,' he said that evening when I pressed him.

How strange that they sent Holy Woman to talk to me, not Priest, nor Constable . . .

That's when I realise that their voices were missing in the church, too.

June 1856

In the afternoon, the hot weather is finally traded for a cooler wind. We are travelling with good speed. The sea stretches vast and empty. There are no foreign warships as far as the eye can see; the war in Crimea is indeed over.

With the evening, the wind dies and the colours of the sky fade as on an aged print. The only person still out on the rear deck is Lovisa. She stands starboard, both hands gripping the railing. She has lost her hat. In my too large coat, with the remaining black shocks of hair pointing upwards, she looks insane. She stares down into the water. She might throw herself in—

No. Lovisa is too selfish and not selfish enough for such an act. I call to my mind one of my first images of her, when she can't have been older than four. She is standing in the middle of the kitchen as I enter, in front of her poor mother, hands fisted, shrieking, face red, tousled ringlets quivering on her back.

Most fathers would have sent that kind of a daughter away a long time ago. But, until now, despite her behaviour getting worse, the minister has fought for her. He has supported her through drunkenness, aggression . . . At fourteen, she renounced religion. The minister had problems with the Church when he tried to settle the matter of her nonattendance. On that occasion, I enquired if I could help. The minister's mouth compressed into a thin line, and his eyes narrowed, but he didn't respond. The whole time, he has acted as if it's been unthinkable to him that, in the end, his determination won't resolve the issue. So what has happened for him to reject her now?

Seven o'clock. I am not hungry, but I am tired. Before I retire, I point out Lovisa to the ship's captain and ask him to find her a cabin. He hesitates, looks at me, then at her. I can't say I blame him.

'She is the daughter of the State Minister of Justice,' I say.

An accommodation is swiftly liberated for her. I ask the captain to show her to it. I will speak with her – I have no choice in that matter – but not yet.

My compartment has two beds along the walls and a mahogany stand underneath the window, with a washbasin. As I wash my hands, I have a view over a flat sea and a high blue sky.

Lovisa will get a cabin similar to mine and not think twice about it. It will seem natural to her that she should have a room of her own and a wide berth on which to lay her head, even in a steamboat, even after having been thrown out. We will be gone from Stockholm for more than two weeks. Surely this is enough time for a father to calm down and see reason? Surely he didn't mean me to leave her up north?

No, he did. He cut her hair.

We could take her in, I think, but Isabella would not have it. 'What about our children?' she would say, and I would look at Ellen and Harriet and Peter and think, what about them?

A convent, then. Or the madhouse.

I cannot picture Lovisa in a convent. And I don't want to commit her to a madhouse, I myself having been offered a second life. I was four when I came to the minister, an orphan. I still don't understand how he came to sponsor me, a tawny youngster with his left cheek mauled. Yes, the minister was from a wealthy family, known for acts of philanthropy, but still, he was no older than twenty-nine, and unmarried. Yet, sponsor me he did; he let me live in his house, taught me, showed his true largeness of spirit the day I told him I wasn't interested in law but in mineralogy. 'Rocks, huh? They interest you more than letters? Why?'

'It's the maps,' I said, surprising myself and making no sense. If it was just about the maps, I could become a cartographer, an engineer, or a steamboat captain, for that matter. Yet I knew with certainty that I wanted to pursue the career of a mineralogist.

The minister let it pass. 'As long as it's something scientific,' he said.

Yes, we share that passion.

I will try and convince Isabella on my return to let Lovisa live with us until I find another solution.

Our first port of call, Ratan, is a hamlet with no more than ten houses. The rocks are dark, in part covered by vivid green mosses. On top of them grow plenty of birch, small willows, and pine. Since I can't see it, the land beyond must be flatter. It is as if nothing exists past the shoreline. 'Peculiar,' I say to the captain, who stands beside me.

He nods. 'You should see it when it's foggy.'

I watch our cargo being unloaded and then restocked with logs for the steamboat engines. Lovisa is nowhere to be seen. It occurs to me that if she has disembarked with the other passengers, I might not have noticed. So be it. If found, she'd be arrested and put in prison. Women must be under the protection of a guardian. In a way, it would solve many problems.

When we leave Ratan a few hours later, most people have gone ashore. On the sofa in the saloon across from me sit two priests; in the armchairs, some men of business, and others who wear the blue uniform of civil servants.

At dinnertime I walk to the dining saloon at the front of the boat. I sit down and am joined by the two priests and a reddish-faced man with a shock of grey hair and a sweeping moustache. We are served black bread and its accompaniments – dried and smoked fish – and beer. The sea lies steady. We could be in a restaurant in Stockholm, if it weren't for the occasional whiff of burned wood from the engines. The priests introduce themselves as Hans Rexius and Fredrik Wetterlund. The ruddy man only uses his first name, Lars. The priests are travelling to 'the most gruesome of places', the younger one, Frederik Wetterlund, declares and his face shines. He is a pale youngster, a 'gruesome place' still carries excitement; the place in question being a hamlet in the mountains close to the border with Norway.

'We're not certain yet how to get there,' he says.

Lars nods. 'It's a long journey. There are no roads, the weather is unreliable, and then there are the predators . . . You ought to find yourselves some fellow-travellers.'

'We're hoping to be able to travel part of the journey with the bishop on his visitations,' Fredrik Wetterlund says.

'Then you're from the region?' the older priest, Hans Rexius, asks.

Lars nods. 'I'm in charge of the new county gaol in Luleå.'

I take a sip of my beer. The drink is cold enough to chill the palm of my hand.

'I've heard about it,' the older priest says. 'A cell-block

33

prison? Criminals isolated rather than housed together? And the custodial time will now be treated as an opportunity for change?'

'We have programmes for reformation.'

'Does your gaol also take Lapps who have broken the law?' the younger priest asks.

The warden nods.

'The Lapps are a different breed,' his older companion says.

I take out my pipe, stuff it and light it.

'The priest we will be replacing has a few of them as servants,' Fredrik says.

'Why the journey to Stockholm?' I ask the warden.

He glances at me. 'Just business.'

'And you,' the older priest turns to me. 'What are your reasons for going to Lapland?'

I decide to chance it. 'I work for *Bergskollegium*, but this time I am travelling on behalf of the State Minister of Justice.' I look at the warden, before smiling to the priest. 'He has asked me to see to it that the new owners of *Gällivare-verken* have everything they need.'

'Once they begin extracting iron in Lapland,' the older priest sounds wistful, 'it will change the region completely.'

The warden stares into his glass.

I stand on the promenade deck leaning against the railing. Our ship passes by silent, wooded islets. The pine forest on shore has darkened to a black frame. The sky, however, remains a light blue.

He comes up behind me, and it is a while before he says, 'Nobody knows I've told the State Minister about the murders.'

'Nobody will hear it from me.'

Lars steps up to the railing.

'Tell me about it,' I say.

I can sense him shake his head. 'It was like a slaughterhouse. The Lapp was sitting in the middle, on the floor. The bodies had already begun to smell.' He clears his throat.

'Who is he?'

'We don't know anything. He refuses to speak.'

'Why did you travel to Stockholm?'

The warden hesitates. 'I got this feeling . . . that something wasn't quite right. The county governor asked that I didn't register the prisoner, asked us not to tell a soul. I met the minister when I was appointed, and I felt' – he shrugs – 'like I owed him.'

The minister does that to people, I think. The county governor is the King's appointed man; undoubtedly astute and knowledgeable about the King's wishes. He has had the same instinct as the minister: save the *Gällivare-verken* agreement. *Shut this down.*

'I want to see him,' I say. 'The Lapp.'

The warden shakes his head. 'The prison lies just by the county governor's residence. You'll have to ask him.'

He hesitates again.

'Nobody will hear it from me,' I repeat.

He nods, leaves.

L

Our third day on board the ship. I stand by the railing. Cold water sprays my face and I taste salt. I lost my hat in a wind gust. It curled through the air to land and bob in the dark blue whirls behind us. Now my skin stings and is turning horribly brown and parched. Large white birds with black wingtips circle overhead, then tilt and glide back towards shore. Far away, what might be the backs of seals gleam.

I have never been north. The year my mother went to the spa in Söderhamn, I begged to go with her and her face became drawn, and she looked out of the window and then at my father with that sorry helplessness of hers. And it was he who had to say, of course not: 'Don't be silly, Lovisa. Your mother feels she needs a rest from us.' I remember the down-turned corners of his mouth and his cold eyes. Disgust. Whether with me, my mother, or having to deal with this eruption of sentimentality, I don't know.

Late afternoon, I surrender. My fingers are stiff and I fumble to open the iron door. Inside, the warm air smells of pipe smoke and liquor. Further away, Magnus walks to sit down in an armchair. I push my head down and march towards my cabin. From the corner of my eye, I see the people in the chairs beside him look up and startle. Magnus appears daunting. Along with his long hair and the scar, his facial features are sharp, his beard is neatly cut, his eyes an intense blue. He's the kind of man people avoid. Then someone tells them how successful he is. And then, of course, it becomes *Magnus this* and *Magnus that*. People forget about the scar. Perhaps they no longer see it. I wonder if at times he laments his appearance. I don't know him well. He left our home when I was little, and then he married my inane sister and that made me not want to know him.

'Have you noticed how children always look you in the eyes?' Eva's voice. We promenaded – strolls that became longer and longer until they lasted whole afternoons and had us arriving back home with red cheeks and clear eyes and leaving us with no time to change our clothes before supper. I had begun to think that, in hiring Eva, my father had made an unusual mistake. Eva was my kind of person, not his. 'They don't notice appearances – they don't care – they look for whatever is in there, deep, deep inside.'

I thought her words profound. When it came to Eva, I thought many things.

I picture her before me now: straight brown hair, blue eyes, the thin bottom lip so unlike her full upper one that it gives her mouth an imbalanced, insecure expression. It hurts to think about her. And so I shall keep thinking about her and remember what it feels like to be betrayed. I shall engrave her face on my retina until I see everything through the light of her image . . .

The breath leaves me and I lie down on the berth in my cabin. The bulging window makes me feel I am looking at a small, dark painting. The sun stands close to the horizon and the sea glows cobalt blue.

I feel numb. I will never feel again. Then I surprise myself by having more tears to cry.

My father sent me away. For good this time. No, he didn't send me away, he threw me out. 'Leave her in the north,' he said. And my mother didn't say one word to oppose him. I realise I must have thought that if it came to this, she would stand up for me.

What will they tell Eva? Will she ever think of me and question where I've gone?

The sounds in my cabin grow weaker and weaker. I lie with eyes open, burrowed into the bedding like a dead bird into its feathers.

The air is cool today, the sky clear. The captain came and knocked on my door to tell me we would be arriving at our destination in less than an hour. I guess Magnus asked him to. I guess Magnus didn't want to alert me himself.

Magnus comes out on deck and stands by the railing; too close, not close enough.

So here I am, forced onto someone who doesn't think me worthy of a polite conversation: a comment upon the territory we are approaching, our journey perhaps, or the day's weather. My cheeks feel hot, the shame, crushing.

We near land. The wind lessens, the water turns a still black. It looks as if the coast is floating towards us rather than the other way around. The chugging of the steamer slows, slows, slows, until it is a weary iron heart beating in the ship's bulk.

B

Blackåsen, Spring 1856

The village lies silent, imprisoned by him who sits with the bodies. Nobody carries out everyday chores, all doors remain shut. For they cannot be certain the beast won't come out; they cannot know what will happen next. Merchant, Long Beard, Giant, and Night Man take turns to guard the vicarage, rifles pointed at the house. They've sent Hunter to the coast for help. I am hiding in the shadows by the far end of the boneyard. Priest is nowhere to be seen, nor Constable. I feel certain they are dead. Who the third man might have been, I don't know. I can't see anyone else missing.

I won't mind Constable being dead, it has to be said. 'Jan-Erik Persson' – Nila whistling his name. Bad seed, that one. We've known him since he was young. We know all the settler offspring, by look at least; running wild on the mountain in summer, reined in by their parents during winter. Sometimes, we happen upon them, often at one of the old sacred sites – good places for telling stories about ghosts and curses, it seems, and we scare them, rattle amongst the stones or hoot like an owl, to laugh when they run away.

One winter, I came across the Constable boy and his brother on Blackåsen Mountain. It was one of those winters when the cold was unbearable, your tear ducts froze and you felt your windpipe burn as you breathed. We were famished, and I set the traps closer to the village than I usually would. I heard voices and found the boys by the old maze; Constable can't have been more than eight at the time, the younger boy, perhaps five. I watched as Constable fooled his brother, said he'd give him the dried meat he had in his pocket if the boy proved himself brave. 'Go straight into the forest,' Constable said. 'Walk one hundred steps, then turn around and come back to me.'

The little one didn't want to go, but he must have been as ravenous as I was. Hunger is a convincing companion.

'I'll be right here,' Constable said.

The boy left, his shoes scraping on the frozen crust. As soon as the small figure disappeared in amongst the trees, Constable turned and ran the other way, all smiles.

Of course, the younger boy was soon lost, everything looking the same in the dark. He shouted for his brother, then began to cry when there was no response, running this way and that.

I didn't want to show myself to him unless it became unavoidable. I didn't know how the settlers would react to me trapping so close to their village, but the boy was panicked. I broke a branch with a snap that startled him into silence. Then I whispered, 'This way,' and, 'Here.' He cocked his head and followed my directions, walking as if in a trance. I led him back home. You can imagine what might have happened if I hadn't been there. I don't know what story they told their parents.

Priest was better. Nothing holy about him as a boy, but he had a good head, and his father sent him away to be educated. He returned after his studies with a white collar and a large black book, and came to find the *sita* at our spring campsite.

His freckled skin had paled from time spent indoors and his hands had turned soft; a fine person. Those large, grey eyes, the way he held his book . . . he reminded me of a much older man. In the past, we'd had missionaries come. And the bishop came regularly – the town priest with him. They made us feel bad about our sins, and cry so much we felt good. Now we were to get a priest. Our own priest.

'Nils.' He smiled.

They sat on the floor in the *kåta*, cross-legged, and drank the soup I had made. Priest told Nila about his plans to build a church in the village.

'I'll need you to attend the sermons,' Priest said, 'once the church is ready.'

'It's a good idea,' Nila told the *sita* later, 'a church on Blackåsen.'

I tried to understand why I had this gnawing feeling in my chest; we were Christians. But the closest church was one day's travel away. There is a huge difference in attending church a couple of times a year and going there every Sunday. I would have expected Nila to need time to think about it. I would have thought he'd ask the views of the others.

That evening, he approached me, said: 'You are thinking something.'

'It just surprises me. You being so in favour.'

Nila smiled, that tilted smile when half of his face lifted. Mischievous or sad, I could never tell. 'We will support them in what they feel they need. Besides, I like a God whose thunder is worse than his strike.'

Next time we came back to our winter camp, the red timber church stood ready in the village, an uncomfortable shape of a wheel with eight corners. That first Sunday, we attended the sermon and were preached to about God and the Devil, and how it was either or, not none, not both. The church smelled of cut wood and paint. We smelled of reindeer and of fire. Our clothes felt coarse against the white planks of the benches. Nila sat with his eyes half-closed, gazing at the cross. After the sermon, the settlers lingered. They nodded at us, faces open. I remember smiling.

Over the years, I saw the shift in myself and the others. Every now and then, I'd hum a psalm or sigh to Jesus. I'd glance at Nila but he'd seem unaware, or nod absently. Almost as if he encouraged it. He didn't mind; not then.

On day eight, Hunter returns with them: six men from the coast with hats and guns. The vicarage windows stay blank. Nobody moves inside. The men speak with the villagers. Then they deliberate at length amongst themselves. They choose to enter the vicarage, three from the front and three from the back. The settlers encircle the house. My mouth is dry.

After a short time, they lead the killer out onto the porch, crooked legs, long black-white hair straggling far down his back. A Lapp? Could be.

The villagers draw nearer each other, become a village again. They watch in silence the man who has slain their own.

The killer totters down the steps of the house. The men have to hold him up by his arms. Then the perpetrator hesitates and sticks his nose in the air, like a dog. He swings his head in my direction. I crunch down. He can smell me. I feel a hysterical bubble in my chest. He knows I am here. And then my blood stills, for, through the branches, I see his face.

The man who stares straight at me, who has sensed me, is the one Nila carved in the tree: the same gaunt cheeks, the sharp nose, the cold eyes.

I watch as they take him away. His steps grow longer and steadier as they walk down the path. By the time they reach the dirt road, he could be a young man.

I find I have grabbed at my heart.

M

June 1856

Three large timber ships loll in the blue harbour water, being loaded and unloaded, barrels rolled into the adjacent warehouses. Beyond the wooden quay Luleå town begins, the church rising high in its middle. The town lies framed by dark green forestland. Thirteen or fourteen hundred people, Gabriel thought, and growing quickly. Luleå rests on sediments carried down by Luleå River; sand mainly. Later, I'll go and see the banks, search for evidence of the uplift of land. The whole of Sweden is rising; once concealed rocks make their appearance, the muddy ground emerges into daylight, breaking free from the restraint of the sea.

Directed by the captain of our steamer, Lovisa and I walk the road leading straight from the harbour in the direction of the white church. In five minutes we are at the central square, where we find an inn.

We are shown our accommodations on the first floor. 'I have some matters to attend to,' I say in the hallway. 'Order dinner in the tavern. Ask them to bring it to your room.'

Lovisa responds in the way she always does when spoken to, or asked a question: she half-closes her eyes, displaying her eyelids and two thin, perfectly rounded, raised eyebrows. I know this look. When she uses it on me, I want to shake her and say, 'Look at me when I am talking to you!'

I find I have clenched my jaw, and I grimace to relax it. I will not let her idiocies get to me.

The county governor's dwelling stands separate from the town on a piece of flat land by Luleå River – just like the innkeeper told me. A straight dirt road leads up to it. The residence is a long two-storey building on a stone foundation, flanked by two similar houses. The frames of the tall windows on the first floor are decorated wood carvings, and the door is in the middle, perfect symmetry.

Workers are carrying crates inside. I enter the doorway, and behind me one of the men stumbles on the doorstep, and he and his companion drop a heavy box. It hits the floor with a bang, and books spill out.

A man opens the double doors on the left and strides into the hallway. He must be close to fifty years old. He looks severe, like most of the men the King appoints; square face, nose bent like the beak of a bird of prey, the corners of his mouth pointing firmly downwards. His forehead has no worry lines, his eyes no laughter wrinkles. It's the face of a person who has surely lived and experienced both struggles and joys, but who hasn't allowed himself to be marked by either. He glares at the books on the floor and then at the two men, who already stand caps in hand, heads bent. Then he sees me.

I, too, take off my hat. 'My name is Magnus Stille,' I say.

The two workers begin to lift the books into their crate – slowly, heads still bent – and we watch them. I feel the urge to add that I had nothing to do with this mishap.

'I have travelled from Stockholm. I was hoping you'd find the time to receive me,' I say instead.

'What chaos,' the county governor says, still looking at the books. 'We have just moved in, and the house isn't even ready.

Well,' he lifts his head, reaches out and presses my hand, 'welcome to Luleå.' He pronounces the town's name as 'Lule'. 'I am Gunnar Cronstedt. So what brings you here?'

'I work for *Bergskollegium* in Stockholm.'

There's a beat of something in the county governor's eyes, then he smiles: 'Up to inspect the discoveries then. And what a peculiar coincidence.'

He walks to the door and gestures for me to follow. 'Frans, look who's here,' he says into the room.

Bergskollegium's regional master of the mountain, Frans Svensson, sits in one of the armchairs. He was born in the region, a short, bulky man with protruding teeth. I have met him once before, in Stockholm, prior to his appointment. Nowadays he resides in Piteå, some twenty-seven miles further south. Frans inhales with a snapping breath, nods. 'Indeed.'

'Unless you knew Mr Stille was coming?' the county governor says.

'Oh no,' Frans says. 'Oh no.'

The county governor walks to a counter laden with liqueurs and crystal glasses, pours three glasses of arrack, hands one to me, the other to Frans, and nods to the armchairs.

The panelled walls in the sitting room are painted red; the tapestry above is French. The square tiled stove has brass shutters. We could be in a mansion in Stockholm.

'You'll want to see the records,' Frans says, 'to get an update? But they are all in Piteå.'

He leans on the armrest with his elbow. His armchair creaks.

'I am not here for the books,' I say.

'So then what does bring you here?' the county governor asks, and sits down.

I glance at the regional master of the mountain, take a sip of my drink, and taste the liquor, sugary, fiery.

'You can speak in front of Frans,' the county governor says.

Truth or untruth? Truth, though I would have preferred to come at it more slowly rather than from the outset.

'I hear you've had some trouble . . . On Blackåsen?'

Gunnar Cronstedt leans back. 'So the news has reached Stockholm.'

Surely he has informed the King? Even if he is trying to keep the murders a secret, he would have to. Unless . . . What if the Lapps are rioting and the county governor hasn't told Stockholm because he doesn't want to be seen as not being in control?

'Who told you?'

I don't answer his question. 'It's important I know what happened because of the mineral discoveries in the region,' I say instead.

Cronstedt circles his glass, making the liquid inside twirl. 'We have the culprit.'

'Tell me.'

He shrugs. 'It happened after a parish meeting. The three victims were in the vicarage when the Lapp came. He had brought a knife. The priest, the constable, and a third man were found dead. The villagers sent a messenger to us, and we arrived eight days after the murders. In all that time, nobody had dared approach the vicarage. We found the Lapp inside, still sitting on the floor amidst the bodies.'

Why wouldn't the perpetrator have tried to flee? 'What did this . . . Lapp say? Why did he do this?'

'He hasn't said one word since we picked him up.'

'Does he speak Swedish?'

'Of course,' the county governor says.

Frans mumbles something, nods and looks at the ceiling.

'Why them?' I ask.

The county governor's teeth gleam. 'What do you mean?'

'The priest and the law enforcement officer.'

The priest and the law enforcement officer would make up the local authorities in a place like Blackåsen. If this was about a dispute – a decision gone against the perpetrator perhaps, he must have realised they would be replaced.

'I guess because they were there,' the county governor says. 'This was clearly not a rational act.'

'But did it look like there had been a fight?'

'I am not certain I would call it a fight. There was a lot of blood . . . Ample signs of men trying to escape.'

He takes a swig of the arrack, scowls, and exhales.

'And the third man . . . Who was he?'

He shrugs. 'Some settler.'

There is a knock on the door, and a girl in a white apron appears. She curtsies.

'Dinner,' the county governor says. 'Add one plate,' he tells the girl.

I will need to know more than this to satisfy the minister. But the evening has just begun. Outside, the sun shines, but with a softer light. Mosquitoes dance on the window pane.

We are served reindeer, a lean and finely grained cut that tastes like beef, only more so. The conversation moves to Stockholm, to the demands for change, the worry that harries the nation.

'Here, too, people join in unions of various sorts,' the county governor says, and fixes his gaze on me. 'But we are keeping tight control of the mob. There won't be any strikes.'

'None?' I smile: how can you be certain?

'None.'

'The King is losing control of the country,' Frans says, mouth full. He tilts his head and puts another forkful in.

I nod to the servant – yes, please – and she serves me more meat. I don't comment. I don't intend to forget that the county governor is the King's man.

'I guess "Kalle Crooked Nose" will take over,' Frans says. This is what people are calling the Crown Prince Karl XV.

Many long for the reign of the crown prince. Some people say he is already in charge. The State Minister of Justice tells me it is not so. The King doesn't want to let go. 'Suddenly, he seems to resent his son,' the minister told me once. 'Sees him as a threat rather than the fine heir he has worked hard to raise.'

The servants bring in a second bottle of wine, a third, a fourth. I light my pipe.

Frans laments the fact that they cannot hunt elk until the autumn. The county governor, speech garbled now, warns him that he and his friends must take great care not to hunt too far inland.

'We don't want to cause problems with the Lapps by straying on to what they feel is their territory.'

The county governor sighs; Frans stares at the glass in his hand. They've opened a door back to the events at hand, and they know it. Why don't they want to discuss this with me?

I turn to Frans, who, in many ways, works for me. 'Was the killer known to you?'

The county governor pours himself more wine; it overflows onto the tablecloth, a large, red blotch.

'Of course not,' Frans says, 'I never met him.'

Why 'of course'? Because of their less pure blood? Certainly, here there is an 'us' and a 'them'.

'Is there any prior history of violence that involves him?'

Frans's hand goes to his shirt neck. He looks at the county

governor. 'We don't know who he is,' he says. 'The forest is full of them, and other vagrants.'

'Any incidents that involve other Lapps?'

'No.'

'But is there unrest amongst them, or—?'

'This interests you that much? Then let's go and see him.' The county governor rises, sways, and has to take an extra step. 'I'll show him to you.'

'I'm not certain—' Frans tries.

'No, no. I'll show the animal to him. You can stay here.' The county governor pokes a finger in Frans's chest. 'We'll be back in time for dessert.'

The county governor stumble-runs down the wooden stairs. We round the building flanking the main residence and turn right. The county governor struggles to keep steady on the uneven ground.

'You are not from around here,' he says. 'The Lapps are like children. Nomads, you know; less evolved. We are trying to help them, but . . . they are unsteady. Most likely, the Lapp had too much to drink, some perceived injustice got hold of him, and then he acted without thinking.

'Bloody mosquitoes.' He slaps his arm.

The gaol is a rounded building in white stone. In the middle of the roof, there is an elevated section. Windows?

As we enter, two guards stand up. Neither of them is the man I met on the boat.

'The Lapp,' the county governor says. 'Open up.'

One of the guards scrambles. He takes us to an iron door and opens a peephole.

'Not that. The door.'

The guard unlocks the door and swings it open. The county governor enters first.

The cell is shaped like a piece of cake – the furthest wall away from us, the shortest. An opening up high lets in light and it falls on the bench beneath it. A man sits on the seat, head lowered, face shaded by a bush of long hair, straggly, black and white. His shoulders protrude, his arms arc behind his body. Chained.

'This is him,' the county governor says.

The prisoner lifts his head and blinks several times.

He is an old man, wrinkled and crumpled. This kind of man should sit in a chair and watch life in the shape of children and grandchildren around him. I try to imagine this man wielding a knife. I can't.

'See?' The county governor says beside me. 'Childlike.' He clears his throat and swallows, his drunkenness catching up with him in this silent space. Now he knows he's inebriated and he doesn't feel well. He leaves the cell.

'Why?' I ask. 'Why did you kill them?'

The prisoner closes his eyes and bends his head.

One of the guards escorts Gunnar Cronstedt home. The guard hovers by the county governor's side, afraid to touch him. The county governor staggers left, then right, all the while ignoring the man beside him.

My chest feels tight and I exhale.

A wave of nausea wells up inside me, and I vomit. Liquids splash onto the ground by my feet. I jerk my legs apart so as not to stain my trousers.

I look around, but there is nobody. I try to slow my breathing. I take out my handkerchief and wipe my mouth. What is happening to me? It's the second time in a matter of days that I feel sickness. Perhaps I am ill. Perhaps it is serious.

No. It must have been something I ate. It might have been the reindeer meat.

I wipe my mouth again.

I begin the walk back to the inn. The sun has lost its power. Dusk hangs in the air. People swarm in the street, laughing and talking. Nobody meets my gaze. I feel as if I am not really here. I have a sour taste in my mouth.

At the inn, the low ceiling renders the tavern noisy and smoky. Sand and juniper twigs cover the floor. A bet is going on in one corner, money on the table; people stand around it, lean forward. A knife glints against a thigh. It won't end well. I cross the floor, and a drunken woman falls against me. I grab her elbow, she laughs, looks up into my face, then pushes away from me as if she's burned herself. I continue towards the stairs. On the first floor, the noise pumps through the boards, but I have slept in worse. As I walk down the corridor to my room, a voice calls for me: 'Master Stille!'

The innkeeper trudges up the stairs, wheezing from the effort.

'Yes?'

'It's the young missus travelling with you . . .' The innkeeper wrings his hands and avoids meeting my gaze. 'Your sister-in-law.'

'Yes?'

'We don't want any problems.'

I wait.

'Something went missing earlier.'

The story is a simple one. Invited for coffee by the innkeeper's wife, Lovisa accepted. The innkeeper's wife went about her work – peeled potatoes, carrots, boiled water, whilst the young lady sat down at the table. They discussed this and that: how expensive everything was in Stockholm, how the size of flour bags had changed for the worse . . . True, the young lady knew scant, but the innkeeper's wife can carry a whole conversation on her own, and she did. It was later, when she was to pay the timber man for the wood, she discovered that with Lovisa, the purse had gone too.

Did she do this? Steal? I wish I didn't believe it so readily.

'I am certain many people come and go in your kitchen,' I say.

'Indeed,' the innkeeper says. 'Indeed. Only we asked her about it, see? Just asked if she had seen anything, and she handed the money over. She had it in her pocket, see?'

I exhale. She is trying to destroy herself. The innkeeper is standing sideways on to me. I look straight into his ear. I imagine it stretching, waiting. He doesn't want to involve the law – probably has his reasons. I could force the issue. It would take Lovisa off my hands sooner, rather than later. But there would be an enquiry, a trial. I would need to stay put.

'Where is she now?'

'We locked her in her room.' The innkeeper digs in his vest pocket and retrieves a key. 'We don't want any problems,' he repeats.

I manage a smile. 'This is most gracious of you. I will deal with her.'

I unlock the door to Lovisa's room. As I close it behind me, the innkeeper disappears down the stairs. Lovisa is sitting on the bed, a bored expression on her face, eyelids towards me, eyebrows raised. The insolence. I want to slap her. I want to shake her and shout.

She opens her eyes and raises her chin.

I force myself not to act. Instead, I turn, walk back out, and lock the door.

*

In my room, anger pounding through me, I fling my hat onto my bed. If she was my daughter, she wouldn't be too old for me to use my belt on her.

I am certain nothing can be said or done to Lovisa that hasn't already been said or done. I have met people like her before, determined to finish themselves off. One of my teachers at Falu mining school, he was like that. The drinking and the rough nights were amusing at first – we all wanted to take part – of course, to drink with a teacher! But this man couldn't stop. The nights turned uglier, the acts grew sordid, the drinking spilled over into the day. The rest of us withdrew. Awkwardly, we blamed our studies, our families, other engagements . . .

I met this man again for the first time in many years earlier this summer. His eyes were sunk into the sockets, black pits. I was surprised to see he was still alive.

What people like that don't realise is that there is no fate. Your destiny has nothing to do with being born with this characteristic or that, it's what you decide to do with your life that matters. I am certain this is why the minister has been unable to let go with regards to Lovisa. Didn't he say, when I first arrived with him and he decided my new name would be Magnus Stille, 'Your life begins here and now.' Hasn't he repeated it a hundred times since: 'Your life began when you came to live with me.' And how wise he was! What would it have been like if I kept pondering my origins? If I thought that the answers lay in those forgotten four first years of my existence?

The minister is right. We had better leave Lovisa to her own devices.

Then the face of my own daughter, Harriet, comes before me, and I shrug, annoyed at my sentimentality.

I walk to the window. Beneath me, a man runs out of the tavern and down the street. I remember the money on the table, the knife. The door is flung open, and two men set off after the absconder.

I sigh. I cannot be the one who lets Lovisa fall. That kind of a decision, the ultimate punishment, must be made and implemented by a father or a husband. The minister shouldn't have asked me to take her on. Dealing with her was his duty. I vow that I won't leave her alone for one minute until we are back in Stockholm, and then I will drop her at his door-step, and he'll have to see to her. And I won't indulge her. If Lovisa is seeking a reaction, she'll have none from me. I shall take her with me as I would bring a piece of luggage.

I had hoped this mission would be easy, but now I am not certain. Since seeing the prisoner, my undertaking has grown. There is the 'why' the killing took place, but also the 'who'. The Lapp appeared ancient. I can't imagine him killing three men on his own, or even participating in the killings. Something is not right. If the county governor is concerned about protecting the *Gällivare-verken* agreement, then why would he not just tell me?

I will have to go back to see the prisoner tomorrow. I'll make sure to speak again with the warden from the boat. If they don't talk, the other people who might know something are those who live on Blackåsen. But if I go there, I'll have to bring Lovisa with me . . .

I stand for a long time by the window, in this silver evening that won't end. What a delight to live with days that merely mellow before growing again into full days.

I put my bag on my bed and take out Hermelin's print – the one that neglects to show Blackåsen Mountain. I have brought it with me from Stockholm. I love maps: the texture of the thick paper, the smell of old books and ink. The drawings are often exquisite – like the angels bordering this picture here. I relish seeing the way the mapmaker has chosen to depict the world, what he has marked upon, what frame he has imposed on a piece of land. I might have been right that time when I was young: maps might be why I chose to become a mineralogist. If you don't know where you're coming from, you want to know where you are going.

The closest large town to Blackåsen lies perhaps fifty miles from Luleå. Gabriel and I estimated that Blackåsen is situated another twenty miles north of that, but through a terrain which is quite impassable: woodland all the way; fens, bogs, rivers.

We are not far away. Desire itches in my chest.

I can't imagine a woman walking twenty miles through the wilderness, but after what's happened, I can't leave Lovisa here.

I try to situate an imaginary Blackåsen on the map.

I realise that what I thought were blonde curls on the painted angels are devils' horns.

$\mathcal{L}$

I don't know for how long I have screamed, pounded, kicked the door.

Magnus can't lock me in. He doesn't have the right. Damn you, Magnus! Burn in hell!

But he did it. Nobody comes to help. Nobody ever comes to help.

When I stop, the sides of my hands ache. I shiver, wrap my arms around myself, stagger to the bed, and curl into a ball. I could die here and no one would know. Breathe. Lie still. Don't think about the door. Close your eyes.

Why did I not care when the innkeeper shut me in? It's because I knew Magnus would come. I waited for him and the ensuing fight. And then Magnus didn't say anything. He ought to have shouted: *What are you doing? What is wrong with your head? Why would you betray everyone like this?* But he didn't look at me.

Magnus is not my father. He'll lock me up. The madhouse.

One of my mother's friends was put there by her husband. It was said she heard voices. She aged ten years in that one year. When we next met her, my mother walked straight past her, but I saw the begging eyes in the middle of the slack, grey features, and pulled at my mother's coat for her to stop. For days afterwards the rims of my mother's eyes were swollen red.

What *am* I doing? What *is* wrong with my head? Why *do* I betray them like this?

I don't know. I have this deadness inside, and whatever I try, I feel nothing. No, no, that's not true. It's the other way around. I have too much pain inside, nothing quells it, and the disappointment I feel after each failed attempt makes it worse.

I thought Eva was the answer. Oh, Eva, in our hallway, stupid yellow hat on that long straight hair, thin arms by her sides, tattered suitcase by her feet. 'I am here,' she said. Not: 'I am here to teach you, Lovisa.' Or: 'I am your teacher.'

Just: 'I am here.'

And I could have cried. Instead, I exclaimed: 'Finally!'

Morning comes to Luleå unannounced. The sky remained blue all night. At one point, the colour deepened, only to lighten again. My window faces a small fenced yard. I can hear the noise coming from the other side of the enclosure, from the street. For most of the night, the town must have been as full of activity as it had been during the afternoon. Then, for a brief moment, it was quiet. Perhaps it lasted an hour. Then, a muted 'good morning', shutters slamming open, a horse snorting, a man's voice: 'Shhh, calm down.' Morning had arrived.

I have dressed and packed. I touch my bare neck with my hand and wish I hadn't lost my hat. It's hard to appear normal with hair like a tuft of grass. For, as I sit here on my bed and wait for Magnus, I want to appear normal. When he comes, I will explain about the pain, and promise to change. Give me one more chance. I will beg him if I have to.

A knock, and the key turns. I rise. My heart pounds in my chest. Magnus bends his head to look in.

'Good,' he says, 'you're ready.'

He is pale. Lines cross the white skin around his eyes. He

hasn't slept, probably because of me. I open my mouth to say the words.

'I guess we can eat downstairs. Well.' He leaves.

I walk out into the corridor. He is already heading down the stairs.

The young woman who serves us stares at my hair. At Magnus's scar. Back at my hair. The wood of our table is marked by what could be stab wounds from a knife.

'Is something the matter?' Magnus asks, gruff.

'No.' She licks her lips.

'Then take our order. I'll have coffee and bread. Lovisa?' It's a command.

I nod.

'Two of everything. And meat.' He frowns after her as she leaves.

He's trying to win my confidence. Someone else tried to do that . . . Oh yes, my Latin teacher; a scrawny man with glasses and bad breath. Poor Lovisa, misunderstood. 'Come and sit here beside me . . .' Pale hand clasping my knee.

They sicken me.

Magnus lifts up his bag and takes out a map.

'There is no need to do that,' I say.

'What?' Magnus uses what looks like two small legs in steel. With two fingers, he walks them one foot to another, across the map.

'You don't have to be nice to me.'

'Why wouldn't I be nice?' he asks without looking up.

Coffee, black as tar; yellow butter. One tears at my innards, the other one soothes.

After breakfast, outside, we walk past a few shops, one of which displays clothes on a stand by the door. My sister would stick her elbow in my side and grimace at the garments to show they are last season's.

Magnus stares straight ahead. Say it now, I tell myself. Tell him you are sorry. Say it!

My hand flies up to touch my neck. 'I would like a hat,' I hear myself saying.

Magnus's mouth sets in a thin line.

'If you don't mind, of course.'

'As you wish.'

As I pick one, any one, the woman tries to sell me a dress, too. She pulls out a brown modest outfit. 'Good both for daywear and evening wear,' she says, decidedly not looking at Magnus, who stands by the doorway, face stony. I could enact the role: large eyes, a fearful glance at Magnus. *My husband is terrible; I am frightened.* But I just shake my head at the dress. I put on the hat and have to admit to feeling better, normal almost, even though it is large-brimmed, and the fabric flowery.

Magnus pays. Outside, he looks at me, scrutinising. I feel a pang of fear.

'I need to go and see a prisoner,' he says, 'and I am wondering if I can bring you.'

A prisoner? 'What has he done, this man?'

'He is said to have killed three people.'

A prick of something different this time. Excitement?

'Three people?'

'That's what they say.'

I nod once, then again. Yes, I can be brought. Magnus nods too. He heads down the main street, taking long steps. I follow. A killer! But Magnus doesn't believe he did it. 'Said to have killed' were the words he used.

'Is this what my father sent you for? To see this man?'

60

'Something like that,' he says, over his shoulder.

We turn left, and then leave the town behind, turning right. We walk towards a lone white stone building. Magnus ascends the steps in one go and pushes open the door, lifts his hat briefly.

'We've come to see the Lapp,' he says. 'I was here with the county governor last night.'

The guards glance at each other. Magnus stands without moving. Yet the fisted right hand behind his back . . .

He is lying. He doesn't have permission. I avoid looking at his fisted hand again and hold my breath.

'Do I have to wake the county governor?' Magnus asks. 'He had a long night.' The way he stresses the word 'long' makes it into a threat.

'No, no.' One of the men hurries to an iron door, head bent. He unlocks it, and Magnus walks in. The shortest of hesitations, and I follow.

A damp but sharp scent, the residue of a cool night and of morning urine. A wooden bench stretches along one side of the room. The cold white of the walls and roof lend a grubbiness to Magnus, to the guards, and to the prisoner.

Deep wrinkles cut through the criminal's face. The bags under his eyes on each side of the outsized nose are so marked they could have been drawn on to his cheeks with blue ink. Underneath the bench, he has crossed his legs by the thin ankles.

Then his full black eyes meet mine. There is no age. There might be indifference, but no frailty. I am looking into the eyes of a wild animal. It's as if the Lapp isn't all human. If they send me to the madhouse, this is what people will be like. I shiver. The Lapp turns his eyes from me to Magnus.

'I have come on behalf of the State Minister of Justice,' Magnus says.

The Lapp tilts his head back. His features remain immobile.

'I want you to know the treatment of you will be fair. The minister himself is taking an interest in your case. Tell me what happened. Why were you in the vicarage?'

He adds, 'I can't help you, if you don't talk.'

The Lapp doesn't respond.

Magnus waits. Finally, he shrugs.

Outside, he turns to the guards: 'Where is your warden?'

One of them is locking up the prisoner. The other one says: 'He's travelling.'

Magnus takes a step towards the exit, but then hesitates. 'Where to?'

'Stockholm.'

'He hasn't returned?'

The guard shakes his head. 'Not yet.'

'I am not sure he was the killer,' Magnus says, more to himself than to me.

I am thinking of white stone walls. Of barred windows. Of being shut in.

'I am not certain he understands what I am saying.'

I remember the Lapp's black eyes. He *was* listening. Perhaps not to what Magnus said. The Lapp's interest seemed to be in Magnus himself. I don't know what I mean by this.

'But they know he did it,' I say.

Magnus glances at me. 'The Lapp was found at the place of the killings. That doesn't mean he did it. The murders didn't happen in Luleå. No one here knows any more about the events.'

'Where did it happen?'

Magnus points with his whole hand. There, far away. Somewhere inland. Far, far, far . . .

A disquiet between us, a tension. How to approach a matter without being seen to be so doing. I feel a lift inside. A very small one.

'And so we'll have to go there,' I say, blandly, as if it is of no consequence.

Magnus's face is immobile. I have dug my nails into the palms of my hands.

'I guess you need to make certain, with my father asking you and all.'

He doesn't answer at once. Perhaps I seemed too eager.

'We could travel by carriage to the closest town,' he says, 'but after that, there are no roads, and the ground is not passable for a horse. We would have to walk through the forest for about twenty miles.'

He said 'we'. I dare not exhale, just gaze straight ahead.

He sighs. 'We ought to be able to cover the distance in two, three days. You are in a good physical condition, aren't you?'

I imagine us as viewed by somebody else on the street. A reedy young woman, large flowery bonnet tied around her neck in a bow, and a bearded man in his forties, stooping over her. Normal people. I nod.

B

Blackåsen, Spring 1856

I dreamed about young Nila last night. He had lost his hat. His black hair lay pasted to his skull by sweat, as he ran in deep snow. He was trying to drive the reindeer into an enclosure, but the leader of the herd wouldn't have it. As the animal circled a grove of birch trees, Nila cut him off. He grabbed the reindeer by his antlers and pulled him along. The creature seemed to be laughing, as if it had been an act. Nila noticed me and he smiled. He tapped the side of his head with a finger. I laughed, too.

Then I noticed the herd had stopped. They weren't following any longer. They set off into a sprint, running towards their leader, towards Nila – one single body moving over white snow.

I woke up, reindeer hide twisted around my ankles.

'How is it possible?' I ask out loud once my heartbeats have returned to normal. I am speaking to young Nila. 'That you carved that face?'

By 'you' I mean old Nila. I don't perceive them as the same person. The old Nila hovers in the forest, but I am not talking to him. Not yet, perhaps never.

Young Nila doesn't respond.

I don't know how many days have passed. After seeing the

man who killed the settlers, the Lapp emerging from the vicarage in custody of the men from the coast, I lay down and slept for a long time. I heard voices, that of my mother, that of my father. I must have run a fever. Perhaps I still am. I am talking to the dead.

My throat is parched. I squat to drink from the rivulet, but my body needs more. I will make myself a hot drink of birch leaves from the trees close to the marsh. It will ease the headache, and if there's any fever left, it will take care of that, too. I take my satchel and my stick.

Perhaps Nila saw the Lapp somewhere, I think as I go down the trail. And as he descended into madness, this face stuck with him and he carved it into that tree.

Only this Lapp killed Priest and Constable, men who Nila was at odds with.

What if, and this thought I cannot bear, Nila asked this man to do what he did?

It cannot be. Nila didn't have it in him. I repeat this to myself over and over, but the carved face, too, reappears again and again.

It was two winters ago that our difficulties with the settlers began. The first few weeks, whenever we came to church the settlers greeted us just like before, with faces open. But before the New Year, Priest came to find Nila. 'Attending sermon is not a choice,' he said.

Constable stood beside him, round eyes trawling us and our camp.

'We attend as often as we can,' Nila said.

The *sita* nodded. It happened that we forgot. Or that we couldn't make it because of the weather or the herd. But we went to church most Sundays.

'Are you still practising your old faith?' Priest asked.

Someone behind me inhaled, a tiny gasp. I wanted to say no. Not at all. Hardly ever. Nila is nothing like his father, or his grandfather before him. You know us, that's what I wanted to tell Priest. We are members of your church.

'It is forbidden,' Priest said. 'Devilry.'

The two men eyed each other. The *sita* stood quiet, unmoving. Then Nila's face eased as if he'd come to a decision. 'But then, your God forgives all.'

It was said lightly. And Priest preached of forgiveness all the time. But Priest's eyes widened, and Constable turned to stare at Nila.

Nila stood immobile until they walked away, behind him the *sita* a wall in the winter darkness. But that evening, I came upon Suonjar whispering with Innga and Aili. As they noticed me, they separated like dry leaves in a wind.

After that visit, we took greater care not to miss sermons. But the difference between us and the other worshippers had been made clear: we were pagan. We had to be watched. I wanted to protest. We were as Christian as they. Perhaps more so. The whole thing made me feel dirty and, I must admit, I felt it was Nila's fault.

'What did you mean?' I asked him.

A week had passed. We were walking back to the site after emptying snares. The moon was small and hard. Nila's fur hat was pulled low over his eyes, his woollen scarf up over his mouth.

'When you said their God forgives all?'

We walked on. I thought he might not answer.

'It is better if you don't know.'

I realised then how much he must be keeping from

me – to what extent this other life still kept him separate. I had thought he too had changed like the rest of us. But perhaps he hadn't. The insight knocked the breath out of me.

Nila stopped. He dropped the ptarmigan in his hand onto the snow, and folded me in his arms. My nose pressed against the cold, smooth leather of his jacket. I was leaning against him rather than cuddling him, which was good because otherwise I think I might have punched him.

The birch grove by the marsh swirls in a faint wind, dressed in glowing green. Thin, white trunks in a grass so light it all becomes a mere shimmer to the eye. Towards the end of the thicket, I find the smaller trees. The sap of the leaves makes my fingers sticky. I fill my satchel.

Returning, I take the detour and circle the village. Night Man sits on a chopping block in his yard, sharpening his scythe. Holy Woman stands bent over her garden patch, weeding, fingers moving fast in the black soil, ripping.

By the church, in the boneyard, there are three new mounds of earth. And so, whilst I slept, they buried their men.

The vicarage windows are open. The curtains flutter in the wind. Priest's Wife, or Widow as she now is, opens the door, and comes out to sit on her doorstep to drink her coffee.

As if nothing has happened.

No. They are waiting. There is more to come. Fear flutters in my chest. I try to swallow it down.

Back at my campsite I make a fire, though I won't be eating. How is it possible? How could Nila have carved his face?

67

What if, just what if, the spirits told Nila?

Jesus.

The forest around me is silent. The sky a thick white.

M

The girl waits on the road out of Luleå, on the other side of the graveyard. Our feet crunch on the ground as we walk across the burial place towards her. Lovisa looks at the girl, her gig and pony. I feel bad. I have tricked her into this journey. But then, I think about her shenanigans and feel less guilty. Besides, have I not also duped myself? For if I wasn't planning to go to Blackåsen, then how come I brought my sextant, my pocket chronometer, and my theodolite?

No, better admit it, I was always going. Though whether for the sake of the murders, the missing maps, or to see for myself the largest iron deposit in Sweden, I don't know.

Once decided, I acted fast. I made all the arrangements and got the provisions. I want us to get away before the county governor knows, I am not certain myself why. The warden was scared it would be known he had spoken with the minister, and the guards said the warden had not yet returned from Stockholm even though I know he has. It's likely nothing. It just makes me feel uncomfortable.

I realise the path we are treading is filled with skulls and bones that snap under our feet as we walk. There isn't a clean patch to step on. I guess it's not strange they can't keep their dead buried, the whole island being nothing but sand pushed about by the wind. I am going to point it out to Lovisa, but then think better of it.

Two days' journey to the town closest to Blackåsen, said the man who helped me organise this trip, but he must be wrong. There is a road, and we have the pony and the gig. Surely, it won't take us that long. When I told him of our final destination, he rolled his eyes. 'Nobody goes there,' he said, before recalling, in fact, that lately there had been a couple of travellers heading for the same destination. I asked him who, but this he couldn't remember.

We set off and soon pass cultivated fields and large wooden houses painted red. The air smells of sweet pine, and the sun shines from a clear blue sky. The light is rich, without being severe. The glittering sea soon disappears behind the teal-green trees. The girl taking us can't be much older than my daughter Harriet. The coach skids, and gravel shoots from under the wheels onto the roadside. I search inside myself to understand the feeling, and then smile. It's as if I am about to revisit an old friend.

I dig in my satchel and find the map I was given last night as part of my provisions, showing Lapland, coloured in yellow and pink. Beside it lies the bottle of aquavit that I was also handed. 'You won't find alcohol anywhere out there,' the man who got my provisions said. 'It's forbidden to sell spirits outside town, but the traveller is allowed to bring his own supply.' He grinned at me.

I shake my map out. Sweden lies in the centre of the drawing, Norway to the far left. The green border between the two resembles the spine of some amphibian.

'Could you please hold your papers to the side?' Lovisa says.

Her shoulder against mine feels hot, and droplets of sweat

glitter across her nose under the hat. I turn further away from her.

'Is that it?' Lovisa asks. 'Is that where we are going?'

'Yes.'

Once we begin walking, we'll have to cross the large river that snakes across the map. There are a number of hillocks to the north of it, all unnamed. We could make our night camp on one of them, and then traverse the flat valley the following day, reaching our destination late in the afternoon. And there, on this map, finally is Blackåsen, faint rings drawn inside one another, like when you throw a stone into water and it ripples on the surface. I can feel the tug of the swirl, and the mountain rises up through it, water glistening on its sides.

We enter a sandy forest. Our carriage creaks as it hits every rut and bump in the road.

I look at the young girl on the coachman's seat and imagine Harriet there instead. It makes me smile. Harriet is strong. Isabella calls it stubborn. She will have to change in order to become a good wife and a mother. Sometimes, secretly, I hope she won't. The world already has so many good wives and mothers.

'Have you ever been to Blackåsen?' I ask the girl.

'No,' she says, eyes fixed on the road.

'Was that your father I met yesterday?'

'Yes.'

'He said people have travelled to Blackåsen recently?'

'Perhaps.'

I fold the map up. 'I will tell people I have come to map the mountain,' I say to Lovisa.

Lovisa doesn't respond. She is leaning back in the carriage, eyes closed. I have to glance at her twice. Her features are interesting: without the habitual scorn, naked and vulnerable, they are almost beautiful. For the first time, I recognise she is no longer a child.

I wrote a letter to Isabella last night and sent it with the steamboat captain back to Stockholm, telling her that I would be away longer than planned, and asking her to talk to the minister about Lovisa. If anyone can convince the minister to take Lovisa back, it is Isabella.

I am tired. When I finally fell asleep last night, I dreamed my dream again. I am in the forest, running, bare feet drumming against the ground. It's not only my feet. Someone else is coming, too. Someone I am trying to escape. I pant and turn, breathless, restless. Then I wake up, chest in a knot. I have had the same nightmare so often I should be used to it by now, but I don't know what's worse: the fear I sense when I wake up, or the frustration that I cannot remember how it ends.

Isabella's voice in my ear, making light of it: 'I guess each man has to have his own nightmare.'

Mid-afternoon: I realise I have stopped thinking. This forest is never-ending. The road is no longer a road, but a mere trickle of a path. The pony struggles up the steep hills, and often we have to descend and walk alongside it. When you sit in the shaking cart, the eye flickers from tree to tree to then still itself. The trees blur. The spirit dulls. It's like entering some other state. The silence is absolute; the stillness, crushing. It has also occurred to me that I might not be able to use my compass. The magnetic iron ore on Blackåsen will likely distort any reading.

It is late by the time the girl finally halts the pony.

'This is where we'll spend the night,' she says. 'At Ove and Anna-Maria Edgrens'.'

We are at a farmer's house. I descend and stretch my arms out to loosen my shoulders. On the other side, Lovisa struggles down from the cart. As the girl begins to unshackle our pony, a woman and a man come out of the house.

'Welcome,' Mrs Edgren says.

Mr Edgren lifts his hat to us, and I respond in equal fashion. In his other hand he holds a fishing rod.

'Ove is off to try his luck,' the woman says to me. She has tied a kerchief over her reddish-brown hair. Her facial features are delicate; the nose small, the chin pointed, her hazel eyes, clear. 'Would you like to join him, or are you too tired?'

Ove Edgren is a heavily-built man in his early thirties, with a neatly-cut beard. The brown eyes under the rim of the hat are lively.

Right now, the thing I would like to do most is sit down and take out my instruments and my diary, but this can wait. I say: 'I'll be glad to come with you.'

Our young guide leads the pony to the barn. The farmer's wife shows Lovisa the house. My host and I walk down the hill behind their property in silence. It isn't long before I hear water. Their farm is situated on a slope surrounded by birch trees. Far down, at the foot of the incline, a river rushes by. We are at the bottom of a set of rapids.

My host lifts the fishing rod and attaches a lure to the hook, dark hands moving deftly.

'Salmon,' he says, and nods to the river. He stands by the water, moves his arm, and sends the line forward and out. Slowly, he reels it back in.

I watch the frothing water throw itself down the rapids and twirl between rocks, touching the strand, where we're standing, as tiny ripples.

73

On his third throw, Ove catches something. He rolls it in, rod bending. A dark silver fish with a pinkish breast lands at my feet. Ove hits it on the head with a rock, puts it further up the shore. 'Want to have a go?' he asks.

Beside his, my hands look unhealthy; white and thin.

'Let the line roll out behind you,' he says, 'and then flick the rod forward.'

My first try gets the line caught in the pine trees on the slope. Ove's eyes are laughing. 'Let the fishing rod travel in a straight track, not in an arch.' He shows me again and goes to untangle the line.

My second effort is only a bit better. The hook and its lure plop in the water no more than five feet out. I roll it in and try again.

We return to the farmhouse with four large fish, all caught by Ove. Ove's wife, Anna-Maria, puts them on a rack over the open fire. Ove and I sit in silence, comfortable with one another. You find affinity, fishing.

'Sofia said you are heading for Blackåsen Mountain?' Anna-Maria says, laying plates with fish and boiled potatoes before us.

Sofia? Ah, our young guide?

'That's right,' I say.

Sooner or later, the event on Blackåsen will be known locally. But it is still not very long since it happened.

Anna-Maria pours us milk to drink. The fish smells of charcoal. Ove uses his knife to put butter on the meal, and I follow suit. Never has a fish tasted better. When Lovisa finishes eating, her plate, too, is empty.

'Blackåsen?' Ove says. He is picking his teeth with a wooden splinter.

'I am a mineralogist,' I say. 'I want to see the iron in the mountain. Lovisa is my sister-in-law.'

Lovisa picks at her cornbread with her fingers and rips a piece off.

'Anna-Maria collects stones,' Ove says.

His wife laughs, and her cheeks redden. She tries to explain it: 'There's something ancient about it. Like holding a piece of the world in your hand.'

Lovisa is giving her a sideways look.

'Which, in a way, it is,' I say. 'A stone can show so many things about the past. May I see your collection?'

She keeps her stones in a broad, flat pail. They clatter against the tin as she lifts the container out. It is clear the stones have been picked for their shape or their colour, not for their value, yet I lift them up one by one. 'This is milky quartz,' I say, and hold it to the light. 'It gets its hazy colour from tiny droplets of liquid gas trapped inside during its formation. This is flint stone, a form of quartz. Flint stone shows that here was once a sea. Isn't it amazing that a stone whose waxy surface makes it so soft to touch can be shaped to form the edge of a knife? This is granite. Its name comes from the Latin word for "grain", and looking at it you can understand why.' I hold every stone in my hand and weigh it, before putting it down again.

Anna-Maria stows her box away and disappears. Perhaps she has gone to add another sleeping place now that she knows we are not husband and wife.

Ove and I go outside to smoke. The glow of the evening sun penetrates the few clouds. The forest is dark, but down the slope the river glimmers silver. I puff at my pipe.

'Someone else travelled through on their way to Blackåsen not long ago,' Ove says. 'Someone like you.'

'A mineralogist?' I ask.

He nods.

I am sure there have been many, what with the *Gällivare-verken* deal.

'Do you remember his name?' I ask anyway.

Ove goes inside and comes back with a book. 'I always ask my visitors to write their names in my guestbook,' he says, pipe in hand. He flips the pages. 'Rune Dahlbom. About six weeks ago.'

Rune?

But I know Rune. In fact, I thought about him only the other day – he was my teacher, the one intent on destroying himself. He came to see me early in the summer at *Bergskollegium*. He didn't mention he was travelling north. He asked to see our maps of central Sweden . . .

I feel cold. We would have left him in the archives on his own.

'Has he returned on his way back south?' I ask, sounding stiff.

Ove shakes his head. 'Not yet.'

I ought to have asked more about that third victim. 'Some settler', the county governor said.

'People on Blackåsen keep to themselves,' Ove says.

'Yes?' Nothing indicates the third man might have been Rune. In fact, we'll most certainly meet him as soon as we get there, full of apologies about the 'borrowed' maps.

'They don't like strangers,' Ove stresses.

He puts the bit of his pipe back in his mouth. I have been warned.

When we come inside, Anna-Maria has returned to the kitchen. She is lifting and looking amongst the books and papers on the bookshelf.

'Something the matter?' Ove asks.

'No.' She smiles at him. 'I have misplaced my sewing scissors, that's all.'

Lovisa sits by the kitchen table, eyelids two white full moons.

L

'What a silly goose that was last night,' I say, and imitate the farmer's wife, 'Look at my stones Magnus "like holding a piece of the world in your hand".'

Magnus stares at me. 'Why would you belittle a woman who has done nothing to you but receive you in her home and offer you dinner?'

The words burst out of me, 'Because she is little! Her life is little. Her mind is narrow, her concerns, petty . . .'

Magnus shakes his head, as if in disbelief. 'And you? What do you have to offer that is so large?'

Our cart drives over a stone. We lurch and bump down hard, and my shoulder hits his.

'She loves her husband,' Magnus says in a calmer voice. 'She is a farmer's wife, she collects stones like so many people. What are you?'

He puts one hand on the cart and jumps down to walk beside it.

He and the girl talk. This and that. Magnus laughs. I close my eyes and lean back, trying not to feel sick.

The town's inn has small windows and low doorways. A single wooden bed with white linen stands on the uneven floor. The chalked stone walls seem to tilt inwards. I can't breathe. The tiny window is bolted with a lock of iron.

Out there, the sky dwarfs the wooden town. At the horizon, thick clouds have swelled into a mauve mass. The wind sweeps through the tall grass around the square. It tears the white flowers off the young tree in front of the inn and they spin through the air. The purple of the sky is approaching. Oh how I wish for a real storm. I hope the heavens will fall down on us. Tear us apart. But as I watch, the clouds pull away and the sky pales. It drizzles. Nothing more comes of it.

There's a knock on my door.

'We've been invited to the priest's house for dinner,' Magnus says.

Behind me, my room feels like a presence, pushing against my spine.

Two other priests wait in the hallway in the vicarage – one old, one young. The two greet Magnus, shake his hand, all smiles.

'Had we known you were coming this way,' the older one says, 'we could have journeyed together.'

'I didn't know it myself at the time,' Magnus says.

'We met Magnus on the steamer from Stockholm,' the older priest says to me, 'but we didn't have the good fortune to meet you. My name is Hans Rexius. This is Fredrik Wetterlund.' A gesture towards his companion.

'Lovisa Rosenblad,' I say.

'My sister-in-law,' Magnus adds.

The older priest has a jovial, round face. His cheeks are pink. The younger one has a sallow tint to his skin. His dark hair is cut off sharply and too high up at his neck. His gaze is intense.

'So what did you think of Luleå?' Magnus asks Hans Rexius.

'Much more progressive than I had expected. Unfortunately,

the bishop had already left, but we hope to catch up with him in one of the smaller towns further on. We have to hurry, though. They tell us few travel this region as well as the bishop.'

Rexius laughs. His upper body quakes and his mouth is wide open, but not a sound emerges. He stares intently at the person he's speaking with, as if to persuade him to join in.

A third priest enters. His hair is white, his shoulders hunched, his expression as he walks, pained.

'Ah,' Hans says. 'This is Axel Bring – our host.'

Bring's grey eyes probe Hans Rexius and Fredrik Wetterlund as he greets them. He is probably not much older than my father, I think, but he has not aged as well. Perhaps he is ill. Bring comes face to face with Magnus. His hand flies up to grab at his chest. He stares at Magnus, and with his other hand he reaches out. For a moment, I think he might actually touch Magnus's cheek.

What is the matter with him? Has he not seen scars before?

Nothing on Magnus's face reveals what he must feel.

'This is Magnus Stille,' Rexius sounds gentle, questioning, 'and his sister-in-law, Lovisa Rosenblad.'

Bring tries a smile and shakes Magnus's hand. 'Welcome, welcome. Please enter.' He walks to open another set of doors to a dining room, faster now, as if to make up for his paltry first acts as host.

'Rosenblad,' he says as we sit down. 'Related to Karl Rosenblad, the State Minister of Justice?'

There is a faint tremor by his chin. I refuse to meet his gaze. I have not forgotten his earlier misstep, and it is Magnus who answers: 'Lovisa is his daughter.'

'Magnus is here on his behalf,' Rexius says. 'Right, Magnus?'

A shadow passes across Magnus's face, but then he smiles. 'I am travelling to see Blackåsen Mountain.'

Oh, Bring nods.

After this, nothing. The men talk about the region: the climate, the geography. Rexius wants to know more about the Lapps.

'They are Christians,' Bring says. 'Many of the Lapps are settling, becoming farmers, rather than remaining nomads. Their children attend Swedish schools. Here in our town, twelve young Lapps board in households during the school year, and they could be any Swedish child. By all means, the Lapps want to be Swedish, but their spirits are weak.' He throws a quick glance at Magnus and at me. 'Well, it's what is said,' he says.

'How will they receive us?' Rexius asks.

'Very well. They want to hear the Scripture being read and preached.'

'Is there no resentment amongst them?' Magnus is looking at him fixedly.

'None.' Bring shakes his head. He doesn't ask why there would be.

We move to take coffee in the priest's study. Heavy purple curtains cover the window and shut the light out. I stifle a yawn. My body hurts after our journey. I don't sit down, but go to the bookshelf abounding with religious volumes, from the large leather-bound ones with gold inscriptions, to the small pamphlets of missionaries. A pen lies, together with a notebook, on a small tray of gold.

'We spent the night with Ove and Anna-Maria Edgren at Tana Rapids,' Magnus says at the table. 'They said another mineralogist passed through here not long ago: Rune Dahlbom?'

'Rune, yes,' Bring answers.

'He was going to Blackåsen?' Magnus asks.

81

'Rune originates from Blackåsen.'

'Oh? I didn't know.'

'Yes, he left to get his education – many did.'

And then, finally, we bid the priests goodnight.

Magnus and I walk in silence towards the inn. The sun, a heavy yellow ball in a light sky, leans on the forest and reddens the wooden house and the church of the town.

'Give them to me,' Magnus says outside my door. He holds out his hand.

'What?'

He doesn't answer, but his hand is still stretched out.

I put my hand in my pocket and take out the pen and the gold tray and give them to him.

B

Blackåsen, Spring 1856

Every morning, Holy Woman wakes early and begins her chores. She doesn't pray. I imagined holy men and women lived differently, but in daily life Nila could have been any one of us. Night Man walks in large circles around the others, avoiding them, until Priest's Widow catches him. After this, he spends two full days working outside the vicarage making wooden crates. Inside, Priest's Widow begins to put her things in the boxes. Every now and then, I come upon Child of Village sitting on a stone, or walking a path, humming as usual. She is no longer a child, of course, she is a grown woman in her middle age, but we never changed our name for her.

They fish. They hunt. They prepare their houses for winter.

The only one who seems to grieve is Constable's Widow. She cries into her apron, her face a puffy red. Her old father, Blind Man, sits on the steps of their house, without any words of comfort. Perhaps he has nothing good to say about his son-in-law. Perhaps he's as deaf as he is blind.

One day, the two brothers, Hunter and Long Beard, come to work on the church. They mend the shutters, they repair the stairs. I watch them from the edge of the boneyard.

I feel it before I see it: a worry in the air, the earth vibrating perhaps. And then they emerge on the dirt road: Merchant and Giant. Hunter and Long Beard stop their work. They wait as Merchant and Giant approach.

'We need to change,' Giant says, his voice like a crash of stones. 'We've discussed this so many times.'

'There is no need,' Hunter says. 'You don't like it, you can leave.'

Giant shakes his head. 'Sometimes I think you believe we will actually go away.'

'Two of yours are dead. This time the parish council needs to reflect what this village looks like,' Merchant says.

'You have a nerve,' Long Beard says. 'They are barely in the ground.'

'I didn't want them to die,' Merchant says, 'but you can't keep deciding things, just because you were born here. We who came later belong here, too.'

Long Beard points his finger at Merchant. 'If I find you had anything to do with their deaths . . .'

The four draw tighter. Any time now, a first punch and then the brawl.

'Gentlemen.'

We all turn. Holy Woman has arrived without us hearing. Her words lay themselves on top of all the others, a layer of snow. Calm down, the voice says. Calm down. 'This is not how to resolve things.'

The group loosens. Just a little bit.

'You were born here, too, Adelaide,' Merchant says.

'Two members of our community have died. People with official roles. They will be replaced. But there is a time and a place for this conversation, Jacob,' Holy Woman says to Merchant, 'and it is not here, not now. Now, we have to stand as one.'

Merchant looks grim. He narrows his eyes. 'We won't wait much longer before we take what we are owed. One way or the other.' And as he turns to leave: 'Don't assume the new council will be as lenient with you as the previous one was.'

He shoots the sentence off, aiming it at Holy Woman, then he leaves. Giant hesitates before following, feet tramping the boneyard, his back a boulder.

Hunter, Long Beard, and Holy Woman stand silent, watching them.

There are so few of them left now. The menace should feel less, but it has become the other way around. Like when you remove stones from a mountainside, the rest might come tumbling down.

I am back at my campsite before night. Tomorrow, early, I will leave for the high mountains. It is not up to me to decide what to think about all that has happened. I have to tell the *sita*. The *sita* will decide.

I fetch my bag and sit down by the fire to pack. I pick up my china cup. I guess Dávvet will be leading us. My stomach creeps.

As a child, Dávvet was earnest. A black-haired tot, he trailed Nila everywhere, watched as the older man went about his chores, trying to anticipate his every act, desperate to help. His parents let it carry on. After all, it is often how things happen if an elder has no children of his own. Nila got up earlier in the morning and left before the boy came. I remember the first time he did it, the pain in that child's eyes when he realised Nila had gone without him . . . The kind of hurt that grows self-doubt and, later, resentment.

'You could try and think of him as the son you never had,' I said.

85

I thought perhaps Nila saw some trait in Dávvet that made the child undeserving of his teaching him the old ways. But how could a child be unworthy? Perhaps Nila just didn't like him.

We never had children, me and Nila. I came to feel he kept them from me. As if it were a choice. On one occasion when we were arguing, I yelled it to his face, and both of us shrank away as if we had been slapped. Me, because my words meant I believed he had those kinds of powers and now I had angered God. And he . . .? His face scrunched up, and he avoided meeting my gaze. For a long time afterwards, I walked away when he reached out for me. We never spoke of it again.

Dusk has grown on me, and here I am still sitting, open bag by my side, cup in hand.

I'll pack tomorrow. I place the vessel back in the moss and fold my bag.

It is strange: apart from that one time, I never prompted Nila to take on Dávvet. Did I know then that we would come to abandon our old beliefs? Come to think of it, Nila never did teach anyone anything. Did he know too?

Dávvet as an older boy became the insolent sort who had roamed without a master since childhood and who needed one. He was too beautiful: blue-black hair, dark-eyed. Many of the *sita*'s girls gave him the eye. Especially one: Livli, a grown woman, already married. We saw how she wet her lips and let her hips sing. The women in our *sita* warned her, the men, Dávvet. 'You have a man,' we said to her. 'Your time will come,' they said to him. But things went the way they went: Dávvet had Livli, or perhaps Livli had Dávvet.

By then, Nila's father had long since handed power over to his son, and Nila sat as our head. Livli said they loved one another. Were we then so unyielding that we could not recognise love?

Dávvet sat cross-legged, slumped, his blue-black hair choppy on his forehead. The muscles on his arms flexed. Shame on us. He was still a child, yet I don't think there was a woman present who didn't imagine him in the act.

'It was the singing,' he whispered.

We shifted. Singing?

'A woman's voice. Tones clear as the wind.' His voice broke in a young man's way, a flash of annoyance cut over his face, and he cleared his throat. 'The song wrapped itself around me, pulled me along. I couldn't fight it.'

Livli's mouth had fallen open in a strange half-smile.

'I am sorry,' Dávvet said.

'Is this true?' we asked him.

Dávvet peeled back his leggings to show legs full of lesions where the bands of song had held him.

At this point, Livli flew at him, began to spit and tear, and had to be restrained.

Was he telling the truth?

I doubt it. But at least Dávvet showed some remorse. Livli didn't. Dávvet could still be said to be a child. And Nila hesitated. Perhaps he felt that if he had paid attention to Dávvet when he was young . . .

It was clever. In a way, Dávvet was getting back at Nila, saying: See, I have the gifts too. You should have taken me under your wing. You should have taught me.

The punishment was harsh and one-sided. Livli shrieked as we shut her out; we stood in a ring around the camp, sticks in our hands, the dogs panting by our sides. For days, she tried to approach us, and each time we set the dogs on her. Hearing her scream and plead with us, I wanted to cry. Leave, I thought. Oh please just leave.

After this, Dávvet lived a quiet life. Perhaps he dreamed of Livli's screams at night. I know I did for a long time.

June 1856

I wait at the inn until I am certain Lovisa's door will remain closed, before I return down the stairs and go out. The air is warm as I cross the square towards the vicarage. *Come and see me*, in unsteady handwriting; that is what it said, the note the priest Axel Bring pushed into my hand when we said goodbye.

The door opens before I manage to knock. Bring stands in the hallway. We return to the study where the coffee has been cleared from the table.

'So Karl Rosenblad sent you here,' Bring says as we sit down. He tucks his cassock in around his thin knees with an unconscious gesture.

I nod.

The slits of his eyes get thinner. 'I know Karl. I know him well. If he sent you here, it is for a reason.'

I hesitate. 'Three men were killed recently on Blackåsen by a Lapp. The county governor wants it kept quiet.'

Bring gasps. 'Who died?'

'The priest, the constable, and a third man.'

'But I know these people.' His voice is choked. 'The third man . . .?'

I shake my head: I don't know.

Bring mumbles: 'What has the world come to . . .? And the perpetrator was a Lapp? I find that hard to believe.'

'Why?' I ask.

'This will have consequences – for them as a people. The Lapps are mindful of this. Unless liquor was involved.' He hesitates. 'Have you . . . come across Lapps, Magnus?'

There are no Lapps in Stockholm. 'No.'

He exhales. It sounds like laughter. He shakes his head, then leans his forehead against the bony knuckles of his hand.

'They don't know who the Lapp is,' I say, 'and he refuses to talk.'

'Gunnar Cronstedt should have brought him here. I might have known,' Bring says, looking at me, as if it was my decision.

'Tell me about the victims,' I ask.

'The priest and the constable grew up on Blackåsen. They returned there after their studies.'

'He was lucky,' I say, 'the priest. They don't normally get to choose where they are sent.'

'Oh, it was more than luck. The village didn't have a church before he arrived. He, Ulf, built it. He came to see me first, said he hoped I wouldn't mind, and, of course, I didn't. Anything that lightens the burden . . .'

'And the constable?'

'Jan-Erik. He wasn't an easy man.' Bring exhales and looks up at the ceiling. 'No, it was worse than that; he was not a good man. He sought advantages, and used them. But it was well known, and people knew to avoid him.'

'How big is Blackåsen village?' I ask.

'Eight to nine households. The village used to be larger, but now a lot of the houses stand empty.'

'Do they mine the iron in the mountain?'

'Perhaps for personal use.'

'Can you think of anyone with a reason to do this?'

'No one.'

Somewhere in the vicarage, a clock chimes. I count to eleven.

'Karl and I go back a long time,' Bring says. 'Too long. We were students at the same time in Uppsala. Why did he send you, Magnus?'

For some reason, I don't like his question. I shrug. 'He wanted his interest in the matter to pass unnoticed.'

'It still doesn't explain why he sent you,' Bring says, mildly now. 'Karl always has an underlying reason for everything he does.'

I don't respond.

I am hoping to find a moment to return the gold tray and pen to their place in the bookshelf without him noticing, but he never leaves the room. So instead, before going back to the inn, I simply hand them to him.

Without a word, he returns them to the bookshelf. He looks at me and shrugs as if to say, 'women'.

The light is growing. It is morning. I am tired. I haven't slept. The sun shone the whole night and my window had no blind. I found myself getting up to look outside again and again – each time feeling more peculiar. Not that the lack of sleep matters. We have nothing to do today but walk.

According to this morning's astronomical observations, our position is latitude 65° 41' N; longitude 20° 38' E. Our elevation above sea level is about 358 feet. I wonder if we'll reach Blackåsen today.

Bring said it was normal practice to send the nearest cleric to care for the parishioners in the case of the demise of a priest. 'Demise'. He himself grimaced at the word. 'I guess eventually the bishop or the county governor will make contact,' he said.

I knock on Lovisa's door. As I hand her the walking boots I bought her in Luleå, she lets out a laughter that twirls loud in the stairs. 'No thank you,' she says, eyes flashing.

I consider abandoning the shoes there in the hallway and then remind her of them later. But that would be unfair. She has no idea what she's up against. I put them in my bag.

As we leave the town, she walks ahead of me on the green. She strolls like a girl out on a pleasure trip; hips swinging, hands reaching for this tall grass and that flower. For a moment, I think I hear her sing. If I didn't know anything about her, I'd say she looked happy.

L

Every breath I take restores me; fresh blood pumps inside my body, my veins expand, at first shocked, then grateful. All is changing. I am made new. My body bubbles with life. The spread of the sky is enormous. Above us, a white cotton ball of a cloud has shaped itself into a lizard straddling two stones. The lizard mutates and becomes a lamb. Two ears, the eyes . . .

I have slept like I have never slept before. This is what the body can feel like after proper sleep!

I want to talk – even Magnus would do. 'Look at nature around us,' I want to say. 'How amazing it is.' And: 'See those colours!' We walk amongst birch trees, the landscape humming and buzzing. I glance at him and remember the pen and the tray. I feel a sting inside, but shake it off.

Eva would love this.

My stomach hardens to a knot. What do I know about what Eva would or wouldn't love?

Our path takes us uphill, and after a while I am puffing. Far beneath us, the township lies buried in the field. The incline continues. The sluggish movement has distorted the clouds into mere blobs of white fluff.

The dark fir trees have taken over and the path is no more. We no longer walk uphill, but through a flat, dull hell. The woodland doesn't want us here; we have to break into this forest every step of the way – walking, climbing, even jumping, vegetation slashing at ankles and wrists. We have crossed several bogs. Wooden planks have been put out on them, like foot bridges, but the boards are slippery. I have fallen twice, and my dress is destroyed, mud all along one side, and a rip across one knee. The last time, Magnus had to pull me up. My shoes have gnawed my feet raw. But I won't complain. I won't say a word. I can imagine his scorn.

The air quivers with heat. If only I had a fan. My sister has a beautiful hand-painted one with a mother-of-pearl handle inlaid with gold. Isabella twirls it, lets it rest on her cheek, hits her open hand with it, opens it, shuts it, lets it speak for her instead of words – the fan a whole language. Magnus probably bought it for her. Men buy things like that for their women. Whereas I get books; it's as if I'll never be considered grown up. I usually make the giver feel there is something wrong with their choice. 'Ah,' I'll say and turn it around in my hands, or flip through the pages. Why would I do that? What meaningless cruelty.

Magnus studies his map as he walks, the unblemished side of his face turned towards me. The knot of hair at the back of his head is coming undone, and a brown lock twirls down his neck. The curl bobs and swings.

The muscles in my legs scream. I am sweaty and have a wet patch between my breasts, and another one between my legs. My ribcage aches with each breath, my lungs feel inflamed. Better not think. I shall take one step and then another.

Magnus doesn't have any problems. Those long legs stride over fallen logs and through bushes. Every so often, he stops to look at the ground or at stones. He puts some of them in his backpack. I can't imagine how heavy it must be.

We pause to drink water, but I have come to dread these breaks, as after them I have to force my stiff, unwilling legs to move again.

Late afternoon, after climbing a mountain, we finally have a view. Ha! A view of nothing. Just trees, trees, and more trees.

Magnus takes off his backpack and puts it on the ground. 'I had hoped we'd make it to the river, but I don't think we will today. Let's set up camp here on this hill.'

'Hill?' I repeat. My voice sounds tart.

Magnus lifts out the walking boots he offered me this morning; ugly coarse things. He places them beside his bag.

I sink down on a rock, my thighs trembling. My lower back feels as if it might be broken. My arms are covered with scratches. If tomorrow is going to be the same, I'd rather die today.

Magnus searches the area until he finds two large wooden sticks, which he drives into the ground. He takes a sheet of canvas from his rucksack, and a rope, and stretches the fabric between the poles supported by the string. I scoff. If he thinks I'll sleep on the ground, he's mistaken. Though it surprises me he knows how to build a shelter. In fact, he seems more natural here than I have ever seen him. Usually, he has this cold expression on his face. I've always thought of him as an observer rather than a partaker, but now his eyes are clear. He looks . . . present.

He collects wood, hunkers down, and lights a fire.

I adjust my position and my legs scream – absolutely scream – with pain. There is a flare in my stomach, red, hot.

'This is absurd,' I mutter.

Magnus is sharpening sticks with a knife.

'I should have stayed in Luleå,' I say.

That's what I should have done. Cool and clean in a nice room at the inn. What happened in the guesthouse feels long ago, the threat of the madhouse has faded. Though I have to remember this is how it is with me. I misbehave, face repercussions, but something or someone saves me, time after time. I promise myself I'll never put myself at risk again, then soon, the event dulls in my mind, the menace feels unreal, and once more the pain takes over. I need to remind myself of what can happen to women like me. What *does* happen to women like me.

Magnus smiles; a motion, not a real smile. He has brought chunks of meat in his knapsack and threads them, setting the sticks up so they lean over the fire. 'As if you had a choice.'

My chest tightens. He's a man. He can choose what to do, when, and with whom, without suffering ill will and small-mindedness. I can't.

'If you only knew what it is to be a woman,' I say.

Fat sizzles in the fire and smells salty.

'There are worse struggles than that one.'

His voice is light, as if he speaks of issues of no importance. What struggles is he referring to then? Professional efforts? The spats of high society?

'You don't know what it is to have no freedom.' My voice has risen. 'My father . . .'

He throws his knife to the ground. 'In the name of God! Freedom!'

My breath has caught in my chest. Magnus is staring at me.

He exhales, picks his knife up, wipes it off against his thigh, and sticks it in its sheath. 'Your father has given you everything. You've never had to crave food or a place to lay your head.

The "freedom" you talk of is an indulgence that you are able to desire simply because you have been given everything else.'

The blood in my veins stills as quickly as it rose and, instead, I am dead, my limbs numb.

'It is what I feel,' I say.

'If you at least had a cause, I could respect that. But your only occupation is yourself.'

The words smart.

'Nobody owes you anything, Lovisa. If you desire freedom, you must earn it.'

He hands me one of the sticks. I want to throw it at the ground and say, 'You can keep your food.' But I am hungry and he won't care either way.

Far out over the valley, a bird of prey soars high. The bird fights the wind until it stalls. It waits. Then, when it is about to topple, it bats its wings, once, twice, and then folds and floats with the current. The sight fills me with an ache that overwhelms me. I wish, but I have no idea what for. A person who knew birds would surely feel obliged to tell me 'it's hunting', or tell me the name of the species. And I wouldn't want to know. I only want to see the beauty in the flight – up once more, battle the wind – hold it, hold it, give in and float.

Magnus picks up the remnants of our food and the sticks. 'I'll get rid of it, because of the bears.' He walks away.

Bears? A sudden gust of wind disturbs the crowns of the pine trees. They rustle and fall silent. I stare in amongst their trunks, reddened by the sunlight. This is silence. This is . . . nothingness.

The sun stands lower. A lake and two rivers gleam in the valley beneath, like debris from a broken mirror.

I stand up, hesitate, then grab the walking boots. I walk to crawl inside the makeshift tent. At first I sit, monitoring the forest, but my back hurts, and I lie down.

'If you at least had a cause.' He is right. There is no substance to me, and I *have* been given everything.

I met one of those women once; one with a cause, a well-known radical writer. She came to one of my parents' parties. She wore a black dress with straight lines and a white lace bonnet; a black crow amongst the vibrant parrots. I studied her large nose, her tilted dog eyes. She kept her hair in a dull style that elongated further her long face. Did she feel she had to be ugly, to be masculine, to make her point? Didn't that mean that already, she could never win? There she was, alone in the tremendous chatter and mingling of colourful birds; unspoken to by the men, avoided by the women. She caught my glance, and for a while our eyes locked.

When my father asked me later whether I had spoken to the author, I understood she had been invited for my sake.

'She was rude,' I said and enjoyed the brief shadow of hurt or perhaps anger crossing his face. 'Unappreciative of the party, of other guests.'

The more I thought about it, the more it felt as if we had spoken. In fact, I was certain of it. And that look on her face – it could have been disdain.

The woman was never again invited to our house.

Now I wonder why my father asked her. Would he too prefer it if I had a cause?

I listen for Magnus. I try to quieten my breaths, but my heart begins to beat faster from the effort, not slower. My fingers lie clasped on my chest so hard, my hands have distorted. Has he left me here? Finally, I hear footsteps. I turn. Magnus sits down by the fire. He lifts a large metal triangle with bolts and tubes out of his bag and holds it to his eye. He looks in it for a long time, occasionally writing in his book.

I will never be able to sleep with him out there. There is no door to close. He shouldn't see me sleep. God forbid I have to attend to some matter of privacy? Will he watch as I walk into the forest? I shudder. He should have told me that we'd have to spend the night outside.

Magnus puts the triangle in his bag. He clears his throat, rises, and comes towards the shelter. Why . . .?

He creeps in beside me and lies down.

I can't breathe. I am lying beside a man, my sister's husband. It's wholly inappropriate. I'll never be able to sleep. I need to say something—

I sit up, heart pounding. Someone was standing right there, at the edge of the forest, tall and thin as the tree trunks. His body grew and revolved with the wind.

A dream. Oh God. Nothing but a dream.

On the other side of the tent, Magnus lies with his arm thrown over his face. He breathes deep and slow. Night. A night with daylight. Day with a tinge of night.

There you are.

PART TWO

PART TWO

I can see it now, Blackåsen Mountain, its body tinted a beautiful golden-red hue by the sun. It is an old mountain, its shape round. From here, its forest makes it look nothing but a large hillock. The ground in the valley has proven wet. It's covered with long, tufty grass, and the few spruce trees stand black and withered. We pass numerous waterholes surrounded by birch and the occasional mountain ash, their dark water adding to the sombre impression. So far, no trace of habitation. We spent the night at latitude 65° 49' N.; longitude 20° 31' E., our elevation above sea level about 195 feet. I was worried about not being able to use my compass, but the sky has been clear, the stars visible, and astronomical readings relatively easy. I have to force myself not to keep stopping and drawing everything I see. It would take too much time and we need to reach Blackåsen whilst we have food, whilst Lovisa can still walk. She's wearing the boots now – of course without acknowledging it – but the damage to her feet is already done and she is limping.

I hear water. We emerge on a riverbank, composed of strata of sand and clay. The waterway itself must be over twenty feet broad. It doesn't look deep, but sweeps away any fallen branches quickly enough.

'There might be a crossing further upstream,' I say, and we follow the riverside until the waterway widens into a shallow green ribbon of a lake. Boulders on both shores extend out into it – we will be able to walk them like a path. In spring-time, with the masses of water from the melting snow in the mountains, these stones would disappear and the river would become a natural boundary to anything north of it. In remote places like this, people can be shut off for weeks. 'Time of waste', they call it.

I walk out on the stones, placing one foot on the dry surface of one, then the next. Through the clear water that coils between the boulders, I can see the pebbly river bed.

As I reach the other side, at a large gap between the stones, I turn and stretch my hand out towards Lovisa. She pretends not to notice, so I walk on and hear her slip and step into the water. Over my shoulder, I see her grimacing and lifting up her wet skirts. I blow the air out between my teeth, a slow, steady stream. I won't let her get to me.

The ground is drier on the other side, the beach meagre and stony. The trees are taller. The underlying rock must be different. The crowns of the pine trees are dense, and beneath them the air feels cool. I lengthen my steps. I feel I know this terrain. Though my whole childhood was spent in Stockholm, I feel comfortable with nature. I realised to what extent on my first field trip during my training in mineralogy. The students walked a boulder ridge in the forests of Bergslagen, large, round stones, and my feet knew how to place themselves. They knew which rocks would be loose and which ones could be walked on, my eyes scanning both the ground beneath me and ahead, finding the best way forward. 'Magnus the path-finder,' my fellow students joked.

I lean forward, the weight of my rucksack on my back. Behind me, Lovisa sighs. I do not ask her why. The girl has a lot to sigh about.

*

Hours later, not far up the side of Blackåsen Mountain, the trees separate; then, in between their trunks, I glimpse a silver wooden wall, a settlement. We walk out into a yard surrounded by grey timber houses with peat roofs, built of material from the surrounding forest, several of them adorned with white horns. Deer? On an empty barn, the doors gape open wide.

'Hello?'

There is no response to my call. On the other side of the settlement is a dirt road broad enough to take a horse with carriage. As we reach it, we both stop. Lovisa bends down, hands on knees, and exhales. I stretch. The dirt road meanders downhill. The sun dazzles from a cloudless sky. It is hot; a dry heat, and I don't sweat. I bake. We pass another homestead – the same houses. It, too, lies silent. The third one, likewise. Each settlement is surrounded by forest. It gives no impression of being a part of a whole. By God, the isolation! You could live in this village and feel completely lonely. If they had built their community higher up, they would have had more light and a view. But perhaps in wintertime, the mountain provides protection against the elements? Or perhaps, they didn't decide. It was only the way things happened.

At the fourth settlement, in between the trees, there is a movement, a branch snapping. In the silence, it is as loud as an explosion. Lovisa gasps, her eyes round in fear.

Was that a person? Running?

It occurs to me that the people here now have a reason to be afraid of strangers. The villagers who died supposedly did so by the hand of someone they didn't know. When I begin to walk again, I scan the sides of the road.

We arrive at a big, red wooden house. A hand-painted sign reads '*Allehanda*'. Sundries.

'The owners will know where we can stay,' I say.

I open the door and a bell chimes. A man stands behind a counter, rifle aimed at me.

I raise my hands as Lovisa bumps into my back. The man sees her and lifts his balding head, but keeps the weapon high. His round face would be jovial if it weren't for its expression, eyes narrow, mouth grim.

'My name is Magnus Stille,' I say. 'I am an administrator from *Bergskollegium* in Stockholm. I am travelling with my sister-in-law, Lovisa Rosenblad.'

The man doesn't move.

'I am here to map your mountain. We need a place to stay for a few nights.'

'Did the parish council send for you?'

'No,' I say.

'Really?'

I shake my head. 'No?'

He stares at us, firearm still lifted. 'Visitors stay at the vicarage,' he says at last. Then his forehead wrinkles, he drops the rifle, and his face goes slack. 'Though perhaps not.'

No. Not now. For the village no longer has a vicar.

'Wait here.' He disappears into the back.

'What a welcome,' Lovisa mutters. She sinks down on a wooden box and grimaces. It isn't much of a shop. The shelves are largely empty apart from tin cases with coffee, boxes of cigars, a container with 'salt' written upon it. A harmonica, some tools. The view from the shop window is over the empty road, at the wall of spruce on the other side of it.

The man comes back. 'My wife and I have two spare rooms upstairs.'

A short woman with dark brown hair tied in a coarse bun joins him, but stops in the doorway. One hand kneads the chubby fingers of the other.

'I don't know if this is the right thing to do,' she says. 'We didn't discuss it.' Her voice has a whining pitch to it.

Her husband searches in a drawer in the counter, hand rummaging.

'My name is Magnus Stille,' I say, as if that might reassure her.

'Helena Palm,' she replies, without looking at me.

'Jacob Palm,' her husband says, mechanically, as if his name always follows hers. He finds what he's looking for. 'Here's the lock.' He looks at his wife. 'Perhaps I should put it on the door . . .'

'I don't know if this is the right thing,' his wife says again.

'It hardly matters now,' her husband says.

Jacob and Helena Palm's house has three bedrooms, wall to wall on the first floor. They give me the room to the right, Lovisa the one to the left. The middle door is closed. It must be where they sleep, the grocer and his wife.

Lovisa turns and looks in all directions. 'I think I'll have a rest,' she says, her voice both resigned and haughty, long-suffering.

Mrs Palm glances at her husband. This is the kind of house where a person always works, the kind of village where people always work. They make their own food, their own clothes, they labour from early morning to night. Lying down in the daytime is most certainly unheard of.

We don't speak any more. Mr and Mrs Palm disappear down below. Lovisa closes the door to her room.

I sit on my bed, feeling the rough hay underneath the woollen bed cover. I, too, should rest, though it would be frowned upon; I haven't slept well for three nights now. But my body is not complaining and my mind feels clear – if anything, too clear – glassy.

The bell rings in the shop. Mrs Palm's high-pitched voice cuts through the floorboards, before turning into a mumble. Maybe she is telling the customer about us. *From Stockholm*, I imagine her whispering, then repeating, 'I am not certain we've done the right thing.' But it is good if people in the village know who we are so there are no surprises.

The mountain tugs at me, but it's too late in the day to start proper work. Besides, asking questions about the murders needs to be my first priority. My only priority. I will, however, go for a walk.

Outside Lovisa's door I hesitate, but I won't be gone long.

I descend the staircase. The door to the shop is slightly open. The grocer and his wife are in the front room, stacking shelves. They haven't yet noticed me. There are no customers with them.

'It's good they are staying with us,' Mr Palm says. 'It's a protection of sorts.'

Mrs Palm doesn't respond.

I take a few quiet steps backwards and then advance again, making certain to walk heavily now.

I open the door and they both look at me.

Protection against what?

I walk westwards, lengthening my steps, feeling the muscles stretch in my legs. I reflect again on the village's position: carved into the low mountainside, surrounded by spruce, and without any tall buildings. Viewed from beneath, there's no telling the hamlet is here. From here, there's no telling there is any other civilisation. Blackåsen is a world of its own.

Further along the dirt road, in an opening in the forest on a grassy slope lies a red timber church, octagon-shaped, with a hipped grey roof. The tall windows consist of small panes, their wooden frames painted white. In most towns and villages, the church towers over the other houses. Not here. A detached timber bell tower stands beside the building. There are headstones and crosses behind the church – a graveyard, and surrounding it all, a short stone wall. The meadow hums with bees and insects. Behind the wall lies a grey wooden house, surrounded by a large garden. Further away, in a small field, barley is growing. Then I notice them, in the graveyard, three mounds of earth not yet covered with grass. Nothing more than temporary swellings on a surface. That is what they have been reduced to, the men who died. That is what we'll all be reduced to.

The village road ends with the church. Instead a tiny path leads in amongst the trees. I follow it for quite a while before arriving at an open area, a swamp full with brown water, a red tone in places. Then the marsh, too, contains iron. Bog ore. It won't be much, enough for them to make their tools perhaps. Close to the shore, the reeds reach as high as my stomach and smell of rot. The marshland lies at the foot of the mountain. I suppose it gets the snowmelt.

My mind is ticking. If this is being exhausted, I don't mind. I feel as if I could go on for ever. I feel alive and sharper than usual.

I turn and walk back past the entrance to the village and towards the other side of the mountain. I remember from the map the man in Luleå gave me that there's a river and a lake. I emerge on a ledge above the rapids. The shores on both sides of the fast-moving water are steep and densely forested. The south flank on which I stand is made out of a vertical black rock wall. Later, I will have to get down by the water. That is where I'll begin mapping. To the east lies a large mountain lake. It reflects the sun with a light that surpasses the original.

*

'So you are travelling together with your brother-in-law,' Helena Palm says to Lovisa at dinner. The first time she said it, Lovisa didn't hear. The second time, she raised her eyebrows. Now, her brows paint a low, thick line above her eyes.

I put my cutlery down.

'I am being punished by my father,' Lovisa says. 'Magnus was told to bring me with him and teach me sense.'

I want to sigh. She exposes herself. But at least now people won't wonder why we are travelling together.

Mrs Palm licks her lips and leans forward. The doorbell tinkles in the shop. Mrs Palm glances towards the door, then at her husband. 'Hello?' someone calls.

Mrs Palm sighs and walks out. 'Good evening,' she says, chirpily.

'Is it working?' Mr Palm has stopped eating.

Lovisa frowns. 'What?'

'Teaching you sense?'

I have to stifle a laugh. Lovisa's mouth twitches.

We sit in the dining room on the ground floor eating char, a local river fish, and potatoes. One door leads to the shop, the other to the kitchen. Further away, the dining room turns into a drawing room. I wipe my forehead. The windows are open, but it doesn't seem to make any difference.

'Is it always this hot here?'

'Sometimes June is hot, sometimes it isn't.' Mr Palm leans back and lays one arm over the back of his chair, his upper body twisted.

'Are you from here?' I ask.

Mr Palm shakes his head. 'I met a man from Blackåsen at a market down south who told me the village had no grocer. We came ten years ago. Of course, it's not profitable. But now we are invested.'

He has told us they have six cows and a horse. They have money, but it is clear their wealth does not come from the shop. What or who do they need protection from? I wonder again. And why would our presence give it to them?

'*Bergskollegium*?' Mr Palm says. 'I thought you weren't interested in the iron?'

'It's hard to mine now, but that won't always be the case.'

'Is it really a coincidence you are here?'

'What do you mean?'

Jacob Palm presses his lips together, as if reflecting. 'This is not a good time to visit. Even for a man from *Bergskollegium*.'

I hadn't planned to tell the villagers why I had come, but I can see it will be impossible to ask questions without people realising.

'That is one reason why I am here,' I concede. 'Blackåsen is important. I want to understand what happened.'

Lovisa plays with her spoon, balances it over a finger and presses with the thumb to make it dip up and down.

Jacob nods, then sighs. 'We don't know. They held their usual parish meeting, we heard screams. They were found dead and the Lapp was sitting on the floor. He didn't leave the bodies until they came from the coast to take him away.'

'I heard your priest and your constable were amongst those killed. But there was also a third man?'

'His name was Rune Dahlbom. He was visiting.' Jacob shrugs.

Rune. It's all I can do not to gasp out loud. But how . . . Why? Lovisa has stopped playing with her spoon and her eyes are fixed on me. I clear my throat. 'Was he visiting family?' My voice sounds shaky.

'He said all his relatives were long gone. He was an old friend of the priest and the constable, and he was staying in the vicarage. He came a couple of weeks before it happened. The three of them spent all their time together . . . Adelaide too.'

'The priest's wife?'

'No, Adelaide Gustavsdotter is another one of those who were born here.'

Rune is dead. I still can't believe it. 'Who is the Lapp?'

'I have no idea. He isn't part of the tribe that comes here every winter.'

'Winter?' My heart sinks. 'I had hoped to speak with them.'

Jacob shakes his head. 'They'll be on their way to the high mountains now.'

I want to sigh out loud. Lapps are nomads, yet it hadn't occurred to me they might not be here.

'Don't you find that odd?' I ask. 'That a stranger would commit such a deed?'

'Insane?'

'You don't think this is the start of some Lapp uprising?'

'That never even occurred to me.' Jacob changes position and his chair creaks. 'One thing is odd, though – that, at this very time, one of the Lapps from the tribe we do know has chosen to stay behind here with us through the summer: Ester.' Jacob's forehead is wrinkled. 'That's never happened before.'

My father taught me that everything was connected: humans, animals and nature; the living and the dead. 'In the underworld, the dead live lives matching ours. If you walk barefoot, you can sometimes feel the soles of their feet against yours.'

I took off my shoes, but felt only the rasping of blueberry sprigs. 'It's a skill,' he said. 'I will teach you.'

Now I am dead. My hands are tied. I need someone to see and hear me. My people are far. My woman has shut her ears. This village has bolted its doors.

You are open like a mountain rift. Many would step straight in, but I won't. I will talk and hope you listen.

I watch you sleeping, your strange black wisps of hair on the pillow. I can't help but sigh. I fear you won't understand what I am about to tell you, and we don't have much time. I don't even know if you'll hear.

My name is Nila.

You stir in your sleep.

My name is Nila and I need you to hear my story. Can you hear me?

ℒ

A bird perches on the windowsill, pecking on the ledge. It has black feathers and a colourful red stripe on its side. I lie for a while and watch its bobbing head, its slick skull. My bed linen smells of grass and sunshine. Morning light streams in through the window, a soft, yellow, burgeoning glow.

When I walk downstairs, every step makes the wood creak. The kitchen is empty, the dishes from last night have been stowed away. Breakfast plates and cutlery lie on the woven tablecloth. The wall clock shows ten past five.

I sit down on the steps in front of the shop. The spruce trees on the other side of the road stretch tall, their lower, heavier branches sweeping the earth. The silence is absolute. It's as if I have covered my ears with my hands. Even the birds' twittering sounds weak. The green around me shimmers: dew on grass, droplets in spider webs. It smells of wet mud, but the earth is packed hard.

'Lovisa?'

A muted voice from inside, rapid footsteps on the stairs, then the door opens and Magnus stands there, hair ruffled.

'I don't want you going out without me.' He has buttoned his shirt wrongly; one of its flaps hangs lower than the other.

He stares at me, eyes remarkably blue. You don't have to

worry about me, I think . . . And then I understand, and my chest tightens. I had begun to think we wouldn't have to speak about what happened back in Luleå and later, or about our fight, but I was wrong. Things always have to be said out loud. People have to dwell on things, take them apart, talk them asunder, bestow guilt. Magnus, like everybody else.

I rub my nose. All this greenery, I want to say. It makes my nose itch, my eyes water.

'I need coffee.' Magnus closes the door.

Heat twirls in the pit of my stomach. A bird with a black skull. I look towards the mud road. Then I take it.

The village sleeps. I walk fast, glance back over my shoulder, have a vision of Magnus hurrying after me with long steps, face distorted. He doesn't control me. I step over a pothole. I should never have come. I could have stayed in Luleå. It's the way men speak, the depth, the certainty; you can get caught and think they know better – it is right that they decide. I catch a flashing image of my father, or perhaps my mother, and I squint.

The red church lies basking in the morning light on tall golden grass. Its hipped roof looks like a hat, a bonnet, from underneath which it stares at me through white-rimmed windows. Behind it lies the vicarage, the timber walls pale silver. I glance back down the road. No Magnus. My heartbeat slows. I am not afraid of him. If he comes I will argue my case. I shall tell him that this is where our paths part, I will set him free from the pledge my father has forced him to make on my behalf. I'll be calm, strong and mature.

The road ends. A trail, reddish with fallen needles, leads into the pine forest. It divides into three and I take the middle path, the one leading up the mountain.

The trees are immense, higher than any building in Stockholm. Perhaps they are a hundred years old. The morning sunshine falls in between the branches and paints paths of light in the air. I inhale the strength of the landscape. The city park in Stockholm that Eva and I used for our walks, with its gravelled paths and shaped trees, now seems a poor imitation of nature. The thought of Eva stings. I won't think about her. Not now.

I don't know for how long I have walked when I come to an opening in the forest, halfway up the mountain, above the spruce tops. The glade abounds with stones that are hard to walk over, but a large grey rock lies at its edge and I lean against its side. Beneath me, the woodland undulates in bottle-green waves. Further away, at the horizon, chains of blue mountains stitch the earth to the sky.

I imagine Magnus out looking for me, angry, asking questions, as if I were a child who has gone missing. When I meet him I'll be calm. Surely, Magnus, you can see this is doing neither of us any good?

As from now, he doesn't get to tell me what to do. And I will refuse to share with him what I do, where, or with whom. If he protests, or tries to detain me in any way, I shall argue that, between us, there is no real family bond, no friendship, nothing but my father's demand. As far as I know, there is no letter spelling out Magnus's rights over me, and thus, effectively, he has none.

The village is hiding deep down there amongst the trees. I push myself off the boulder, turn, and climb it, digging my fingers and the toes of my shoes into crevices.

Now, should Magnus wish to send a message to my father asking for such a letter, he will have to travel back to Luleå, and he cannot force me to go with him.

Even standing up on the rock, I find the settlement remains concealed. I look down on the stone field. Such a peculiar . . .

The rocks in the glade form long rows with a path in between. Together, it becomes a shape, a heart, perhaps . . .

A maze! It's a maze. Oh, how amusing . . .

I shuffle on my bottom down the boulder.

Where is the entrance?

There, at one end of the glade. The field is awkward. The boulders are not large enough to walk on, the path between them, narrow. I have to place my feet sideways as I step over stones.

The entrance, too, is small. Perhaps this maze was made by children. I take a first step into the labyrinth, balancing with my arms stretched wide, then a second.

Behind me, the sound of a stone hitting other stones. I swirl around and lose my balance.

Oh.

Pain shoots through my hip as it hits the rocks on the ground.

Slowly, I get up and touch my hip and my thigh to feel the damage. The palm of my hand is scraped red.

Someone is watching me. I don't see anyone, but I am certain I am not alone. My heartbeats are loud in my ears. Don't let them see you are frightened, I think, uncertain as to whom 'they' might be. I straighten my dress, smooth it down, and then walk towards the edge of the clearing, my back erect. I glance over my shoulder once, twice. The glade remains empty. Yet I walk quickly back towards the village as, with every step I take, I am expecting someone to touch my shoulder.

★

Mrs Palm, the grocer's wife, measures sugar, pours it into paper bags, then ties a piece of string around each one and places them to one side of the counter.

'Good morning,' she says. 'So you, too, are an early riser?'

The road outside lies still. My hip pulsates. Without bending, I stretch one hand down and nip at my skirt to shake off some dust. 'Where is Magnus?'

'He left. Said he wouldn't be back until dinnertime.'

The bird with the black skull returns to peck in my chest. I had expected him to search for me.

The doorbell rings and a blonde girl in a yellow dress enters. She turns to close the door behind her. Poking from her sleeves, her arms look like sticks. The lace around her neck appears frayed.

'Good morning, Sigrid,' Mrs Palm says. 'What a surprise.'

All of a sudden, her voice has assumed a mean tone. Her hands rest on her hips.

The girl turns, and I realise she is not young, but a woman, older than me, probably Magnus's age. She, Sigrid, doesn't seem to notice Mrs Palm's manner. Her face is battered with a violent profusion of freckles, and her large eyes shine a translucent grey, with a darker ring at the edge of the iris. I turn and pick up a box of cigars from one of the shelves.

'Yes?' Mrs Palm says.

'I need salt,' Sigrid says.

Mrs Palm hesitates. 'I'll get smaller bags then,' she says, mouth no larger than a coin. 'One minute.' She disappears into the back.

The doorbell rings again. This time, it's a woman with brown hair that reaches far down her back. Her colouring is vivid; blue eyes, red lips, and white skin, with a nose too large for her fine face, a mouth too wide, wrinkles that form an X between straight eyebrows.

'What are you doing?' the new woman asks Sigrid.

'I am getting salt,' Sigrid says. There's something final about how she says it, as if she's expecting to have to defend herself. She's still looking at me. The dark-haired woman follows her gaze.

'What is your name?' Sigrid asks me.

'Lovisa.'

The woman nods several times. 'Lovisa,' she repeats.

Mrs Palm comes back. 'Sigrid and now Adelaide. What a surprise indeed.' Her mouth twists.

So this might be Adelaide Gustavsdotter of whom Mr Palm spoke; friend of the deceased. Adelaide purses her lips.

'Salt, you said? How much would you like?' Mrs Palm lifts the salt bucket up onto the counter and removes the lid, exaggerating each movement. She takes out a small bag and a spoon.

'Oh, just a little,' Sigrid says.

Mrs Palm waits, spoon hovering above the white salt.

'Give her two spoons,' Adelaide says.

Mrs Palm measures the spoons, stroking off the surplus with her fat finger.

'I assume I'll put this on credit, as usual?'

Adelaide takes the bag from Mrs Palm. 'I'll pay for it.'

She hands the bag to Sigrid, who seems oblivious to both Mrs Palm's rudeness and Adelaide's response. Adelaide digs out two coins and throws them on the counter. She places her hand on Sigrid's shoulder and guides her towards the door. In the doorway, Sigrid turns around. 'Come and visit us, Lovisa.'

Adelaide pushes at her to leave, but Sigrid stands her ground. 'Come and visit us soon.'

Mrs Palm mutters as the door closes. She throws the lid on the salt pail and puts it back on the floor.

My face twists. I look through the window at the empty road in front of the house. 'Who was that?'

Mrs Palm scoffs. 'Sigrid Rudin. Her mother, Susanna, died when Sigrid was little. She did away with herself. In fact, this' – she makes a sweeping gesture – 'used to be their family's house, but when Susanna died, Sigrid moved in with Adelaide. They all stick together, the ones who were born here. Ever since her mother's death, Sigrid hasn't been quite right in the head. Sometimes she falls down, gets the shakes.' Mrs Palm trembles and makes her eyes bulge, to demonstrate. 'They say she has visions, not that I've seen any proof of that.'

'I meant the other one,' I say, and enjoy Mrs Palm being wrong. 'Adelaide.'

The name has got a peculiar ring to it when you pronounce it. Like the name of a dance.

'Ah.' The grocer's wife pushes things around on the counter. 'Adelaide Gustavsdotter is the leader of a religious group here. Separatists.'

Mrs Palm takes the flour sacks and pushes them onto a shelf. She lifts the salt container and carries it out into the storage room. Inside, she mutters, moves things around. Then the shop falls silent. The sun shines in through the window and onto the wooden counter with its broad, grey boards.

The coins lie grubby against the wood. I pick them up and put them in my pocket.

I go back to my room and sit down on my bed. I should open my window to get some air into the room, but standing up again feels an impossible act. I wonder what Magnus will do when he comes back. Whatever energy I had, whatever resolution, it is now gone.

Part company? What nonsense.

I don't even have any money.

B

I didn't leave. It was all that thinking about Dávvet that put me off. I don't yet understand what I have seen and I don't want Dávvet to decide the meaning for me. For Dávvet was close to them, in particular to Priest.

I stand up and take my satchel and my knife. Every night I have heard a *rievsak* squawk, trying to impress some hen. A few days ago, I set two traps. Last night, there were no bird calls. The image of the bird's tender meat makes my mouth water.

Yes, attending Blackåsen's new church we all changed, but Dávvet changed the most. His skin became clear. There was a new light in his eyes. I saw how he washed before sermon, how he put on his finest clothes. I saw how deeply he bent his head. He had finally found his master.

One night, at the fire, he said: 'We must be whiter than the snow. Look at me, see what can happen when you let sin enter.'

I wondered whether this meant he admitted to telling lies that time with Livli.

But above all, we rejoiced in his change. We felt he was finding himself, becoming who he was supposed to have been all along.

Then one day, not long after Nila and Priest had had their

first dispute, I came across Dávvet, Priest, and Priest's Wife in the forest. Priest's Wife was picking branches, seemingly not for wood fire – these were thin, twirled branches, silvered by water and wind. Dávvet and Priest walked in silence, shoulder to shoulder, like old friends. At one stage, Priest let Dávvet pass ahead of him, and, as he did, he put his hand on Dávvet's shoulder. They were close. I felt a sting of something I realised was jealousy. I, too, would have wanted to walk there with them. Then it began to nag me, how come we didn't know about their bond?

I would have asked Dávvet about it, but he came back late. That same night, the attack took place.

It was one of our dogs who woke us: Láilá. Her shriek cut through the still night and we were on our feet and outside at once.

For a brief moment, nothing. Then, dogs howling. Not our dogs. Egel, who was guarding the reindeer, cried out.

We ran towards the herd, but the beasts were already amongst it, setting upon the animals, driving the group apart.

It took us the whole night to gather the flock again. One of the animals was still missing; the spayed one, who makes sure the herd follows as we walk. We finally found the tracks: that of the missing animal and those of clumsy men.

The reindeer hung from a tree. In the snow underneath it, a wild blood spatter, and then a patch of deeper red.

'Who could do such a thing?' Beahkká said. 'Not take it to eat, just . . . kill it.'

Nila's face looked white. 'Lift me up.' The men hoisted him on their shoulders. He cut the rope and the dead reindeer fell into the snow with a thud.

I used to scratch this reindeer under its chin. It liked to have its ears tugged gently. I stared at the spatter of blood, at the small patch. I know how much a reindeer can bleed. Then I realised what the pattern meant. The hole in the animal's neck was small. The animal had struggled. It had suffered.

My stomach churned. Beside me, Suonjar grimaced and wiped her mouth.

Whoever did this, I thought, and I had a face in my mind, a face with round, unblinking eyes, hates us. Really, really hates us. And the glimpse I got of that hatred was so strong, it blinded me.

'We don't know who it was,' Dávvet said later as we sat down by the fire. He was leaning forward as he spoke, elbows on knees, speaking against us, not to. 'We don't know.'

Nila sat immobile.

'We shouldn't let this separate us from the villagers. Instead, we need to approach them, become more like them.' Dávvet spread his fingers wide. He looked like Priest on his pulpit.

'It's punishment for our sin,' Suonjar said.

'This has nothing to do with *our* sin,' Nila said.

'We have to—' Dávvet began.

'Enough!'

It startled us. Nila never raised his voice.

'We are not at fault,' Nila said. 'From now on, more of us guard at night.'

I looked around our little circle of dark men and women in tattered clothes, at the few children. We had nothing on our side. They had numbers, and the law. They had God. This was a warning. But to kill an innocent animal to force us to go to church? It didn't make sense. I felt the rift in the *sita*.

We have let the dogs in amongst us, I thought. We are letting them scatter us, and if we're not careful, each of us will find himself alone.

'Perhaps we should leave Blackåsen,' I said. I sounded as if I had breathed too much fire.

'No.'

Dávvet and Nila spoke the word at the same time. They stared at each other, then at me.

'We are needed here,' Nila said.

Dávvet nodded.

I knew what they meant. Apart from one miserable winter, our tribe has always had its winter camp here. My mother, my grandmother, her mother, hers before her. We cannot go elsewhere. We are as braided into this mountain as it is braided into us.

I find the *rievsak* in my snare. As I twist it loose, its reddish-brown body still feels warm in my hands. Its thick white wings fall limp, and its head hangs over my finger. There is a weight in my chest. 'You sang too loud,' I tell the fowl, 'that's all.'

Things will never be like they were before, that's what I think, and I long for my father, my mother, my aunts and uncles; for that period when I, too, could imagine singing aloud. Now I am the oldest alive. There is no chanting to be had, and there won't ever be again. The bird twitches, not yet quite dead. I break its neck and gut it with my knife so as not to bring filth back with me to my camp. I will cook it, pack up, and then I shall leave Blackåsen. I have to share what I have seen. I have to trust the *sita* to draw the right conclusions. It is like the reindeer herd; if we let ourselves be divided, we have no chance.

Did Priest know Dávvet was the crack that could be used to enter the *sita*?

Oh, if Dávvet had spoken with the others, if he had schemed with them against Nila, I would have sided with my husband and fought.

But Dávvet came to me.

Close to my campsite, a tiny rasping that doesn't belong to the forest and I stop. There it is again: *scrape, scrape*. I circle a rock, step over the rivulet.

A stranger – a man – bends down by the far end of my site. The material of his white shirt looks fine; his long hair is gathered in a tail. He has placed a wooden box on the ground beside him. He scrapes at the surface of the boulder with his nail. Then he holds it still and begins to hammer it in.

A branch lies beside me and I step down on it hard. The man turns, glimpses me, and rises.

Good God. The left side of his face is eaten away.

Something powerful did this to him; something unforgiving. And he survived. He must be strong. Strong like a bear.

I have covered my mouth with my hand and let it drop. But my mind beats at the same pace as my heart.

The man looks at me, too, at my hat, my dress, the dead bird in my hand. Perhaps he has already told me his name.

The box on the ground is full of metal sticks, strangely shaped wooden spoons, a hammer, a pair of shears. He stands on the birch twigs I use for a bed. By his feet, my reindeer hide lies. He follows my gaze and takes a step to the side. For a moment, his apparent awkwardness does remind me of a bear. It sparks a glimmer of light inside me, and a brief easing of the ache in the pit of my stomach for the first time since I came to Blackåsen. I wish I hadn't reacted upon seeing him. I am certain he knows how he looks.

'I came to find you and then I saw the *brachiopods* . . .' he says, and studies my bedcover as if he's considering folding it.

The what? I look at my stone and can't see anything. Then I realise he said he came for me. That does not bode well. I walk to the fire pit and squat down, placing the dead bird and my stick beside me.

Bear – for this is how I will come to think of him – puts his hammer and his nail in the box and closes it. He glances again at my cover, but leaves it.

'They say it was one of your people who killed the men in the village,' he says. 'A Lapp, I mean. Was it?'

I lean sticks against each other and stuff grass underneath.

'How would I know?' I ask.

I light the fire. The grass turns black before it gives me a small yellow flame. I tend to it, blow on it.

Bear has turned his face. I see his unblemished side. In the old days, his appearance would have claimed our deepest respect. I sigh. 'He was not part of our tribe,' I offer.

He nods, still looking away. 'I thought your kind left for the high mountains in the summertime. Aren't you far away from your family?'

'Your kind.' I repeat the words in my head, but then my eyes fill. My kind. I blink. The others will have arrived now at the place with no trees – only heath, lofty sky, and cold air. I miss them. Even Suonjar, a little. If I leave today, I could soon be with them. Why 'if'? I *will* leave today. I *will* soon be with them.

'So are you,' I say.

Bear puckers his brow, as if he has only just remembered his own family and he's surprised at himself.

'My husband died,' I say. 'I am choosing our winter site.'

'Oh.' He pauses and rubs his forehead with the back of his hand. 'I thought you always used the same camps.'

I push one of the wooden sticks further into the fire.

'Do your people have grievances against the settlers?' he asks.

I think of cut trees and burned forests. Of land that has changed possession. Of feeling dirty in church. I shake my head.

'I work for *Bergskollegium*,' he says, 'we are in charge of the Swedish mountains.'

I force back a smile. Nobody is in charge of mountains.

'Before coming here I discovered we have no maps of Blackåsen. And, even stranger, the mountain is not on the official map, either.'

That ends my amusement. We are not on the map. As though we don't exist.

'I thought I'd draw the mountain before I leave. If they'll let me.' He gives a teasing smile. 'The settlers are afraid of strangers now. With good reason, too.'

'Not of strangers. They're afraid of each other.'

It is hard to think things and not say them. I was never good at it.

Bear purses his lips. 'You must know Blackåsen well.'

I know what he is about to ask. I am not staying. I am leaving, walking away and joining 'my kind'.

'I wonder . . .' he begins.

I shake my head.

He nods.

As he turns to leave, I can't help myself: 'Why are you interested in that stone?' I nod towards it.

'It doesn't belong here. That's all.'

M

By the village entrance, I sit down on a stone and take out my writing book. My thoughts are racing. I want to try to sketch the clothes Ester was wearing whilst I am certain to remember them. Her shoes were made of light leather, boat-shaped with the toes pointing upwards in a tip. Wound around her legs, woollen bands in vibrant colours – red, blue, yellow – connected the shoes to the trousers. She was wearing a blue woven frock with red edges, and, on top of this, something like a bib, heavily embroidered around the neck. Her hat was red and cone-shaped, like a sugarloaf, and her long hair was braided and reached far down her back. Her knife and a small pouch hung from her leather belt, and whenever she moved, she made a jingling sound, for at the back of her belt were thin leather ribbons with small brass rings. In her hand she held a stick that she was using as a cane. But most amazing of all was her face: the brown eyes, the small broad nose, the sallow skin. It was a face full of wisdom. Impossible to tell her age, but as her hair was white, I guess she is of a certain age. And that dead bird beside her on the ground . . .

At this, I feel light-headed. Will I be sick again? I wait. No. No, the wave subsides. Once you've been unwell your mind can trick you like this. It keeps waiting for the illness to return.

I bite the end of my pen and then write in my book that she was still using steel and flint stone to light her fire.

I should ask her to help me map. She could be of great assistance. I'll go back and see her again in a day or two. Of course, I'll focus on the killings for now.

I probably gave her a strange impression of myself, studying the brachiopods, but when I saw that stone . . .

I put my pen and my book in my satchel. Jacob said the village has a night man. I will go and see him next. He would have been the one to take care of the bodies, among the first to see the place after the murders happened. And then I shall see the widows.

The night man's homestead is the last one eastwards, the one furthest away from the church. It's hot. I take out my hand-kerchief and wipe my forehead. Above me, the sun is a ball of fire.

I have met a Lapp. I chuckle. She didn't strike me as childish. On the contrary. And the way she moved, lithely, with a quiet force. To think that people can live with only a fire pit.

It can't be a coincidence, her being here at the time of the murders. And I am certain she lied when she said she was here to choose a winter site. Jacob, too, said the perpetrator did not belong to her tribe, so why the lie?

I find the night man sitting on an overturned bucket outside his house, holding a mug in his hands. His scalp is bare. In his thin face, his eyes sit deeply and his nose tilts to one side – broken. A blow this way, and, at some other time, that. On the laundry line hang only men's clothes.

'My name is Magnus Stille.'

He takes a sip of his coffee. I can tell he already knows. Villages talk.

'I am told you took care of the bodies of the men who died?'

'That is what I do,' the night man says.

I look at his brown, strong arms, and wish I hadn't put on a white shirt. 'Did you see the Lapp?' I sound annoyed.

The night man shrugs.

'You didn't think he was old? Frail?'

He sips at his coffee again. 'I've seen older and frailer men do worse things.'

'Answer the question,' I say.

The night man sighs, a long push of air, then rises. Our eyes lock. I don't move. He jerks his hand and throws his drink into the grass. But now he seems sulky, rather than fierce. And he doesn't walk away.

'Who died first?' I ask.

'The priest.'

'Why do you think that?'

'He had not risen from his desk. The others had. Or, at least they had tried to.'

I can't help but squirm.

'What were they killed with?' I ask.

'An ordinary hunting knife.'

How fast the killer must have been, then, to succeed in murdering three able-bodied men before they could overpower him, manage to escape, or call for help. I think of the old Lapp in the prison in Luleå.

The night man nods as if he has read my mind. 'There was glass on the floor, glasses on the table. They had been drinking.'

Alcohol, I think. Rune probably brought it with him.

So, childhood companions having a drink together ending up dead. Jacob said that . . . Adelaide Gustavsdotter also spent time with them.

'Was there a woman with them?' I ask. 'Adelaide Gustavsdotter.'

The night man shakes his head. 'She was the one to find them, but she wasn't there when it happened.'

'If the Lapp killed them . . .' I begin.

He tilts his head. 'Why "if?" It was him.'

Probably. 'Why did he stay with the bodies? Why didn't he try to escape?'

'Perhaps he had done what he came to do and now he no longer cared?'

Yes, perhaps. But then the perpetrator would have had a purpose and not have acted on impulse, not out of insanity.

I take another look at the laundry on the clothesline. Like all the others, the house lies isolated. You can't see or hear anything from the next settlement.

Something strikes me. 'This is a small place,' I say. 'It's hardly a village, and yet you have a priest, a constable, and a night man.'

'I guess our parents used to think this would grow into a large community,' he says.

'And then?'

'And then it didn't.'

The night man bends to pull up some grass, which he uses to wipe his cup clean.

A fly buzzes close to my chin and I swipe at it. 'Do you know what Rune Dahlbom was doing here?'

'Visiting.' He shrugs.

'Was there anything – anything at all – that seemed strange to you?'

'Like what?'

'I don't know . . . Something about their bodies, or the room . . .'

The night man pauses and frowns. I hold my breath.

'Per?' A woman's voice.

By the blood of Christ! I turn. She comes towards us. Her features are sharp, her nose downturned, her lips a full red.

'Have you seen Sigrid?' she asks, her blue eyes on the night man, her gaze so intense it shuts me out.

'No.'

The woman nods. She reaches out to squeeze the night man's arm and leaves. The night man has turned his head. He is looking into the forest.

'Anything else?' he asks, voice gruff.

I want to laugh. His house is the last one on the road – she wouldn't come here to ask if he'd seen anyone. No, she came to tell him not to speak to me. And whatever the night man, Per, thinks he saw, I reckon he is more scared of this woman.

'Adelaide?' I ask him.

His nod is so imperceptible, it's almost not a movement.

Another night and I can't sleep. How can anyone, in this perpetual sunshine? Without blinds, the light floods the room, makes my soul itch, and my legs ache. It can't continue like this. I haven't slept since I set out on my journey. I turn onto my side.

Mrs Palm told me Lovisa came back and went to her room without dinner. I regret what happened this morning. When I walked out and saw the door to her room was open, I over-reacted. But the fact remains: I gave her an order and she disobeyed.

I turn again.

I wonder what Lovisa would have said, seeing Ester.

'They're afraid of each other,' Ester said. Why would the settlers be frightened of one another? Though Adelaide told the night man not to speak. She has probably done the rounds in the whole village. It will make it even more difficult to talk to the widows. I didn't manage to see them today. When I left the night man, it was already late.

That light!

I get up and take one of my shirts. A nail sticks out from the wall above the window and I hang my shirt on it and put my rucksack on a chair beneath it.

Pointless.

I take the bedspread, rip down my shirt and pierce the blanket on the nail – I'll reimburse Mrs Palm for it later. I position my bag so that it holds one corner of the material to the side, and use a chair to do the same on the other side. The bedspread forms a triangle in front of the window. At least it's a bit darker.

I lie down again.

Everyone claims not to know the perpetrator. Frans did say that there were lots of vagrants walking around in the Lappish forests. But why kill three men without anything personal at stake?

'Insane.' I repeat Jacob's words to myself, but my mind's voice sounds hesitant. Why those three? Why not anyone he met on the road before or after? And why stay to be caught?

Somewhere in the house, a door closes.

I don't know what I'll tell Lovisa tomorrow. I have to punish her for not heeding my word. Only I can't think of any punishment that will make a difference. Perhaps, when things have gone that far, there is no option but the madhouse.

Stop now, I tell myself. Stop thinking. I have to sleep. My body aches. It burns.

The bedspread is not helping. The uncovered areas seem to glow even stronger. I turn onto my stomach and put my pillow over my head.

Think of home. My daughter Harriet's face forms in my mind, the way she laughs when I hurl her up into the air. She is much too big for me to do that now – it is not appropriate and it breaks my back – her mouth wide open, her black hair in the air, a fan.

I try to raise an image of Isabella, too, but can only see her blonde, parted hair, her face nothing but a hazy spot in the middle.

I need to tell you a story. It is not pleasant, but it's important. You see, everything has a spirit – the stones on the ground, the trees around you. Some are good, some are bad. Some are helpful, others not. You learn to navigate.

When I was twelve years old, my father taught me a lesson. By then, I had seen how he was always able to find prey, how the spirits warned him when danger was close, how they helped him find passage when snow closed the mountains. We all knew that the spirit in Blackåsen was the most powerful, and I had begun to think that if a person could tame that, nothing would ever stand in their way. I hadn't said anything, but my father knew. I guess They told him.

One winter day he took me out into the forest. The sky's fires above us, sounds of a giant blaze. We made a fire and sat down, my father with his eyes closed, singing a song of old. Spirits came to sit with us. I saw Hare, Hawk, and Wolf. But my father was looking for something different.

'Come, come, spirit of the marsh,' he sang.

The spirit animals left us, and I understood how different this one was.

It took time, but she came. A girl child, with greenish skin. Her long hair hung wet down her back. Her eyes glowed black. I must have smiled at her, for her lips separated like a mirror of my expression. I noticed that where she should have had fingers, there were white, thin claws.

How we fought! She ran circles around us, giggling, as if it were a game. One of her strikes sliced my arm from my elbow all the way down to my wrist. I still have the scar.

We had to call on Bear to help us tie her, and even with his help I wasn't certain we'd manage. When the girl was finally gone, my father and I lay on the snow. My arm throbbed, the pain so great that my breath came out in jerky gasps. I didn't dare to look at the wound.

'This is nothing compared to Blackåsen,' my father said, with his eyes closed. 'If you call on something you cannot master, it will master you. Remember this.'

Remember this?

Oh, how I wish I could forget! But a person cannot un-see. He cannot un-live. That night would come to change me more than my father understood.

We came back to the camp, and it was early morning. People went about their chores, laughed and teased. But I was changed. I had been set apart. Nothing could ever again be the same.

I didn't want this. The gift is a burden, a curse. But there was scant choice. The spirits are as real as you and I. And what do you think they'd do if they thought you were no longer listening?

L

I comb my hair, and the tufts poke up in the air, leaving my pink scalp visible. When I was a child, one of our roosters at our country mansion had some disease and lost a lot of his feathers. I remember the ugly, granular skin, and how the fowl twitched when he walked. He knew what he looked like. I press my hand to my scalp to try to flatten the bristles, and the hurt in my chest pulls my face together into something unrecognisable.

It will grow out, I tell myself. It doesn't make me feel better.

Downstairs, the breakfast plates sit on the kitchen table, ready. Here, everything is the same, day out and day in. I look around. A bar of soap lies on the kitchen counter. I hesitate, then take it and put it in my pocket. I push open the door to the porch and expect Magnus to come running, calling: 'Don't go anywhere without me!' I mimic my gaoler's voice in my head, high-pitched.

I sit down. The wood is cold against my buttocks. A mist loiters over the tiny field beside the house in a last futile effort before the sun burns it off. Some birds screech: thrushes? For a while, I thought I was interested in nature. I asked my father for a book about birds. He studied me, and I could tell his mind was trying to work out whether any benefit could be gained by refusing. I made myself blank; not too eager. My mouth felt dry. He must have found no reason to decline, for then he gave it to me, and Eva and I carried it with us on our walks. 'What can that be?' 'A nightingale?' 'No, no, look at its colouring.' What nonsense.

I imagine Eva's face before me on that last day: large eyes, distorted mouth – shock. No, not shock: distaste. It was distaste.

Damned be the impulse that got hold of me! And damned am I for acting upon it! Allowing my fantasy to roam for months and not reining it in. I am undisciplined, childish.

I am trivial.

I dig the heels of my shoes into the grey wood of the porch and push them out, scratching the timber. I hate it here. Here, there is nothing but trees and mud and insects. I want to go home. Only now I have no home.

We are alone at breakfast, Magnus and I. He hasn't looked at me once. My coffee spoon clinks against the china. I put it on the table, then adjust it so it lies straight. Magnus is looking through the window, his face cold. I take a bite of my bread, chew, but find it hard to swallow. I lift my cup, then put it down again.

'I went for a walk yesterday.' I sound hoarse. 'There is this stone field up there. A maze.'

Magnus stretches across the table, reaching for bread. His hand has grown tanned, his shirt is buttoned tightly around his wrist.

'I wanted to look more closely at it, but . . .'

Magnus puts butter on his knife and spreads it onto the bread.

To my horror, my eyes fill. Even a dog under the table would be shown compassion, offered a caress or a pat. But not me. It is acceptable to leave me unspoken to, ignored. My chest flutters. I knot my hands together in my lap.

'The Lapps used to build labyrinths a long time ago,' Magnus says. When I peek up, he's turned his head. 'I thought we'd go and see one of the widows today. Her name is Frida Liljeblad.'

We walk in silence down the dirt road. I put a name to what I am feeling: gratitude. Why would I be grateful? Am I then not human like him? Oh, my thoughts are too muddled. I'd better not think at all.

Magnus waits for me to draw level, and we take the path towards the vicarage. We leave the shadows of the trees, and, despite my hat, I have to squint against the light.

The widow opens the door herself. She feels very familiar, but I know why. You meet women like her everywhere in Stockholm: round, soft faces, and startling blue eyes, mildness in every feature and every gesture. The only unusual thing about her is her hair. Her blonde curls have been braided, but not recently. The plait is untidy and is coming undone by her shoulders. As if she knows what I am thinking, her hand to her head and her fingers try to work the loose strands in.

Magnus lifts his hat. 'I am Magnus Stille. This is Lovisa Rosenblad, my sister-in-law.'

We enter the drawing room, where Adelaide Gustavsdotter, the woman from the shop, is sitting in an armchair facing the sofa. She rises. Magnus sees her and his lips curl.

Behind Frida Liljeblad and Adelaide Gustavsdotter, a maid wipes the windowpanes. She glances at her mistress, but, when there is no sign, she continues with her work.

'I heard about the recent events,' Magnus says to Frida. 'I am so sorry.'

Frida's face twists and she sinks down onto the sofa. This

woman is grieving. Not all marriages are as loveless as my parents'. I want to apologise, though I have said nothing.

Behind the widow, the maid rubs at a spot with the cloth, but her movements have become tiny and she hunches her shoulders.

Adelaide speaks. 'It is a loss. For our whole community.' The deep wrinkle between her eyes is back. 'Then you are here because of what happened?'

'Not directly. I am the administrator at *Bergskollegium*. I am here to map Blackåsen Mountain. I was told about the murders by your governor.'

Adelaide looks down, but not before a flicker of something runs over her face. Dismay? As though it would bother her more to think Magnus has come for the mountain, rather than for the dead men. But when she lifts her head, her face is empty, her gaze direct.

Magnus takes a step forward. 'I was told it happened after a parish meeting,' he says to Frida. He hunches, makes his towering figure seem comforting. Perhaps he does care.

'Yes?' Frida says.

'A Lapp entered.'

'Yes?'

'And it happened in your husband's office?'

She nods and looks up to the ceiling. I guess that is where the priest has his workplace. *Had* his workplace.

'How did he enter?'

'Well I . . . He just walked in.'

'And nobody saw him?'

Frida shakes her head. Another wisp of hair falls from her braid. I wince. Stop it, Magnus. This is enough. She is hurting.

'Then what happened?'

'He killed them.'

146

Adelaide moves, but Magnus shakes his head. Stand back. 'Where were you?'

'I was in the church, tidying up. I heard screams, so I ran back.'

Magnus nods and pauses. 'Was your husband worried about something?'

'No.'

'Nobody he mentioned being scared of?'

'No.' The widow sounds shocked. 'This is a peaceful community. Things like this don't happen here.' She half-turns to Adelaide.

'He didn't talk about the Lapps?'

'No!'

Adelaide stares at Magnus, nostrils flared. 'I think that next Magnus will ask to see the room where it happened,' she says in a cold tone.

Magnus nods, as though his request is neither rude, nor unusual.

By the window, the maid has stopped moving.

The priest's study on the first floor contains a table with four chairs, and a wooden bookshelf full of books. Two windows face opposite directions; one overlooks the church, the other the meadow behind the vicarage. The priest's desk stands beneath the one that looks out over the field. He could sit there and forget he was a priest. The room has an acrid smell, like that of metal.

Frida waits in the doorway.

'Tell me where they were found,' Magnus says, quieter now.

'Ulf, our priest, was here, by his desk. The others were close to the table,' Adelaide says.

I can see it: the priest, writing at his desk. The door edges open. No, it is flung open. They all look up, at first not understanding. Then they raise their hands, try to stand, all too slowly.

'How do you know?' Magnus asks Adelaide.

'I, too, was at that parish meeting. I had left, but heard the screams and returned.'

'And then you saw . . . him, the Lapp who killed them?'

Adelaide nods to the floor. 'Me and Frida both.'

Frida has entered the room. Her white shoes look dainty on the dark pools that stain the wooden floor.

Is it blood? My stomach rises. It is blood. Why haven't they cleaned it up? I half turn to Magnus, before comprehending. For several days, the Lapp sat here with the bodies and the blood seeped out of those men, into the wood, soaking too deep ever to scrub out.

Oh God. I want to put my hand over my face. I glance at Frida and hope she won't look down, hope she won't understand.

'The parish meeting; what did you discuss?' Magnus asks.

'The usual things . . . Church finances, the mill needs repairing – nothing out of the ordinary. You don't think he did it,' Adelaide says. 'You think he's innocent. But I saw him. He sat right here.'

Frida has walked over to the window. She adjusts one of the curtains so that it hangs straight.

'Rune was staying with you here in the vicarage,' Magnus says. 'Do you still have his things?'

The clothes in his brown leather bag lie neatly folded. I try to swallow, but my mouth is dry. Frida goes to stand by the bed. Magnus lifts up shirts and trousers. So few things. I look away.

'Nothing,' Magnus says.

'What did you expect to find?' Adelaide asks. She has remained in the doorway, arms crossed. Her eyes are on the bag and its contents.

'I was thinking that, being a mineralogist, Rune would have had maps of Blackåsen.' Magnus rises.

'I knew Rune from Uppsala,' Frida says. 'The three of them: Ulf, Rune, and Jan-Erik came there for their studies. My father is a professor, and I kept meeting them at various gatherings, at celebrations. They were different from all the other students. Serious, diligent, and then that slow way of speaking. We all grew fond of them.' Her voice trails. 'I can't imagine that they are gone,' she whispers.

Outside, a bird calls and we all startle. It sounds like a scream.

Once outside, Magnus takes a large step off the path and continues into the graveyard. I hesitate, but follow him, stumbling on earth and tufts of grass.

My chest is tight. How can the sun be shining? Three men died a few steps away. Adelaide said she heard screams. Men screaming.

'That woman,' Magnus mutters, 'Adelaide Gustavsdotter. She is everywhere.'

'Mrs Palm said she leads a religious group . . .' My voice sounds thick. 'Separatists?'

'Oh.' Magnus nods as if that explains something to him. 'Their members have left the Church. There are many similar groups. They're still forbidden, though. Gathering to pray without a priest is deemed heresy.'

We have come to the wall of the church. Magnus stops and then leans out from behind it to peer back at the vicarage. I feel dizzy. I want to go back to the shop. I need to sit down. The blood on the floor. A stain that can never be removed. How could anyone kill another human being? A person, flesh and blood, with scents and sounds, breathing next to you, and you turn, press a knife into that living body, extinguish all light. How is it possible? My legs tremble. I lower myself down onto the ledge by the wall and put my head between my knees. And that poor woman, Frida.

Though something about Frida, or perhaps it's Adelaide, irks me.

Magnus tenses and I look up.

The maid from the vicarage. As she crosses the graveyard, Magnus grabs her and spins her in towards the wall of the church. I scramble to get out of the way. Magnus holds her, covering her mouth. The maid fights, then, all at once, she stops and goes floppy in his hands. My breath comes in puffs, as if I'm the one who has been caught.

'Shhh.' Magnus turns the awful side of his face towards the maid – sinewy red and white.

The maid pants. Her chest heaves.

'Who was at that parish meeting?' Magnus asks, and lets go of her mouth.

'The vicar, my brother, Rune Dahlbom, and Adelaide,' she rattles.

Magnus hesitates: 'Your brother?'

'Jan-Erik, the constable. He was my brother.'

Magnus sighs. When he speaks again, it is softer. 'Was Rune at the meeting, or did he arrive later?'

The maid's eyes are round. She swallows. 'He was there . . . I had to prepare more coffee.'

'Where was Adelaide when the men died?'

'I don't know.' The maid's voice quivers and rises.

'Hush,' Magnus says. He pauses. 'Hush,' he repeats. 'Now, think yourself back there that day. What were you doing?'

She nods several times and gathers herself up. 'I was in the kitchen, preparing soup.'

Magnus bends his head: *Continue.*

'It was too thin. I needed to use more flour.'

'What did you hear?'

'It was noisy.'

'It?'

'They.'

'They were fighting?'

She frowns. 'Perhaps. They were loud. Then the soup boiled over. I worried Frida would come and see it. I wiped it up.'

'And after you were done, were they still fighting?'

'No. The house was quiet. Then, footsteps. Up the stairs. Then, a crash. Screams.

'And?'

'More footsteps. Above me, up the stairs. Then a woman's scream. Perhaps Frida's.'

I close my eyes.

'Who is the Lapp?'

'I don't know.'

He takes a step towards her.

'They were not being truthful, sire,' she whispers. Her upper lip glistens. 'Things like this always happen here.'

'What do you mean? What has happened here?'

The maid kicks him on his shin. She runs through the graveyard, skirts flying, turns the corner of the church, and disappears.

Magnus leans towards the wall beside me. I can smell the cloth of his trousers: warm wool, grass, earth. I rise, knees still weak. He holds my gaze with serious blue eyes. '"Things like this"?' he repeats. 'And Adelaide . . . What kind of a woman would enter a room full of screaming men?'

I think of how Adelaide and Frida were sitting opposite each other. That's what irked me earlier. Why opposite, not beside? And when Frida faltered, Adelaide did not reach out to touch her. They are not friendly.

B

Yet another clear evening. The chirps of birds are soft, the colours melt into each other. I stayed. Bear will come and find me. Whether I like it or not, we are not yet done. It's the mapping . . . I need to understand more about what he's going to do and why. Nila used to say Blackåsen had powers. We were to take great care not to disturb the mountain.

I light my fire, and, using birch bark as tinder, I blow at it, nip a little here and a little there, to strengthen the flame and then to focus it. I place the kettle on two stones.

Nila had a verse for every site that stated what was important about it; what you had to remember, or look out for. I've been trying to recall the one for Blackåsen, but can only think of the first line. *Beyond The One Who Binds Water. By The One Who Sees* . . .

I don't force it. It will come back to me.

Bergskollegium, he said. 'In charge of the mountains.'

I chuckle.

Though people like Bear open the mountains. They dig out their treasures and then force our people to help. A Lapp can be kept with his reindeer and her *akja* – sleigh – for years, pulling minerals here and there in the snow, waiting at some outpost without his tribe. He'll come back to his *sita* changed. For this reason, any Lapp who reveals something new to these men, or helps them, is deemed a traitor.

Soon, the water boils. With my stick, I lift the pot off and remove the lid. I am just putting in a pinch of salt to clear the coffee, when he comes.

'I am sorry to disturb you again,' he says.

I nod towards my reindeer hide. He hesitates, then sits down. First, he supports himself on one arm, then the other, straightens his back, then, finally, crosses his legs and settles down. Some people forget how to sit on the ground. His face looks ashen. When the sun doesn't set, some people forget to sleep, too.

I pour the black liquid into my china cup slowly, so as not to spill. I put some reindeer cheese in the coffee to soften it, and a couple of pieces of dried meat, and hand it to him. The cup looks more comfortable in his hand than in mine. He stares into it as I prepare my own drink the same way. Then he takes a sip, and I know what he'll taste: the fat from the milk and the salt from the meat. His features relax a little, his colour returns.

We drink in silence. I nod to the coffee pot – more? Bear shakes his head. I make myself a second cup.

'I've begun asking the settlers about what happened.' He stops there and sighs.

Then they told him nothing.

'I think I might be able to begin mapping the mountain in a day or so,' he says. 'I was hoping you would consider helping me.'

'Consider helping.' I want to chuckle again. I slurp my coffee. 'How will you . . . map it?' I ask.

'I'm interested in the iron,' Bear says. 'I'll try and draw its formation.'

That will be easy enough for him. It's a black road straight through the middle, sloping slightly east.

Bear drains his cup. 'Don't answer now, but promise you'll think about it.' He nods, willing me to nod back.

People like him . . . People like him, usually don't ask.

I pick at a piece of meat in my teeth, get it, chew it again.

'Adelaide Gustavsdotter.' He changes the topic. 'Do you know her?'

Know and know. In the same way I know all of Blackåsen's children. I shrug.

'I think she has something to do with this,' he says.

It takes me a while to realise he's talking about the killings.

Holy Woman? Never. She was fond of both Constable and Priest. Without them, she'll be on her own. There are still other settlers, yes, yes, but somehow I am certain that to her, it's not the same.

Bear is trying to get up from his seated position. He has to turn over on all fours. He mutters. I bite the inside of my lip not to giggle, but when he looks at me, my eyes are far away.

'Think about it,' he says again, and stretches tall.

He leaves, and I can't help but laugh. I won't help him, of course not, but I like him, this Bear. In fact, he reminds me of someone. I try to think who, but I can't.

I make myself another cup of coffee, emptying the pot.

Someone is coming. At first I think it is Bear returning, but these steps are lighter, smoother.

It is Holy Woman. I wonder if she heard.

No. Her cheeks are red. She has just been walking. She squats down beside me and stares into the fire. When she folds her arms around herself, the waves of her ribs become visible on the side of her dress. I wipe my cup clean with moss. I rub Bear's cup, too, and glance at Holy Woman, but she hasn't noticed that there were two of them.

155

'I am so sorry about Nils, Ester,' Holy Woman says.

She is still staring into the fire, and I put in another branch, to give her some heat. It awakens her and she looks at me. 'How did he die?'

My insides clench. 'He drowned.'

'Drowned?' Her eyes are on my lips.

'Yes.'

'Ester, did he send you here?' she asks.

Send me? What do you mean 'send me'? Nila is dead.

She gives a quick smile and stands up. 'Don't listen to me. I can't believe he's gone, that's all.'

M

Blackåsen Mountain, latitude 65° 57' N.; longitude 20° 29' E.
Elevation circa 300 feet at the mountain's base.

It's early morning and I sit at the desk in my room. Tomorrow I'll start mapping.

I smile, then think of the minister. But clearly this is no Lapp uprising. It might well have been the Lapp I saw in Luleå who committed the act. Perhaps he was indeed crazy. This will die down on its own, and it's unlikely it will make waves enough to threaten the *Gällivare-verken* deal.

Today, I'll speak with the constable's widow. But then I will stop enquiring.

Lovisa waits for me in the kitchen, hat on her head, hands in her lap. Perhaps she is learning. Perhaps this will be the journey that changes her.

I feel hopeful.

We find the constable's widow in her garden patch, clearing weeds. She's a thin-lipped, wiry woman. An old man sits in the shadow on the porch. The woman hears us, stands up and shades her eyes with her hand.

'My name is Magnus Stille,' I say, though I am quite certain she knows who I am and why I've come. 'This is Lovisa Rosenblad.'

Neither she nor the old man move at first. Then she lets

her hand drop. Her eyes surprise me; they are a gentle brown, and seem to belong to someone younger and softer.

The sun is hot on our heads. 'You're growing potatoes,' I say. The earth is dry.

She looks down at the plants as if she sees them for the very first time.

I sigh. 'I am trying to understand what happened to your husband.'

Her eyes fill. She takes out a handkerchief and wipes one eye, then the other. The priest in town, Axel Bring, said the constable, Jan-Erik Persson, was not a good man. He must have been good to his wife. 'It was his fate,' she says.

'Why would it have been his fate?' I ask.

'Why else would it have happened?'

I don't say anything. Most people still think there is a preordained trajectory to human life. A drop of sweat trickles down my chest. Peeking out from under the hat, the tip of Lovisa's nose looks red. I take a step to the side, into the shadow of a spruce.

'Did he know the killer?'

'I don't think so.'

'Your husband was a constable. Did he have any papers? Or a register of wrongdoings committed here?'

'We have no crimes.' It's the old man on the porch. His eyes are a bluish white. He is blind.

The widow frowns at him and turns to me. 'He had no papers, but you're welcome to look inside,' she says.

'Yes, please.'

The widow walks ahead of me, and I step up onto the porch, turning sideways, careful not to knock against the old man. Lovisa remains outside. The house consists of two rooms: a kitchen and a bedroom. A spinning wheel stands by one of the walls, two balls of yarn resting on its base. The woodpile by the fireplace is neatly stacked, the hearth clean. There are no papers or books.

'He had a sister?' I ask, when we come out onto the porch again.

'She lives with us, too,' the widow says. 'She is working in the vicarage today.'

'No point in asking questions,' the old man says. 'No one will talk.'

'Why?'

'It wasn't their fault. It got to them. It will get to you, too. You'd better leave while you can.'

I look to the widow and realise I'm expecting her to hush the man, or make a gesture to me to ignore him, but she doesn't.

'It?' Lovisa queries.

Oh nonsense. 'What really happened here?' I ask. 'It'd be much better if you just told us.'

The old man grins toothlessly. The widow shakes her head – to him, or to me, I am uncertain. As we leave them, I hear him chortle behind us.

The meeting has left a bad taste in my mouth. The villagers might be enjoying this: seeing us fumble in the dark, asking questions that no one will answer.

'She said it was his destiny.' Lovisa's eyes are round.

I sigh. We are back outside Jacob and Helena's house. In the bright light, the hand-painted sign with '*Allehanda*' written on it looks tired. The wood has cracked, the paint, at places, faded.

'Something is awfully wrong,' Lovisa says.

'The only thing amiss is that people are wasting our time.' I take a step towards the shop.

'You don't feel it?'

I stop. 'Feel what, Lovisa? They are keeping things from us, certainly. Does it have anything to do with the murders? Unlikely. Small places like this are rife with rivalries and old fights – some amongst them probably see the opportunity to get even.'

'The old man said "it" got to them. That we had better leave whilst we still could.'

'He was trying to scare us. He laughed when we left.'

This is where I need to stop: I know that, and yet I don't. 'Don't become hysterical, Lovisa,' I say. 'You are somewhat educated, after all.'

She exhales and her eyes narrow. 'You're just like my father; you don't respect women.'

My heart begins to pound in my chest, my whole body tenses, and, by God, I do want to hurt this female beside me. 'That's ridiculous. Why wouldn't I respect women? Why wouldn't your father?'

'The way you treated the priest's widow, without any regard for what had happened to her!' Lovisa is yelling. 'The way you talked to the constable's widow. You look down on us.'

'I have nothing against women,' I say. 'Most of them are not like you.' The hatred in my voice surprises me.

Lovisa's cheeks have reddened as if I've slapped her. I sigh and rub my forehead with my knuckles. I want to say that I am sorry. I *am* sorry.

'Tomorrow we will begin mapping the mountain,' I say, and, for a moment, I despise myself.

She doesn't meet my gaze. The red cheeks, bright eyes, black tufts of hair . . . I relent. 'Tell me one single thing that is amiss here.'

Now, she stares at me, chin lifted. 'There are no children,' she says, strides past me and pushes open the door.

No children?

Lovisa walks straight through the shop and runs up the stairs.

Surely, we've seen children? I walk inside.

'I found the papers.'

I am still looking after Lovisa. At first, I don't recognise the priest's widow, Frida Liljeblad. She is wearing a green dress and hat. Then I see her blue eyes.

She digs in her basket and takes out a brown paper folder. 'Rune's maps, or at least I think that's what they are. He had them stuffed under his mattress.'

'Thank you very much.' I open the folder: documents with annotations, a couple of maps. I flip through the papers, most of them indeed bear *Bergskollegium*'s stamp.

She shifts her basket from one arm over to the other. 'It will make your stay here easier,' she smiles, 'if you don't have to map the mountain.'

'Yes,' I smile, too. 'It certainly will.'

Mrs Palm hands her a paper bag, which Mrs Liljeblad puts in her basket. The doorbell rings as she leaves.

Mrs Palm busies herself, sweeps something invisible off the counter, moves a package further away. 'He should have married someone who came from the village.'

'What?'

'The priest. He shouldn't have brought the poor woman here.'

'Mrs Liljeblad?'

She nods. 'She could never be happy in this place.'

'Did they have children?' I ask so as to have something to say.

'No,' she says. 'They didn't.'

L

I hate him. Hate! I catch a glimpse of myself in the mirror on the chest of drawers in my room – black wisps of hair, wild eyes. I hear muffled voices in the shop. *Bla. Bla. How nice and how good.* A few steps and I am by Mr and Mrs Palm's bedroom door.

Their room resembles mine. The window overlooks the back of the garden, the bed is made with a rough woollen blanket, the wooden planks are varnished and have yellowed, and the wallpaper is pale with small red flowers. I turn to look behind me. The stairway is curved. If someone comes up, as they are certain to do in a minute, I'll have time to make it out of their bedroom, but I'll be caught in the hallway. I take a step and the floorboard creaks. I tiptoe to the dresser by one wall and open the two top drawers. The bureau rocks and a decorative vase standing on top of it tips to the side with a crash. I freeze and wait. Nothing. The vase didn't break. I put it back and my hand is trembling. In the right drawer, Mrs Palm has her things: some handwritten papers and cards. I open her jewellery box: a couple of beaded necklaces, two gold rings. I pick a brooch – a small one in pewter – and put it in my dress pocket. Beside Mr Palm's threadbare undershirts lies a large, sturdy pocket watch with a gold chain in a green leather box. There are pens, coins, a small pin with a steel foot and a red circle at the top. This is the one I take.

As I close the door to my bedroom behind me, I exhale.

I walk to the window. My legs feel unsteady. Outside, the field's long grasses and ferns look silky in the soft evening light. The trees' foliage floats unconnected to their solid, grey trunks. Behind them is a different type of forest, thick and black.

'Hysterical.' The mere word makes my heart pound harder.

I open the window and lean on the sill, staring into the forest, then at that empty road that stretches left and right, but leads nowhere. A line, a nick on the mountain's side.

I keep hoping when I am with Magnus; for some reason, I keep thinking that I could speak with him. I have no idea why. He's my father's protégé, my sister's husband, so why would he be different from them?

It's that scar. Someone who has been hurt like that, who has lived with men's reactions to his looks his whole life, wouldn't they turn out different . . .? Human?

Laughable.

My grandfather had a painting in his home of a young woman. It was hanging above the mantel in his office, and it was different from any other portrait I'd seen. The woman was dressed in a blue and grey silk gown, wearing a hat with feathers and beads, and holding her gloves in one hand. It was clear she was about to leave. She wouldn't remain standing there in the doorway any longer than it took for the artist to sketch her quickly, or perhaps not even that long; perhaps he had to paint from memory. I could gaze at the portrait for hours. Her face was irresistible: dark, serious eyes under thick eyebrows, the straight nose, the mouth with full lips. Her expression was one of impatience or irritation. It wasn't until I was eight or nine that I realised that the woman in that painting was my mother. I kept comparing: the fixed gaze – the shifting eyes; the lips firmly set – the weak mouth; the rosy cheeks – the grey complexion. Even at such a young age, it was clear to me that what had changed her was the fear of my father. And this man, her husband, my father, raised Magnus in his image. No, there is no hope to be had with him.

No children, I said. I didn't know I had noticed it until the words came out of my mouth, but now it is obvious. There are no children. This village is full of adults.

Someone is coming along the road, a figure in a pale dress. A yellow dress. She comes closer, and yes, it is Sigrid. She sees me and lifts her hand. I respond in the same way. She doesn't stop walking, but I know she is smiling.

The house is silent. Beside the window stands a wooden chair with an ornate back, a cross carved in the middle. A prayer chair, my mother calls them. I sit down on it and look at the shadow we cast on the floor, the chair and I.

Once, I tried to speak with my mother about that painting, about how she had changed. She leaned close to me and I got a glimpse of the woman she'd once been. 'Perhaps when you're older, you'll understand,' she'd said.

I swore I'd never become older.

I went about it all wrong. What do I know about her sorrows? What do I know about what he did to her?

I close my eyes. If I could pray, I would.

I don't believe anything is 'meant to be'. I don't believe in destiny in that way.

But should you act or speak, there will be a response. You neglect something and that has consequences, too. The universe responds.

And so, wherever we find ourselves – whether we like it or not, whether we join or not – we are a part of the unfolding of events.

Me, I always felt better letting things be swayed by my deeds rather than my inactivity. It made me feel more in control.

B

I find Bear by the river with a girl. She is pale, with black eyes and hair like tousled feathers. She reminds me of an animal, some bird perhaps. Bear stands by the water balancing on two boulders. He leans towards the wall of the rock, which reaches higher than him, and looks at it through a piece of glass. His box sits on a stone by his feet, a brown book on top of it. He has begun his work. The girl sees me and rises. 'Magnus?' she says.

Bear straightens his back. 'Ester.' He lifts his hand in a wave.

It was the stone, that's what I have planned to say. *I forgot to ask why you said it didn't belong.*

In reality, I want to keep an eye on what he's doing. Someone ought to make certain this doesn't get out of hand; this is what I keep thinking. Someone ought to . . .

And I am the only one here.

The girl looks from one of us to the other.

'Ester will help us map the mountain,' Bear says, and puts his glass piece in his pocket.

I let him think so.

We follow the river upstream, Bear by the water, the girl and I on the bank above him, careful not to make stones or other debris fall below. Bear stares at the rock. He keeps stopping

167

to look at it through the glass piece. He chisels pieces off, holds them to the light, turns them, twists them. Then he puts them in small cloth bags, writes on them, and lays them in his rucksack. Sometimes he sits down on a boulder to draw in his book. Mapping the mountain like this will take a long time.

A south wind blows. I can't feel it, but I can smell it, a notion of wetter, sweeter scents, carried from afar. The girl often glances over the edge, perhaps making certain Bear is still there. She looks at me, too, glowers, eyes black and round, but when I catch her at it, she drops her gaze. A baby raven. That is what she reminds me of.

We walk around an outcrop, and there it is: a grey stone shaped like a figure with outstretched arms. My eyes search for the white bones of hare, but they are, of course, long gone. Nila and his father sacrificed to this stone in spring after a harsh winter, before we were promised to one another. It was a hot day for early spring. The masses of snowmelt had come crashing down, water everywhere underneath us. Nila's father was worried about crossing the river with the reindeer. Nila conducted the ceremony on behalf of his father for the first time. *Call on yours to bind the water.* Nila's black hair gleamed in the sunlight.

Afterwards, his eyes didn't find mine. I knew it had to do with the rite. I stared at him, my eyes demanding a meeting with his. When he didn't obey, I turned sideways. Still he didn't seek me out. An order had been established, one not to be discussed. His practice first; me second. When it came time for the crossing, the river seemed to hold its breath – it floated rather than ran. Nila walked first and pulled the lead reindeer with him. The herd followed, hundreds of animals, spitting, eyes rolling, legs kicking. Nila, a man who calmed water. I turned and found Nila's father watching me. That evening, after the crossing, after helping my own parents, I hung Nila's father's clothes to dry and made a fire for him to warm his bones. I am sorry, I thus said. Never again will I demand what cannot be given. You can trust me.

This was before we became Christians. Now, we know the irregular pattern of ice melting. Sometimes the river runs high, sometimes it doesn't; there's nothing one can do about it. Apart from, perhaps, pray to God, but I don't think God cares much about reindeer crossing rivers.

The figure-stone is part of that verse about Blackåsen. Its name is in the first line: '*The One Who Binds Water.*'

Raven Baby sits down on the head of *The One Who Binds Water*. She is peeking at me again. She nips at the moss growing on the stone.

'Don't annoy it,' I say.

Raven Baby stops sharp. Don't destroy the moss, is what I meant. I sigh and shake my head. Old traditions have long roots.

'Here!' Bear calls from somewhere below. 'Come and see.'

Raven Baby and I make our way down to the river.

'This is iron.' Bear points to a division in the vertical rock face, with speckled white-yellow and black stone on one side, and shiny black on the other. He has already sketched it in his book.

He taps the spotty stone with his pen. 'Quartz mixed with iron,' he says, and then taps the black, glittery one: 'Pure iron.'

His voice is soft. It's a good voice. Warm . . . I press my lips together. People like him are not warm. I need to remember what they do to the mountains and to our people.

Bear talks of earthly plates colliding, layers that used to lie down rising up, the wear of the elements grinding them down again. He presses his hands together as he speaks and I can feel the force. Raven Baby watches, eyes clear.

'Feel how heavy the iron is.' Bear hands us in turn a white stone and a black. The black one weighs my hand down; the white one doesn't, though the two are of the same size.

Then, eyes glinting, he places his pen against the rock wall and removes his hand. The pen remains there.

Beside me, Raven Baby gasps.

'Magnetic. Any compass would also be affected. It would point at the mountain instead of to the north.'

Then this mountain does have powers. I would never have imagined to what extent.

'I want to continue to the end of the iron deposit,' Bear says. 'And then perhaps we should rest.'

Raven Baby and I climb the bank.

I realise we are no longer alone. Someone else is here in the forest, watching. Whoever this is, he doesn't want to be seen. Now, as we start to walk again, I hear him. A branch breaks. I catch a glimpse of a shape between the trees.

Bear has not noticed, nor Raven Baby.

I bend down and pretend to adjust my shoe. There.

Merchant.

Why would Merchant be following us?

Not us, I correct myself, but Bear. Merchant is trailing Bear.

I walk differently now. My eyes go this way and that between Bear and Merchant, as if I have to decide with whom to side.

We pass the winter glade where we bring the younger ones to see the sky's fires dance on the river.

A hundred steps up to the right is the clearing where Nila asked me if I'd have him. I was hunting and he had followed. I heard him approaching and, not knowing it was him, I hid behind a spruce. My heart beat hard, and then he grabbed me, arms around my waist. I gasped, he laughed. He said, 'Hush, hush,' as though talking to a baby. I tasted his mouth for the first time. It was strange and hot and soft.

Bear, Raven Baby, and I have arrived at *The One Who Sees*, a large pine tree in the middle of the many spruce. It has spread itself wide. Heavy branches wind their way to the sky while the lower ones dip. Two holes mark the tree's trunk, watching eyes. Before, whenever we were setting out to lay snares, we used to ask this tree which way the prey were headed, to decide where to set our traps. The leaves of its crown would sway, this way, or that . . . It was a helpful tree. When I stood close to it, I would imagine its branches wrapping themselves around my spine. It made me feel calmer. Nila knew of many such trees. We said that was why he always found prey.

Bear climbs the bank. 'The band of pure iron finishes here. It is two hundred and sixty feet broad.'

He makes a note in his book.

Merchant is a darker hue by a spruce tree further away.

I nod towards a gigantic black boulder similar to the one in my glade. 'You see, they do belong.'

'Black limestone,' Bear says. 'These are brachiopods.' He points to patterns on its surface. 'Or, "lamp-shells", as they are also called. They are fossils that resemble pottery oil-lamps.'

He takes out a hammer and chips a piece out of the stone, which he puts in his bag. Then he digs with the claw of the mallet at the vegetation on the ground underneath it, to lay bare the rock.

'Can you see?' He gestures to the ground. 'They are decidedly different. One originates from here, the other does not. All of this land used to be under the sea at one point.'

Bear stands up. I use my stick to turn the grass and moss back into place and push it down. 'The Great Flood.'

Bear's eyebrows lift. 'Some things in the Bible might have been more . . . symbolic.'

'Symbolic,' I repeat. The word rolls in my mouth.

'It is the rock type which is interesting. There are naturalists who claim there was a period when all of our land was covered by ice. I have seen rocks like these in the south, and I reckon a giant ice sheet would easily be able to transport a boulder this size from one place to another and leave it there as it melted.'

Raven Baby opens her bag, retrieves a crusty loaf of bread, tears off a piece with her hands, and offers it to me. I shake my head. Symbolic?

'It must be over ten feet wide.' Bear bends his head backwards to see the top of the tree. He writes in his book again. 'I am going to have a look over there,' he says, and leaves us.

'He said "symbolic",' I say.

Raven Baby takes a bite of her bread.

'As if not everything in the Bible was true,' I half-whisper.

'Oh, I don't believe in God.'

Priest will be furious, I think. Then I remember Priest is dead.

'Do you usually live in a tribe?' Raven Baby asks, and I see the mangled bread in her mouth.

I look towards Merchant, but he has gone.

'Of course the rock belongs here,' I say, and my words come out sounding like a bark. 'Just like the settlers. Making a point of whether it was born here or not. Why? It's here now.'

I take a breath. Then another.

'So where are your . . . people?' Raven Baby asks, and glances at me.

'In the high mountains.'

'Why didn't you go with them?'

'My husband died. Some things he used to take care of have now fallen to me.'

'Nila.' Raven Baby takes another bite of the bread and squints towards the river.

My heart is in my ears. 'What did you say?'

'Nila?'

'How do you know his name?'

She chews more slowly, then shrugs. 'Someone said it.'

No. The settlers all use his Christian name: Nils. No one would have said it, because they don't know it.

Bear and Raven Baby returned to the village. I had a task, a chore I thought I'd do, but now I can't remember what it was. I came to the marsh and I don't know why.

She knows his name. The bird girl knows Nila's name. How can that be? We never give the settlers our real forenames.

And Holy Woman asking if Nila sent me . . .

This is a warning. Or a threat. Old Nila is talking to me. I can feel his eyes on me. 'Watch yourself, old woman. Watch yourself.'

A crow's *caw* startles me into motion, back towards my camp.

I search in my mind for a psalm to hum. None comes to my lips.

'*Beyond The One Who Binds Water. By The One Who Sees . . .*' I mumble instead, but can't recall the rest of the rhyme.

All at once, there's crawling in the forest. Croaking, baying. Everything is alive, laughing at me.

M

Blackåsen Mountain. I sit at the table in my room, flip the pages in my book, and look at my field sketches and my notes. Elated, I have no other word for it. I am elated. How should I draw this mountain? I don't touch the pen yet. My thoughts are large, the details intricate. There is nothing more pleasurable than this moment before beginning . . . deciding what to include, what to exclude.

I'll make two maps. One topographic, the mountain seen from above, that shows the river, the village, and the marsh. Then one that outlines the iron formation. For that one, I think I will select the orientation north to south. But I need to see the south side before I make up my mind.

The river is not young, it has had the time to erode the bank in places, but it still runs with full vigour. The snowmelt from the mountain keeps it moving fast.

On the vertical mountain wall, created no doubt by the rock breaking and one part descending to where the river now flows, there is quartz with dark iron veins which eventually lead to pure iron. The band of purer ore stretches about two hundred and sixty feet wide; the one mingled with quartz extends another forty feet on the east side and thirty on the west. Occasionally, I saw the apatite: lighter crystals with angular tops. It is magnetite-apatite all right.

We have at least one day's walking left in order to map the

rest of the fault, but, looking at the shape of the mountain, the way it leans towards the east, I have a feeling there won't be any more iron further along. The question now is how long the metal stretches up mountain. Once I have drawn it, I'll try and quantify it. It's more iron than I had realised, but it doesn't change anything. It's still too far away and too complicated to transport to the coast. But to have the chance to map it for myself is hugely exciting.

I pick up my pen and tap it at the desk. It won't be easy to map the iron formation. Although the mountain is not large and not particularly high, probably about 2,100 feet, the topsoil looks to be about forty inches deep, and the forest on the mountain itself is dense. The vegetation is a real nuisance. I'll try to see the rock type on outcrops and in holes. Then, once I have a rough draft, I'll dig trenches to lay bare the edges of the iron block.

I find myself smiling. I had forgotten how I love all this: minerals, their origins, their patterns. To feel rocks under my hand that were created millions of years ago. Or, like she said, the farmer's wife at Tana Rapids: 'Like holding a piece of the world in your hand'. The destiny of us human beings becomes irrelevant. I find comfort in the thought that beneath us, the earth will continue to be steady and unmoved, despite everything, and above us, the procession of the sun and the stars will never change. If Lovisa and I ever spoke properly, I would tell her that a person has to find something similar, a constant, that can comfort him, keep him sane, and then hold on to that, no matter what.

I put my pen down. I won't do anything this evening. I will savour this time, allow my thoughts to swirl and land on their own. In a day or two, we'll begin walking the mountain north to south. Then, perhaps, I'll begin sketching.

Outside, the sun hovers above the treetops, casting a white tinge across the grass and the trees. This sun is not the sun I know. This is a moon in disguise: cold and aloof.

A clanking from downstairs yanks me into motion. Dinner. I rise. Dinner, and then bed.

Lovisa and Jacob sit in the drawing room, Jacob at his desk and Lovisa in a chair by the window.

'It must be difficult,' Lovisa is saying to Jacob, her tone empathetic.

I have brought my bottle of aquavit and raise it to show Jacob: do you want some? Jacob lights up and nods and I pour us a glass each. The liquid burns my throat and chest. This should do it. One glass of drink, a heavy meal. Sleep.

'They always draw attention to how they grew up having to hold the fort against the wolves and the bears,' Jacob says. 'They cleared the ground for farming, they fought the beasts . . . We, those who came later, reaped the benefits of their work.' He quaffs his drink and exhales.

Is Lovisa querying because of the murders? I have to admit I haven't thought about them all day. I didn't even ask Ester any questions, though I had intended to.

'The beasts?' I ask, joining the conversation.

A shrug. 'You know what I mean. Those who were born here stick together. They make up the parish council. They decide. The rest of us do not belong.'

He sighs. 'So you were on the mountain. Anything interesting?'

I smile. 'I think so. But then I am interested in mountains.'

He doesn't return my smile.

'Who was born here?' Lovisa looks Jacob in the eyes, enticing him to go on. She sits straight-backed, hands in her lap.

Jacob responds to her charm and persistence, for that is

what it is, charm and persistence. 'Half and half. Half of the settlers come from here, the other half came later.'

I remember the night man, and how he reacted when Adelaide arrived. 'What about the night man . . .?' I ask.

'Per Eriksson was born here.'

Lovisa has lowered her eyelids, her foot is kicking. We are on the same path.

'What did Per Eriksson do to be punished with the night man's role?' I ask.

'Well, now that is a story. Per killed his father. The man was a drunkard. He was rough with his boy, beat him plenty. When the boy grew up, he'd had it. The old man didn't have a chance. Per was sentenced, and after serving his punishment, he returned here and became the night man.'

Killed his own father? It's hard to imagine after having met and spoken with the man. He appeared sensible. And Adelaide does not fear him. Rather, it seemed the other way around.

'I'm surprised he came back,' I say.

'Most people think the old man got what he deserved.'

'And Adelaide is a separatist?'

'They say that as a young woman, she had a vision on the mountain after which she left the Church. She preaches about each person's right to a relationship with God. Calls the Church "oppressive".' Jacob snorts. 'She's lucky, I say.'

I shake my head. 'Why?'

'She's not married. She inherited her farm from her parents, but if she didn't have this "following" of hers helping her out, she'd never manage.'

'And the priest wasn't opposed to her?' I ask.

'He was . . . influenced by Adelaide. She is quite captivating. And things were said to happen at the gatherings, at least before; unusual things. The priest partook.'

'Really?' I have heard of men of the Church becoming fascinated by the separatist movements, but to participate in them is a different matter.

Jacob scratches his chin as if it now strikes him how strange the priest's involvement was. 'I guess he and Adelaide went back a long time.'

'What do you mean by "unusual things"?' Lovisa asks.

'I don't know . . . People being healed from sicknesses. There were visions . . .'

'Have you . . .?'

'No, no. Only the people who were born here attend her gatherings.' His voice has turned gruff.

You weren't welcome there, either, I think. You would have attended had you been allowed. 'I'm amazed your priest attended separatist meetings. His bishop must have been furious,' I say.

'Oh, he was. Whenever he came, he brought it up, preached about it.'

'And there were no consequences?'

'I guess none of us was willing to tattle on our priest.' Jacob sighs. 'The ones who were born here wouldn't, and the rest of us didn't want trouble. The way things have turned out, we will get a new priest, and I am certain that this time, the bishop will select one who stays away from Adelaide.'

'They all came back,' Lovisa says, 'or they stayed. Did anyone ever leave for good?'

Jacob taps with the fingers of one hand on his desk.

Rune. The third man who died. He had left.

I lie down on my bed. I clasp my hands behind my head and stare at the window. My books and papers lie on the desk in the shadows beneath the sill. Lovisa has spotted something.

I have to hand it to her – she managed Jacob well. And, while I am at it, I admit that not many women would have managed the march from the town to this village. Not many would be able to share a makeshift tent with a man, or meet a Lapp. In fact, Lovisa has shown qualities I love: passion, strength and, yes, insolence. If Lovisa had been encouraged, given responsibilities as a young girl, if she hadn't been asked to conform, what would she have been like today? I'd like to ask Lovisa about what happened to her, what made her the way she is, but I know some things are better left alone.

My stomach spasms and I squirm.

What if I'm never able to sleep again?

I swallow my panic. Surely, sleep will come eventually? I'll lie here. I'll think of Isabella. The way she looks when she sits by her mirror in the evening, braiding her hair, tilting her head, pulling one strand across, then the next.

In the night, footsteps moving around the house, up the front porch, and later, descending again. I don't think I have slept yet. I am too tired to open my eyes. The village is growing restless. I don't like it.

Someone is below my window. Get up, I tell myself, but I can't. A voice, low, but persistent. 'He is not telling the truth. It can't be a coincidence. There must be more.'

I need to make sense of it. But I am so tired.

L

It is morning. Yet again I sit outside on the porch and watch nature realise it has to wake up. Inside, someone descends the stairs. There is a pause, then Magnus steps out. The wood creaks and he sits down beside me. For a while, we don't speak. His body is warm against my arm. I can't remember when I last sat this close to another person. Was it with Eva? No, in fact, we rarely seemed to sit down.

Magnus yawns and strokes his beard with his hand. 'Why did you ask Jacob about who was born here and who wasn't?'

'I don't know . . . Ester said the settlers made it an issue.'

'Did she?' He frowns.

'You walked away to look at something.'

He leans away from me, so as to see my face. 'You handled Jacob well last night.'

I snort.

'No, you did. Jacob was upset. You kept asking, but in a nice way. And clearly, there is something to it.'

He doesn't mean it, but it is a kind thing to say.

Magnus nods and yawns again. His shoulders slump. His beard has grown since we left Stockholm. The dark hair gathered in its habitual pigtail needs a wash.

'You look tired,' I say.

'The light doesn't bother you at night?'

I shake my head. In fact, I sleep better here than I've ever done.

Magnus sighs and says no more.

We follow the river. The Lapp woman's face is grim. She walks to the side of me, pokes her cane in the ground every so often, bends, looks – as if there is anything to see. At her every move, the brass rings on her belt chink. I have decided I don't like her. She's just a grumpy old woman.

Once we reach the western edge of the mountain, we'll begin crossing it, or so Magnus says. I don't care what we do. I find the sound of streaming water lulling. My skirts catch on bushes and make it heavy to walk. I take one step, then another. When I catch a glimpse of Magnus, his blue eyes shine. I wonder if Isabella has ever seen him like this.

I can imagine her raising an eyebrow. 'In the forest?'

Their union surprised me. My father had always adored my sister, but not long before her engagement to Magnus was announced, they had a terrible argument. My father felt she had dallied with one of the young men who had visited us for supper. 'You behaved no better than a fallen woman!' he yelled and leaned over her as if he could print his words on her with his breath. 'Will you be going to visit him tonight, too?'

I was so young, I didn't understand what his words meant but I could tell it was bad.

My sister didn't cry. Not one tear. She just sat, hands in her lap. When he was finished, she bent her head – once, slowly – it looked as if she was saying she recognised his wisdom and she was learning from it. And then she looked up and said: 'Everything I know, I have learned from you.'

She said it softly. It took a moment for her words and their dual meaning to register with my father. Then he gasped. It was weeks before the two of them spoke again. It surprises me that he gave her Magnus. My experience of my father is that he doesn't forgive or forget. Ever.

My beautiful sister.

My sister's skirts rustle when she turns, her hair holds the light of any straying ray, her scent enters a room ahead of her.

The day of the fight, after my father left, and my sister was standing by the window, I drew close to her. I stood by her side, pressing my arm against hers with some foolish notion of showing solidarity.

'Step away from me, you little savage.'

She grabbed the skin of my upper arm with two fingers and pinched – pinched until I cried out in pain. Then she let go. All the while, her face had remained mild. I couldn't understand. I still can't. Why did she hurt me? But I began to realise then the extent to which she and I were different breeds. I resemble my mother; anything I think or feel is written upon me like a sheet of paper. My sister is much more durable.

Down below, Magnus steps from one rock to another. He looks up, catches my eye and smiles at me. For some reason it hurts.

Will I ever have somewhere or someone I can call 'home'? In my mind's eye, Eva is looking at me with disgust.

No, I will always be alone. I know this. And yet still, in any moment of connection, no matter how meagre, how faint, my puny soul will hope. In that perhaps one day, there will be someone or something to call 'mine'.

Pathetic.

Power. To speak and be heard – be heeded. To be revered. Asked for advice. To decide, for it to be so. Whether that command is over one, or many – to be above, to be more.

All power comes to an end; I realise that now. And, then, afterwards, you see that without those who follow, you are not whole. You cannot be yourself. For the self you created, was for them.

What do you think someone would be willing to do, to recover a single grain of what they had before? Who or what would they sacrifice? How far would they go?

Power. The old ways gave me mine. Not once did it occur to me that I would grieve the loss of it. But then I am human. Or, at least, I was.

ℬ

The mountain lies glum; a grey lump sweating in the sunshine. My mouth feels dry.

I shake my head as if that could bring order to my thoughts. Like the church on Blackåsen Mountain came to stretch the *sita* in different directions, since coming back here, I, too, am being torn. I keep thinking about old traditions. I am letting myself become scared.

The Lord is my shepherd. I shall not want.

Beside me, Raven Baby stumbles. Her nose is white underneath the hat, her mouth half open. It gives her face a vacant expression.

Perhaps she didn't say Nila's name after all. Maybe my mind is playing tricks on me. Nila always said I could make a lake out of any little drop of rain.

Bear has begun criss-crossing Blackåsen. He stands for a long time staring up at the mountain, then sketches a wiggly line in his book. Then he walks his line all the way to the top, stopping often to draw a correction or dig at the ground. From what I can tell, he is trying to get to the solid rock underneath the vegetation. He looks at every bare stone, and into rabbit holes. He digs with a pick, and chips at the rock. He draws. Each outcrop, each cliff face, each stream, he sketches. He measures dips and slopes. By the time he has finished, nobody will know the mountain like him.

People are not supposed to look at mountains the way Bear does. He strips it, embarrasses it. He picks it apart, his demeanour cold.

If Nila were here, he'd know what to do.

A cool draught against my legs. I have no right to wish for Nila.

When we left Blackåsen last spring – not long after the dogs had attacked the herd, we travelled to the high mountains. There, the nights were light and food was plenty. The reindeer calved. We were not in each other's way all the time. We settled down. After a few weeks, I began to believe things had gone back to normal. But the seasons passed too fast and the days yet again became shorter. Darkness grew. We returned to Blackåsen Mountain, and whatever we had left behind was still there, waiting for us.

The first day in our winter camp on Blackåsen, Nila had left by the time I woke up. I knew where he had gone and what he was doing – the tradition was to sacrifice whenever we set up at a new site. How I wished he hadn't. When I came out of the *kåta*, the others nodded; then, as they noticed I was alone, their faces hardened. And I saw it in their gazes: rein him in, their eyes said. He's your man, control him. Dávvet was the only one who would speak to me that morning.

Resentment. I could no longer look at my husband without it eating me. I know what resentment looks like. I see it in Innga: the harsh gaze, the downturned corners of the mouth, the false smiles. It isn't pretty.

And, like the others, I was afraid. Afraid of Priest, of Constable, and, most of all, of God.

'Stop now,' I said when Nila returned. I had planned to be

nicer, but I didn't have it in me. I didn't want to give him anything.

'It's not that easy, Biijá.' The whites of his eyes ran red.

I should have asked questions, but my resentment felt like blistering water in a pot.

'You are shaming us,' I said.

That is what I said: 'shaming us'.

In the evening, like all other nights, the *sita* gathered by the fire.

'Another winter, a new season,' Nila said. 'I have many hopes.'

Right then, someone snorted.

I gasped, looked around, couldn't tell who. Had Nila heard it, too? I don't know. If they mocked him now, it wouldn't be long before they opposed him openly. Him, or us? Dávvet's eyes on the other side of the flames caught mine.

When the fire died, Dávvet and I remained. Perhaps I stayed because I knew the conversation to come. Perhaps I wanted it.

'The members of the *sita* are one and the same. Whatever one of us does goes for all of us,' Dávvet said. 'The old ways must go.'

I felt a hot surge in my chest, whilst the weight in my stomach remained cold. Then, I thought of how Nila had looked before he left the fire: his eyes searching. I felt a wave of the old tenderness for him.

Dávvet nodded, rose, and left.

Why, oh why, did I tell Nila he was shaming us?

I have reached the peak, ahead of Bear this time, I turn, and as I do it, I realise that I am looking to him for comfort. Why! Why would I look to him for anything?

He comes up beside me and I frown, as if I'm angry with him, but he doesn't notice. Raven Baby dawdles further away.

'I'll sketch the east half of the mountain today,' he says. 'Later, when I am done drawing, I'll dig trenches down to the solid rock. To delineate the iron.' He stares into his book.

I don't know what he means. All I can think is that he said 'dig', and he shouldn't be digging anything. Not here. He mustn't.

Bear pencils in an outline of the other side of the mountain, eyes flipping between his book and the view. Up. Down. Up. Down. Then he closes his book and sets off downhill.

Nila said we must never disturb this mountain.

I stare at Bear's straight back in the white shirt, the long hair underneath the hat. Bear stops, pulls up the glass piece from his trouser pocket and leans against a rock side. He sees the wrong things. There is the landscape he is drawing, but there is also a second one, one that he cannot see.

We reach the bottom and Bear goes further westwards – thirty, forty steps – and then draws his line. I imagine the mountain growling now: 'There are trails already. Why would you go around breaking new ground?'

'Ten or twelve steps to the left, there, behind those trees, is a good spot to set a trap for grouse,' I say.

'Oh yes?' Bear's voice is neutral.

We pass the gravel. 'When the birds return after the winter, they fly above this mound of stone. This is how we know the time is coming for us to leave for the high mountains.'

Raven Baby gazes at the sky, hands at her waist supporting her back. Bear doesn't respond.

I point to the den, 'One of our young ones, Joel, got bitten by the mother fox here one year. His arm swelled to the size of a log.'

Bear halts. Then he takes his pickaxe and begins poking in the den.

'They come back,' I say. My voice comes out a whisper. 'Year after year.'

Bear glances up at me and stops digging. Too late. No fox will return here now.

After this, I keep my mouth shut.

We reach the yellow cliff outcrop, and I can hear the voices of the *sita* now: 'Hawk! Look a hawk!' Gáhte, my brother, running, screaming and pointing, that severe winter when we were competing with birds of prey for food. Noisier, noisier. By this bare patch, where the wind once swept down like a giant hand and flattened three spruce trees to the ground in one go, I hear the words: 'How I miss him.' My mother. By then, my father had been gone for a year.

The mountain, too, is talking: 'The rain is always heaviest on the south side. It has smoothed out the stones.' 'The north wind passes here. Look at the bent trees.'

I want to press my hands to my ears and scream.

When we arrive at *The One Who Sees*, the afternoon sun leans on the treetops.

'The pure iron bed ends right here.' Bear double-checks his notes. 'This is where we stop today.'

As he says it, the next line in Nila's verse comes to me: '*Beyond The One Who Binds Water. By The One Who Sees. Night turns day, weight turns light . . .*'

I think about the line between the speckled and the black that Bear showed us yesterday. The verse might be truer than I thought. And then my heart compresses, for at this point the voice that read the verse always turned grave. What came next?

The words are gone.

189

Nila was the last one. I have had this thought before and I felt relief then. But now, I realise what it means: Nila was our mapmaker, the keeper of our memories, of our legends, and he was the last one. Never again will our people have a *noiade*. Without him, we have no past.

'*Beyond The One Who Binds Water. By The One Who Sees. Night turns day, weight turns light . . .*'

How does it continue?

I have no idea.

'*Beyond The One Who Binds Water. By The One Who Sees. Night turns day, weight turns light . . .*'

On my way back to my site, I repeat the lines, over and over. I wonder if anyone remembers the whole verse. I think not. We've tried hard to forget.

I hear voices. They stand in a half-circle in the glade by the old maze: Hunter, Long Beard, Night Man, Constable's Widow, and her father, and Child of Village; all of them facing Holy Woman.

'And so we must continue to praise God,' Holy Woman says. 'For in praising him lies a magnificent power.'

Holy Woman sounds tired. Her face is pale and her eyes so dark, it looks like all life has left her.

'Let us pray,' she says.

They bend their heads. Everyone apart from Child of Village – she stares up into the sky. A single Bluethroat twirls in the forest to the west. After a while, Hunter glances up at Holy Woman. Constable's Widow does the same. Then Long Beard. They expect her to lead them in prayer. But she remains quiet, her cracked lips moving in silence.

At my site, I sit up until my head lolls, and I wake. I long for someone to put logs on the fire for me, to keep it burning.

I long for good light. I yearn for morning. I hope that what-ever is stirring in the shadows will stay there. At one point, my mother comes to sit with me. I want to rest my head in her lap, but instead, I close my eyes and blink her away. I can't talk to you, I think. God wouldn't allow it.

M

Night lasted fifty-two minutes. I looked at my clock when the sun went down. For precisely fifty-two minutes, darkness held sway. Oh, darkness. God, darkness. I felt my body go. My legs twitched. Ah bliss . . .

Then the sun soared again and my body sprang up. I was wide awake.

I don't know what to do to. I have to sleep.

In the early morning, I stand by the river. The spruce forest on the other side spreads in bands of different greens. The river runs black or silver, depending on which way I look.

Yesterday, Lovisa and I had barely begun walking before Ester was by our side. This morning, Lovisa is probably still fast asleep and I have already walked a whole length of the mountain on the west side of the pure iron band, but Ester has not arrived. I miss her presence. She is a pleasant companion; potters about, stops to look at some tree, or bush.

I look in my book. The base of the other side of the mountain displays that same surface rock so, at this point, I am assuming the vein of iron goes straight through. The middle of the mountain is entirely composed of it. How far the deposit descends into the earth, I can't tell. Eventually deep pits will have to be dug to understand. One day, we'll mine it.

★

Late afternoon, I begin digging a trench halfway up the mountain using my pickaxe, and then the spade I've borrowed from Jacob. I've chosen an area without trees to avoid having to deal with the roots, but it is still hard work for a single man. I am forty inches down before my spade hits rock. I expose the rock, make the trench about a foot wide, and then continue digging uphill, along the iron margin. I'll dig one trench by this east margin, one on the other side, and then one in the middle so I can sample the core. High above me, a hefty outcrop casts a long shadow. The incline leading up to it is full of loose gravel.

The forest is silent but for the sound of me putting my shovel into earth. The sun is scorching hot, and sweat drips into my eyes. I push my hat further down on my forehead. I like this part of my work less: days and days of hard labour when you are often gripped by a sense of hopelessness. You start doubting your own abilities to read the land. You have to keep reminding yourself that there is only one way to find out whether your theories are correct. And once trenches are dug, I'll be better able to estimate the quantity of iron. Perhaps, for a small payment, some of the men in the village would be willing to help.

Mid afternoon, I stand up and stretch. My throat is parched and my back aches. I have managed to dig a twenty-foot length. The bared iron glitters in the sun. I am done for today.

I swing my bag onto my shoulder and begin climbing, planning to circle the large outcrop, and then walk down to the village on the other side.

I don't know what makes me look up.

The huge boulder comes towards me, falling through the air. For a fraction of a second, I doubt my eyes, then I throw myself to the side. The stone scrapes past and hits the earth with a crash, felling two pine trees before it settles.

Dear God. Oh God.

The peak of the mountain lies still.

That was too close.

My ankle hurts as I stand up. I am panting. If I had died here, no one would have known where to find me.

How on earth did this happen? The boulder is as big as me.

When my breathing is calm again, I climb up to see where the rock was situated before it fell. On the peak, I find a hollow amongst the other stones; it wasn't sitting solidly. It was waiting to fall, and I walked underneath the mound of stones without thinking twice.

It's the tiredness, the lack of sleep. If I am not careful, I'll make a mistake.

On the other side of the crest, at a turn of the path, a man stands. The sight of him startles me. His beard is long and his eyes, bloodshot. He scratches his neck and then his armpit.

'Now they're dead,' he says.

'Excuse me?'

'The angel of vengeance got them,' the man says and nods.

He takes a step closer to me, and I smell urine and sweat. 'I saw him,' he whispers. 'The *noiade*. Lakeside. He has been here all spring.'

'Who?'

'I've seen him squatting by the cairn, catching pike with his bare hands. Not many people know that's where the larger fish hide.' He chortles. 'But then he was no stranger to this region. I recognised him. He used to be here long ago. Shared history. Shared destiny.'

He takes a big step past me and disappears into the forest.

*

'How are you?' I ask Frida Liljeblad, the priest's widow.

'There are days and then there are days. We are approaching harvest, and that will keep me busy.' She pauses. 'I guess I should be asking you how you are doing.'

I follow her gaze to my torn trousers, bloody at the knees, at my filthy arms and hands. I can imagine what my face must look like. I want to turn and see if my boots have made marks on the vicarage floor.

'The mountain is a trial,' I say.

She laughs. 'You are mapping it? Were Rune's maps then of no use?'

'They are good.' I shake my head. 'I think it's inevitable – being a mineralogist you simply have to see for yourself. You have to draw it, understand how it arose . . .'

She nods and looks out of the window. 'I think it's the only place he ever wanted to be, Ulf; back here on Blackåsen. After finishing his studies, he served in another parish before the Church let him return here. I thought this was just another posting. I didn't realise we were coming here for good. Later, I understood he always planned it that way – he would get his training and return here to never leave again.'

That is rare. These days young men see the world, travel, live in different towns, in different countries.

Perhaps it's not possible for us outsiders to understand the draw this place has on those born here,' she says.

How apt, I think. Blackåsen village having magnetic propensities, like its mountain.

'Me, I am going back down south,' she says.

'When?'

'As soon as possible. I am hoping someone will make the journey to the coast so I can travel with them. Worst case, I'll

195

have to wait until market-time, then lots of people will go. You see, I have forest fear.' She smiles.

She asks if I am leaving soon.

'Jacob said your husband attended Adelaide Gustavsdotter's sermons,' I say instead.

She nods. 'Though not recently.'

I raise my eyebrows: Why not?

'They fought. I think they had words about her teachings.'

'How?'

'I don't know. I never attended Adelaide's gatherings myself, but Ulf said her teachings had changed. They were . . . deviating, that was the word he used.'

They would always have been deviating. I remember the maid saying there had been fighting at the parish council meeting. 'Do you think this had anything to do with his death?'

Mrs Liljeblad smiles, genuinely this time. 'Hardly. It was likely one of those fine religious points a priest has to worry about, but which doesn't mean anything to anybody else.'

I say, 'You know, I met this strange man in the forest. Bearded, wild-looking . . . I haven't seen him in the village.'

'Anders, most likely.'

'Anders?' I ask.

'He lives on the other side of the lake,' Mrs Liljeblad says. 'He keeps to himself. I think he's not quite right in the head.'

Lovisa is in the garden when I return, and I join her. She holds flowers in her hand – a northern version of *Campanula rotundifolia* – bellflowers. I light my pipe, and enjoy that first inhalation and the rush of tobacco. The sunset isn't a real sunset. The sun shines the same, and yet I know evening has fallen. How? A smutty tinge to the sky. The grass darkening against the blue.

The day's events play through my mind. 'Angel of Vengeance', and this man . . . Anders, said he had met a noiade? I have no idea who that is.

Lovisa bends to pick another flower.

'How was your day?' I ask her.

She shrugs. 'How was yours?'

I shrug, too. That makes her laugh.

I puff on my pipe. 'Can I ask you for something?'

She tilts her head.

'Could you go and see Adelaide Gustavsdotter?'

'Why?'

'I met this strange man in the forest, and he said that the "angel of vengeance" had got to the men who died. I wonder what or who might be seeking vengeance. Nobody in this village talks to me. Perhaps they would to you.'

I already regret my request. I shouldn't ask her. She is a child. The minister's daughter. My wife's sister. My protégée. The minister asked me to find out. He'd be furious if he knew I sent Lovisa to run my errands.

She looks at the flowers in her hand. 'I'll go.'

'Be careful,' I say.

She makes a face, pushes her hand in her pocket, and lets out a cry.

I grab her wrist. On her finger is a large drop of red blood.

She withdraws her hand. Her eyes look black as she takes something from her pocket; a steel pin with a red circle at its top. My heart beats faster.

'Whose?' I ask.

'Mr Palm's,' she mutters, without looking at me.

I hold out my hand and she puts the badge in my palm, followed by a brooch and a bar of soap?

*

I wait until after dinner, when Lovisa disappears up the stairs and Helena into the kitchen. Jacob and I are alone.

'You are a mining man,' I say, 'a mineralogist, like me.'

He stiffens, then nods.

'I am curious,' I say. 'Why you didn't tell me?'

'They wouldn't let us break the mountain's surface. A few weeks' work would be enough to supply one of the ironworks by the coast for a season. We could have done it together. But the parish council wouldn't allow it. They wouldn't even discuss it. And then, when I said that it wasn't theirs to decide, they threatened me.'

His stare is intense, his tone scathing.

'Why?'

'I don't know! No reason at all. Adelaide, Ulf, Jan-Erik – all of them in wonderful agreement.'

Mining the iron wouldn't have made Jacob wealthy. But it would have provided for him and his wife. Perhaps he is venturous, or perhaps he came here for some other reason. But once he was here, being a mining man, seeing the mountain day in and day out, it would, in time, have appeared irresistible. Jacob said he'd been in the village for ten years. Ten years is a very long time . . .

'I didn't kill them,' Jacob says.

'Then what happened?'

'Rune came. He was here for ten days, and spent all of his time doing exactly what you are doing.'

'You know what it's like; being a mineralogist, he would have wanted to study it.'

Though Rune hadn't begun digging trenches to delineate the iron. Perhaps the existing maps were enough for him.

Jacob's mouth is a thin line. The skin by his lips looks green. 'There must be more to this than that.'

I shake my head. 'The parish council did not ask me here.'

'Then what is going on?'

'If it wasn't for the men being killed, I would say "nothing". I have taken samples of the iron – it is magnetite-apatite, just as all the records show. Nothing is different from what I expected to find. It's a magnificent deposit, too far away to be of real value.'

Jacob's forehead creases. 'I don't understand why they won't break it?'

Yes, it doesn't make sense. I remember what Anders said about an 'angel of vengeance', but I don't tell Jacob this.

Jacob shakes his head. 'How did you know about me?' he asks.

I have Falu Mining School's pin stuck to the inside of my lapel, but I can't tell him this without giving Lovisa away. Later, I'll try to put it somewhere where he can find it.

'Just a good guess,' I say.

L

Sigrid opens the door and her face lights up. She takes a step forward and gives me her hand. She smells of some flower, a light, green scent, too fleeting. Her fingers are thin, her skin dry. I want to lean in and smell more. Apple blossom?

Adelaide sits by the table bent over a book – the Bible? She looks up, but doesn't say a word.

Sigrid tilts her head. 'I'll make coffee.' In the faint light inside, her freckles make her face seem grey.

I hesitate in the vestibule. People do this all the time – call on strangers, introduce themselves, exchange pleasantries.

People do. I don't.

I guess I had imagined a womanly room, soft, full of pretty things, but this room feels masculine, with its heavy wooden furniture – a table, chairs, a stone fireplace, and the absence of decorations. A photogene lamp stands on the windowsill. Up against one wall, a lone bed, strictly made. Against the opposite wall, the same thing. A house inherited from her parents that she could never refurbish, or hadn't had the time to. 'Lucky', Mr Palm had said. Mrs Palm said Sigrid's family used to live in their house, before things turned bad, and Sigrid's mother, Susanna, did away with herself. I wonder if Sigrid laments that big, red house with its two floors.

The smell of coffee wafts through the cottage, and Sigrid hands Adelaide a mug. Adelaide buries her nose in the cup, inhales, closes her eyes and opens them again. 'I feel better already,' she says.

Sigrid smiles. She hands me a mug, too, the liquid black and hot.

'Sit,' Adelaide says and nods at the table. 'Sit,' she repeats.

I take a sip of the coffee and burn my tongue.

'Do you like it?' Sigrid asks.

I nod. I touch the roof of my mouth with the raw tip of my tongue.

'I put in a pinch of dirt. My mother used to say it gives it the strength of the earth.'

I make a face. Sigrid laughs out loud, and Adelaide, too, chortles. I smile, take another sip of the coffee, and now I taste the grit.

Sigrid pushes off the table and rises. She can't be going?

'I will see you, Lovisa,' she says, walks to the door, opens it, and disappears.

The room falls silent. As if Sigrid carries a humming with her, audible only by its absence. Outside, the light has changed from the thick, yellow glow of morning, to become whiter and sharper. People must be waking up, rising, going about their early chores.

'Where is your fellow traveller?' Adelaide asks. 'Magnus.' In her mouth, his name sounds foreign.

I shrug. 'He is probably on the mountain.'

Adelaide frowns and looks down. I study the way Adelaide drinks from her mug: she twists her wrist and takes her mouthfuls in a roundabout way. She has tucked her dark hair behind her ears and it makes them stand out slightly.

This is ludicrous. To think that I would be able to initiate a conversation about her past and ask her questions. No, we sit in silence. I have nothing to say. My heart begins to beat harder. This woman opposite me has a following. She preaches on Sundays to men and women. She was born amongst them, and rose above them. Now, many of them abide by her.

I find her looking at me.

'I . . . It's hard to leave the Church,' I say.

Adelaide raises her eyebrows, waiting.

'I left, too,' I say. 'I mean, my reasons were probably different, but . . .'

She nods, as if saying, Ah, you too. Then you know. 'I believed in callings. This one was mine.'

I realise that in bringing up Adelaide's faith, I am expecting an attack of sorts; convincing arguments, sharp questions. Perhaps, I am hoping for it.

'You don't try to . . . convert people?'

'It is not for everyone.'

It is said mildly, but there it is: the shut door.

I swallow. My mouth is dry. She is shutting me out without giving me a chance. She knows nothing about me.

'You make a distinction between you,' I say, 'between the ones who were born here and those who came later.'

Adelaide twirls her cup in her hands. 'Don't you think it is always the case, Lovisa? We share different memories. We have different pasts. How could we be the same?'

She places her cup on the table and sits up. I can imagine her, in the pulpit – the way she must look when she preaches. Fierce, eyes on fire.

'What brought you here?' she asks, and the X between her eyebrows is back.

'Magnus was asked . . .'

'Not him. You.'

I hesitate. 'My father sent me away—'

She jerks her head: No. 'What really brought you here?'

At once, Eva is with us. Long, brown, straight hair, large blue eyes, stupid, stupid yellow hat.

I am there now: in the library, on that last day, leaning forward, my hands on the desk between us, placing my lips against Eva's. The silence, as I look in her eyes. Her empty face. I kiss her again, bite her lip. Eva rises. A book falls to the floor. Then she leaves to tell my father.

'Many have searched for answers in different things,' Adelaide says, eyes squinting into mine. 'There is no shame in that.'

I can't breathe. Things have slowed down. I stand up.

As I walk away, I wonder if she is watching me from her window, stumbling down the path.

She got it wrong.

To have kissed a woman doesn't frighten me. Why would I be ashamed of that? It means nothing.

There it is – the thing that frightens me.

Six months of trying, of longing. Of coveting. Six months. And then, in kissing Eva, I yet again felt nothing.

I am in my room. The small field in front of my window is empty; the leaves, still, the grass immobile. I wrap my arms around myself. Early evening, there's a soft knock on my door. In the hallway dusk, Magnus's scar makes it look like that side of his face is missing. He smells of smoke. His scent overpowers mine.

'I wanted to ask –' He sees my expression and interrupts himself. 'Did something happen?' He touches my arm. 'At Adelaide's?'

And here it is again – a connection with another human being, thin, faint, perhaps an illusion, and yet my soul rises, opens. I don't belong anywhere, I want to say to Magnus. I am not like anybody else. I wish . . .

No, he's just hoping I found something out for him.

'I didn't go to see her,' I say. 'You have no right to ask me to help you in this. Don't ever ask me again.'

He doesn't shy away. 'I was going to tell you,' he says. 'You must try and find a constant . . . something steady and unchangeable, that you can hold in your mind and revert to, when things around you feel uncertain.'

At first, my heart soars; he understands. But something is different about Magnus. It's not what he says, it's how he says it.

My heart begins to thump in my chest.

Magnus speaks more slowly now, each word a weight in his mouth. I am certain his accent has changed, too. There is that same whistling in his pronunciation that people from around here use when they speak.

The stairway creaks. The grocer or his wife. We startle into motion. As I close my door, Magnus does the same on the other side of the hallway, still looking at me.

My room seems cooler. I walk to the window and close it, as though I could shut this chill out.

After a while, bedsprings squeak in one of the rooms. Then the merchant's house falls silent and not so much as a breath can be heard.

Every man is a map. Each significant choice, each meaningful event, etching itself on the landscape of the heart. You only need to understand a few of those markings to guess the remaining land, to understand the origins.

Some people have a flair for it. 'They are reading my thoughts,' you say. 'They see inside my head.'

It is a skill and thus it can be taught.

How, then, to read the map of another?

Ask questions. Think deeply about the person by your side: What does he see? What does he do? And most importantly: Why?

You say you could never do this. You think you are already made. I am telling you: inside of you lies a vast uncharted territory. Do something with it. Something useful.

B

Once, the priest preached 'seek and ye shall find'. Beside me, Suonjar cleared her throat and winked at me. Everyone knows that if you have lost something, the last thing you must do is seek. Forget all about it, step away, and what you look for will eventually come and tap you on the arm, demanding your attention. Yesterday, I did everything I could not to worry about the forgotten verse. But the few lines I did remember kept running through my mind; water on a wheel, faster and faster. I even woke up mumbling them.

'I missed you yesterday,' Bear says beside me.

'It was Sunday.'

Nobody works on Sunday. It's the day of rest.

'Oh?' he says. 'I thought it was Friday?'

'No, Sunday,' I say, sharply.

The incline is steep. Raven Baby leans forward to counter it. Bear pushes his hat far back over his neck. I exhale. He got the days wrong. That can happen to anyone.

He stops at a large boulder and draws it on his sketch. He did the same thing further down. He squats and squints back towards that first boulder, and draws the line on his sheet between them. He meets my gaze.

'Landmarks. Signposts that can easily be seen from a distance. I'll use them to take cross bearings later.'

Just like *The One Who Binds Water* and *The One Who Sees* are for us. Landmarks. Marks on the land.

Raven Baby's face is brighter today. She knows Nila's name, I think.

'I tried to get one of the men in the village to help me dig,' Bear says, 'but I couldn't get anyone, not even for payment.'

That surprises me. People here like money. Priest was forever preaching about the camel and the eye of the needle. Suonjar explained that a camel was a reindeer with humps.

'Be careful,' Bear says at the peak. 'Yesterday, when I walked below this spot, a large boulder came tumbling down and just missed me.'

Really? Blackåsen is quite steady.

We pass over to the other side, and I stop.

Jesus. My eyes well up.

Bear has scarred Blackåsen. There is a deep cut in its northern side all the way down to the gleaming iron. The mountain underneath me awaits my reaction. This is why the boulder fell. It was a warning.

Bear scampers down the side, pebbles showering his feet. Raven Baby hurries behind him. He puts his bag by the wound in the ground. Oh, how can I make him see?

'I met someone yesterday,' Bear says when I reach them. 'Anders. Long beard.' He indicates mid-chest with his hand.

The ground pulsates with the shock of the cut, its edges trying to heal up. Bear unfastens his spade from its place on his bag.

'He said an "angel of vengeance" had got to the men who died.'

Oh, never mind Lone One. 'It's not a good idea to dig here,' I say.

'He also talked of someone . . . the noiade?'

The short hairs on my neck rise. 'He talked about a *noiade*?'

'Perhaps. Does it mean something to you?'

I hesitate. 'The *noiade* were our religious leaders. A long time ago.'

Raven Baby is studying us, eyes narrow, face pale.

'Anders said this *noiade* was not new to the region. I think he meant the Lapp who was caught after the murders. But you didn't know him?'

A memory at the back of my mind stirs and wants to get out.

'There was a second tribe.' The wound by Bear's feet looks like an open ear. I am talking straight into the mountain.

Bear nods to me, indicating that I should continue. He thrusts the shovel down into the ground, kicks it deeper with his foot. My chest shudders at each strike.

'It was about forty years ago.' I clear my throat. 'One winter, our *sita* didn't come here. When we returned, there were signs of another tribe on our winter site. We never met them. A Lapp whom I don't know, but who is familiar with the region – he might have belonged to them.'

The winter after that with Dávvet and Livli, after we pushed Livli out, we stayed away. Perhaps Nila worried we'd come across her dead, or worse. 'Nothing but problems to us, Blackåsen,' he muttered. I was troubled. It wasn't up to us to make that kind of choice. I was right to feel fear. It became the worst season we had ever had. The weather was harsh. The animals faltered.

If that Lapp was another *noiade*, that could be why I didn't know his face and Nila did.

'And then what happened?' Raven Baby asks. 'When you came back here, I mean?'

I shrug: nothing. Nila's father died there, in a foreign country, a bit like Moses. Not that Blackåsen is any promised land, exactly. And then we came back, and . . .

No, there is something.

Suonjar remarked upon it at our arrival. Something about the children?

'When we came back,' I say, 'things had changed in the village.'

'How?' Bear stands up.

'The children were different.' I have to think hard to remember their real names. 'Adelaide, who was a young girl then, had had her vision. Per had killed his father and run away.'

I stretch my memory further back. Was this when Singing One – she is dead now – turned in on herself? Yes. Was there more?

'As for the others . . . it was as if they were no longer friends . . .'

The verse – something about bad echoes over the mountain? The elder said that whatever was uttered on Blackåsen would echo for ever. It was one of those things they used to scare us children: *Don't scream, it will echo for ever.*

'Who else was young then?'

I try to remember. 'Anders, Ulf, Jan-Erik, and Rune . . .'

My list hovers above us. Three of them are dead now.

'An "Angel of Vengeance",' Bear leans on his shovel, arms crossed on the handle. 'But if something happened back then, why wait so long to seek vengeance?' He creases his face, bites his lip. 'Perhaps Rune needed to come back here for it to happen. It can't be a coincidence, his return and the murders.'

Grating on the peak, feet hitting loose stone: Hunter and Long Beard step out above us. I hadn't heard them coming.

They skid towards us on the gravel. Hunter holds a rifle in his hand.

'Magnus, right?' Hunter says.

Bear stands up tall, his expression turning grim. 'Who am I speaking to?'

Judging by their expressions, they won't be giving out their names.

'What are you doing on the mountain?' Long Beard says.

'I am mapping the iron ore.'

'Some things are best left unmapped,' Hunter says.

'Is this a threat?'

Long Beard looks at Bear, at Raven Baby, and then at me, and begins to laugh. Hunter joins him. 'Just a bit of advice.'

'Who are they?' Magnus asks me, once they're gone.

'Matts Fjellström and his brother, Daniel,' I say.

'Were they born here?' Raven Baby asks.

Yes.

The three of us watch after them, standing side by side.

M

Early in the afternoon, as I thrust the shovel in the ground, my vision distorts. A flickering flares up all around the edges, limiting my sight to that of a mere tunnel. I push the shovel in the ground again, heave earth to the side, and then stop. I drink water and blink. Ester and Lovisa sit further away. My ears have blocked, I yawn to release the pressure and drink more water. I have finished one trench – it is about thirty-five feet long – and I am one third of the way through the second one at the opposite rim of the iron band. Meeting those villagers up here made me more resolved. I won't let anyone think they can frighten me.

But I have overdone it. I might be about to faint. I glance at Ester and Lovisa again, I should tell them.

'I think we are done for today,' I say instead.

As we walk back, I have to watch where I put my feet. I try to breathe slowly and walk at a steady pace. The flicker is still there.

The sun's rays, long white legs that wheel across the earth, ready to scorch us if we get in their path. I am hallucinating. I don't look at the sky again, but at the ground by my feet. One step, then another. We leave Ester behind and enter the village. I avoid looking at Lovisa.

We reach the dirt road and I feel better. The flickering stops. What a relief. I will have to be more careful in future.

Then I realise I've wasted a whole afternoon when I could

have been digging. The extent of my anger with myself is ridiculous. I promised the minister to find answers. The mapping is secondary. Only, it doesn't feel that way.

'Let's go and see Adelaide Gustavsdotter,' I say to Lovisa.

'I am not going,' she declares.

Fine. I shrug.

Adelaide rips open the door while my hand is still raised to knock. She hesitates, then takes a step backwards. The two men we met up the mountain are with her, the brothers, Matts and Daniel Fjellström. A hole gapes in the window and shards of glass litter the sill and the floor.

'What happened?' I ask.

'Someone threw a stone,' Adelaide says.

'Who?'

She shrugs. 'It's not the first time and it won't be the last.'

Matts Fjellström, the one who held a rifle, begins to sweep together the glass fragments. They clink. His brother, tall, long bearded, fetches a bucket.

'Things don't get any worse here than this,' Adelaide says.

A buzz comes from outside. A bumblebee or a wasp.

'Only it did,' I say.

'That wasn't one of our people. It was that Lapp,' Matts Fjellström says.

Adelaide squats down to pick up the larger glass pieces. She throws them in the bucket.

'Someone said the three men who died were killed by an "angel of vengeance". That something happened years ago that involved them. Would you know what that was?'

Adelaide gasps. She holds her wrist. A deep slash crosses her whole palm. Blood begins to pour, down her arm, onto the floor.

Matts Fjellström grabs her under her elbow, helps her onto a chair. Daniel, tears a strip from a towel and ties it around her hand. Her face is white.

'Are you all right?' I ask.

'I cut myself,' she says.

After a while, she shakes her head. '"An angel"? Who would say this?'

'Anders.'

'Anders.' She nods, and says, 'Many things have happened, but I can't recall one thing in particular.'

Her answer sounds somewhat feeble, but then she has just hurt herself.

'What about that summer, when you got your calling?' I ask.

Matts bends down to pick up glass shards, but slower now, more careful. Daniel holds out the bucket for him to put them in.

'Was it not the same summer that Per killed his father?' I ask.

'You know that Per has paid his dues.' Adelaide's voice is mild.

As I leave her house, footsteps behind me make me turn. Daniel, comes after me, face contorted.

'Stop digging,' he hisses. 'Stop asking questions.'

I can feel the muscles in my arms tense.

'Daniel?' Adelaide's voice, still mild, calls him back.

Daniel Fjellström glances towards the house, looks at me again, and then leaves, walking backwards. 'Stop,' he mouths.

Lovisa and I sit on the bench beneath the kitchen window in Jacob and Helena's garden after dinner. The sleeplessness that first brought on elation and energy is now killing me. Though

Lovisa is sitting right here, I can't quite make out her features. I lean my head against the wall behind me. The evening sky is covered by clouds. The outline of them glows and shimmers, displaying the strength of the sun behind.

'Do you think it will rain?' I ask, at the same time as Lovisa says: 'This is not a Lapp uprising.'

'No.'

'No.'

The minister asked me to find out if this was an uprising. If I already know it isn't, why are we still here? Most likely, the Lapp did kill those men. Perhaps for something that happened in the past. But it was an isolated incident.

'We'll just finish mapping the iron,' I say.

We have found the missing maps. But they are old. What I am doing is important. All finds have to be mapped, again and again, as we learn new techniques and skills.

A bird's chirp twirls in the tree above us. Another one responds. One more—

'Angel of Vengeance.'

I startle, hair snagging against the wood. I realise I had closed my eyes. 'What?'

'You're thinking that the men who were killed once did something so bad they died for it.'

'I guess.'

'Including a priest.'

'Yes.'

Adelaide said the villagers are harmless, but I am not sure I trust her. I remember Daniel's contorted face. If she can't be trusted, and if the villagers are not harmless, then we should not stay one minute longer. We should pack tonight.

'We'll just map the iron,' I repeat.

The evening smells sweetly of lilies and warm water. Underneath Lovisa's chin there is a triangle of white skin. I want to close my eyes again and lean into her, put my nose against that patch of bare skin. I have a family, I think. I have a wife. Her name is Isabella. She braids her hair and pins the plaits up at her neck.

In the middle of the night, hammering on the door. *Bang-bang-bang.*

'Wake up! Wake up! Adelaide's house is on fire!'

My head is muddled. I dreamed about a yellow sun sinking into a red sea.

I open my door as Lovisa opens hers and our eyes meet. Jacob and Helena are already on their way down the stairs, out of the door, and we follow.

Fire in midnight sunshine, how strange it looks. In the light, the flames seem benign. But the land is dry as bone. Soon, black smoke rises to cloud the sky.

We create a line and move water in buckets from the small river behind Adelaide's house. In the beginning, the pails move fast, but it is not until morning that we manage to extinguish the blaze.

My eyes sting from the smoke. My arms ache. We are all black-faced and hollow-eyed. Adelaide rubs her forehead and stares at the charred remains of what used to be a house.

'You could have died,' Matts Fjellström says to her.

'What happened?' I ask.

Adelaide meets my gaze, then shakes her head, 'I don't know.' She takes a step forward, puts her arm around another woman, pale, freckled.

'It hasn't rained for weeks,' someone says.

The constable's sister, the maid, is standing by one of the

bushes. She bends down and lifts up a thick bunch of hay. She raises it high, then discards it. But I haven't seen hay anywhere else.

Matts Fjellström looks at the maid as well. 'You could have died, Adelaide,' he repeats.

I went to see him, the Lapp, in his gaol. I don't know what I had expected. Perhaps I thought the act would have left him strengthened; righteous, even proud. Perhaps I thought it would have left him deranged. I was certain there had to be some kind of a fierce emotion. But he was as if dead; wilted, hair hanging all over his face. I don't think he even realised I was there.

I first came across this man, or the trace of him, at my sites of worship when we returned to Blackåsen. I would compare him to myself, note similarities and differences. Through the years, every now and then, he would come to my mind, this parallel life somewhere out there in the forest.

That night the spirits woke me, showed him to me, told me of the evil he was about to do, I recognised him at once, though I had never before seen his face.

He'll hang for this, of course. It's fine. He wants to die.

L

'You have been most kind to us,' Magnus says to Mr and Mrs Palm, 'but in view of what happened last night, Lovisa and I will move to the vicarage.'

I am watching Magnus. I realise I worry about him. He has changed since we came here, but, for the moment, he is the old Magnus, my sister's husband.

'You are making a mistake,' Jacob says. He is sitting by the kitchen table, while his wife stands behind him.

'I have a responsibility for Lovisa to her father,' Magnus says.

'I know what you are thinking. But I had nothing to do with the fire.'

Magnus doesn't respond. I feel nauseous. Adelaide and Sigrid could have died.

When we leave, I see them through the window. Mrs Palm has put her hand on her husband's shoulder.

'I am not certain any place is safe, but Frida Liljeblad was not born here, nor is she a newcomer who will stay. She doesn't belong to either group,' Magnus says.

'You think Jacob did it?' I ask. 'Why?'

Magnus shakes his head. 'I don't know that he did, but he wants to extract the iron in the mountain and the parish council won't let him. Yesterday, someone threw a stone through Adelaide's window.' He shrugs. 'Perhaps he didn't realise how quickly the fire would spread.'

They are all living in wooden houses; the land is as dry as tinder. How could it not spread?

I think of Helena Palm's hand on Jacob's shoulder. How much can you forgive a loved one? How much could you tell? Could I tell another person everything I have done? The queasiness feels worse, and I swallow. I wonder if one has to.

I peek at Magnus, the long black hair in its tail, the short beard, the blue of his eyes, the scar.

'Tell me about you,' I say.

'Tell you what?'

'About you before us . . . before you came to our family.'

'I think there was no me before your family.'

He doesn't meet my gaze.

In my mind's eye, I see them: Magnus and Isabella, tall and erect, standing side by side without touching, but nevertheless closely, staunchly together.

'Come in.' The priest's widow walks ahead of us into the sunlit drawing room. 'Please sit down and I will get you something to drink.'

Normal life.

'No, thank you,' Magnus says. 'We have work to do.'

I sink down into one of the armchairs. 'I think I'll stay here,' I say.

Magnus closes his bag and puts on his hat. 'Then I'll see you later.'

He could show some disappointment over me not accompanying him. Instead his eyes gleam at the prospect of his beloved mountain.

Magnus departs. Frida Liljeblad hands me a glass of lemonade. She opens one of the windows, and leaves. She closes the door behind her when she walks out, as if she understands that what I desire most in the world right now is solitude in a sunlit room surrounded by books and beautiful furniture, bird song in the background. I lean my head back and close my eyes. I won't think one solitary thought about this miserable place or about what happens here. No, I will pretend I am at home instead. My mother has gone clothes shopping. I will join her. In the afternoon, we'll have tea at a ladies' cafe. We are having a big dinner tonight with guests. But before that, I am going to have a long bath, put on a new dress—

The door opens. I sit up. I must have fallen asleep.

'Did I wake you?' Sigrid asks.

'No.' My voice sounds thick. I rub my face.

Sigrid sits down in the armchair beside me. She is so small she has to stretch her thin arms to reach the armrests. Her cheeks are flushed. How can this woman be older than me? She looks like a child.

'I am glad you are here,' she says.

'What?'

'I knew you would come. Before you and your fellow traveller arrived at the village, I knew you were on your way. I waited for you,' Sigrid says.

I think of Eva.

'I don't think it's me you've been waiting for,' I say, carefully.

Sigrid stares at me, wants something I can't give her. I shake my head. Her eyes darken.

'I am sorry,' I say. I really don't want to hurt her.

'Do you hate him?' Sigrid asks, after a while.

'Who? Magnus?'

'The man who cut your hair?'

My hand flies up to touch my head.

'I would have hated,' she says.

I shrug.

She nods. 'I thought you were like me, but we are different.'

The open window moves. Its hinges squeak.

'Where are you staying now?' I try. 'After the fire?'

'There's an abandoned homestead across the road.' She shrugs.

'You were lucky to escape unharmed.'

She rises. 'This village deserves to burn.'

It is said lightly. Mrs Palm was correct: Sigrid is not all there. She doesn't understand they could have died. The villagers have taken care of her; she has never had to grow up. But perhaps, it won't matter. They'll continue to look after her and she'll never know that life can be quite different from how she imagines it. She'll never have to be disappointed.

'I thought you came for me,' Sigrid says.

'I am sorry,' I repeat.

'It is awful,' Frida says that night at dinner. 'People who have been neighbours for years, eyeing each other with suspicion.'

She leans forward to squeeze my hand and smiles at Magnus. 'I am glad you are here. Last night, I considered asking my maid to stay in one of the guest rooms.'

'How long have you been on Blackåsen?' Magnus asks.

Magnus has dressed up. His shirt is clean; he has washed. He speaks more rapidly. The whistling sound is gone. I try not to think about it, but when Frida let us in this morning, Magnus sounded like one of the villagers, and she, with her accent from the south, like the visitor.

I lean back in my chair, the padded support comfortable against my back.

'Twenty years now.' Frida laughs and shakes her head. 'Twenty years,' she repeats.

She doesn't like it, I think, but she had no choice. She had married into it.

'And before your husband came, there was no church here?'

'The only church was in town.'

Frida lifts the wine bottle and Magnus holds out his glass. 'You like it.' She beams. 'It's the county governor's favourite, too. When we first travelled here from Uppsala, we stayed a few nights at his residence – he introduced us to this wine. Later, when he came to the village, he brought us a bottle.'

Magnus lets the red drink swirl in his glass. 'Have they always fought, the ones who were born here and those who weren't?'

'When I arrived, there were no quarrels. But when more newcomers came and they still held onto all the old rules, the injustices became clearer. When I pointed it out to Ulf, it shocked him. Because he was born here, he couldn't see it, either.'

I suddenly realise why Frida feels familiar. She reminds me of my sister. But why? The two women are diametrically different: one soft and pleasant, one forceful; one tactile, one reserved.

'I am going to give you the same room Rune had,' Frida says to Magnus. 'I hope you don't mind.'

There is a knock on the front door. It opens and someone calls: 'Good evening!'

A man steps in, and removes his coat. It's the priest from town, Axel Bring.

He wipes his woolly head with his hand. 'I've come without notice,' he says.

225

My heart soars. I feel he brings the town with him, its sanity, sensibility, and civilisation.

Frida pulls out a chair for him. 'Please. I will fetch you something to eat.'

Magnus rises and shakes the priest's hand. I can't stop smiling. Axel Bring meets my gaze and smiles back.

'It's official now,' he says to Magnus and falls serious. 'The bishop contacted me and asked me to travel here and remain until a replacement is sent for the priest.'

'What did he tell you about the murders?' Magnus asks.

'An act of lunacy committed by a deranged person, a Lapp.' Magnus nods.

'Is it?' the priest asks.

'Yes,' Magnus says. 'Most likely.'

Frida returns and puts a plate and cutlery in front of the priest.

'"Most likely",' the priest repeats.

'One thing still puzzles me,' Magnus says. 'How long have you been in the region?'

'My whole career,' Mr Bring answers. 'I only intended staying a short time before moving to a new placement, but I've remained for over forty years.'

'Then perhaps you know . . . One of the villagers, Anders, seems to think the murders were committed as an act of vengeance. And Ester, a Lapp woman, said the children changed when they were about eleven or twelve years old . . . How old do you think Adelaide is now?' The last question is for me.

'Fifty?' I say.

'Yes, or a couple of years older. So if she was eleven or twelve at the time, that would bring us to around . . . 1815 or 1816 or thereabouts. Did something happen then that you recall?'

226

The priest clears his throat. He shakes his napkin out and places it in his lap. 'Per Eriksson was sentenced for killing his father . . .'

Magnus nods; we know that.

The priest hesitates. 'I can't think of anything else that would have resulted in this act,' he says, finally.

Frida is watching. She remains quiet. If her husband once did something he later died for, would he have told her, his wife? If he did; she could tell us, now that he's dead. If he didn't, she must wonder what it was.

My father would never have told my mother. He thinks her a lesser being. I am not certain he ever shares anything of importance with her.

What about Magnus and Isabella?

I have no idea. In a crowd, my sister always looks for Magnus. She watches him. Watches over him. She knows where he is at any given moment.

I take a sip of wine, feeling the spicy liquid in my mouth, the heat in my throat, my chest.

'What is your relationship to Ester, Magnus?' the priest asks.

Magnus's eyebrows rise. 'Ester? Her husband died and she remained on Blackåsen.' Magnus shrugs. 'I asked her to help me map the iron deposit.'

'Nils is dead, too? How did he die?'

'I don't actually know,' Magnus says slowly. Then he sighs. 'I am making too much of the murders. I want an explanation that I like more than the one I already have.'

'But things don't add up,' I say. 'Why don't we go and ask him, Anders, what he meant?'

Magnus lights his pipe. Frida is looking down. Only the priest nods.

B

We are at the bottom of a crag. This part of the mountain is solid black, without vegetation. Bear wants to go over to the other side. We should find another route, but he insists.

It won't change, I think. Not between here and up there. Iron here, iron there. You know that. This is too steep.

But Bear doesn't want to let any part of it be. He can't. I have to see all of it, his thin body says. I have to make sure I have touched all of it.

And I, too, am a part of this now. I'll stay until . . . Until, one way or another, it is over.

Bear swings his legs up, finding places to put his feet where I saw none. His fingers disappear into crevices.

Raven Baby didn't come yesterday, but she's here today. She stares after Bear, her face drawn. Her spikes are growing out, becoming tresses that coil around her face. So Raven Baby has wavy hair. I wouldn't have thought. Though who knows what things are like underneath, when all you see is prickles.

Bear's foot slips and a stone falls, hitting the rock beneath. 'I'm all right,' he calls.

'Be careful,' Raven Baby mumbles.

I don't know their relationship. It doesn't concern me. Youth can be attractive. And age is experience, which can be appealing, too. Bear disappears up the side of the stone block.

'This way.' He reappears and waves. 'Climb that boulder and you'll find a path.'

Raven Baby and I step forward. I push ahead of her. I'm not that old. Though I have to scramble on all fours to manage the climb. When I reach the top, I turn and give her my hand. She takes it and I pull her alongside me. Underneath, the three wounds on the mountain's side gape black.

'Speak with him,' I say. Raven Baby's mouth is half open. I see her pink tongue against her teeth. 'Tell him things are getting dangerous.'

Bear is already down on the other side.

'Make him stop this,' I say. 'Please.'

She nods. Then, probably thinking about Bear, she shakes her head. 'I will try.'

If I could only remember the verse . . . I wonder if I'm supposed to warn him.

'Nila was a *noiade*,' Raven Baby by my side.

Did I tell her? I can't remember. The descent drops sharply down.

'I am trying to imagine it,' Raven Baby says. 'Did he wear a robe like the priests in church?'

I picture Nila in a long cloak by the fire.

Raven Baby catches my eye and smiles. 'I guess not,' she says. 'So who is your *noiade* now?'

'Nobody.'

'Nobody?'

'No. We're Christians like . . . like your people.' Nila was the last one, I think, but I don't say it.

'Funny, I imagine your old faith to be . . . more truthful than the Church's.'

Some people are like that. They always believe others have better answers. We begin to walk, and Raven Baby's foot slides. A cloud of pebbles rustles down the slant. I grab her arm.

'The priest from town is here,' Raven Baby says. 'He arrived last night.'

The church hall is balmy. The windows are dirty, their surface dull in the sunshine. A small vase of dead flowers stands on one of the windowsills; the blossoms have dried heads down, white, parched balls. The priest is at the front, arranging the cups for the Holy Communion. He turns and I startle. Last time I saw him, he was conducting the Christmas sermon; his hair brown, his bearing tall. Now he looks as old as me; the two of us resembling those white, parched balls.

'Ester,' he says. 'How nice to see you.'

'Thank you.'

'I heard about Nils. I am so sorry.'

For a brief moment, I worry that he'll ask where we buried Nila, but he doesn't.

This man used to be my priest before Blackåsen's church was built. I want to tell him everything, about Bear on the mountain, about the settlers . . .

Instead, it is he who speaks, 'You haven't told him?' he asks.

I don't understand. 'Told who what?'

I see him pale. 'I assumed Nila had spoken to you,' he mumbles, before turning away, busying himself with the large cup, almost toppling it over.

Dampness breaks out on my chest and back. Embarrassment. Hurt. My heart swells until it's too large for my chest.

When the priest turns back to me, both of us have composed our features.

'I plan to hold a sermon in the next few days,' he says. 'I hope you will attend.'

'Yes,' I say.

The unsaid towers like a wall between us.

I sit on my rock, the black one, the one Bear says doesn't belong. Nila . . . My heart squeezes tight. Why did he keep things from me? Perhaps he always knew that in the end I would fail him. The sun is hovering above the marsh, and its light reaches me through the trees as a red glow. There is a breeze tonight. A warm wind, running over my arms and my neck, making all the hairs stand up. My mother used to say that time was a circle. 'At some point, the ends meet, and time begins to eat itself.' That is where I am. I have spent time in my history, and now I am back where I began.

I find I have clenched my jaws, and relax them.

Tonight grief will find me. Grief and something stronger. Guilt.

M

I am in the forest. Patter of bare feet drumming against the ground. Mine. Someone else's. Someone's after me. I have to run. I have to—

I sit up.

Oh God.

A dream. My dream. I must have fallen asleep at last. Isabella's voice rings in my ears: 'Each man has to have his own nightmare.'

I exhale. It's nothing. Only it felt worse than usual. I look at the clock. I haven't slept for more than a couple of hours, but it is morning. 'Time to get up.' I hear Isabella's voice again.

I get dressed and walk downstairs with a thundering headache. Lovisa sits at the kitchen table. Her hands lie clasped in her lap.

'We can't stay here for ever,' she says. 'Let's go and see Anders and then let's prepare to leave.'

Annoyance flares inside me. I wonder how long she's been sitting there waiting to pounce on me. What is it to you anyway? I think. Are you planning to go somewhere afterwards?

'Tomorrow,' I say.

'That is what you said yesterday,' she says. 'And the day before.'

Really? How many days has it been since the priest arrived? I am trying to remember what day it is, but I'm not sure.

Lovisa crosses her arms over her chest. 'We go today,' she says.

I turn and pour myself coffee, taking care not to let her see my face.

Axel Bring is coming with us. At the horizon, the high snow-clad mountains shimmer white. The lake lies silent, its dark surface still. A haze lingers out on the middle that the sun ought to have burned off by now. The path is black, and the tall grass fringing it, pale with dew. Yes, the landscape might be wet and dark, but the sun is up, relentless. It makes me want to laugh.

On the other side of the lake, the mountain hovers. I had planned to begin digging trenches on the south side today. Visiting Anders won't take long. Perhaps we can still manage to do it. But Axel is going to slow us down. Already, he is walking further behind us.

'He walked the whole way here from the town,' Lovisa says in a low voice. 'I wonder how long it took him.

'You are still not sleeping,' she says after a while. 'I heard you up last night.'

I feel a jolt of anger. Is she spying on me?

'You have to sleep, Magnus,' she says.

What a stupid thing to say. There is nothing I want more than a few decent hours of blissful sleep, with no tossing and turning, no thinking, and absolutely no dreaming.

'I'm fine.' The words come out harsher than I had intended.

She pauses, but not for long. 'Magnus, do you have to continue on the mountain?'

'What do you mean?' I ask. I know what she means.

'I don't know . . . The settlers don't want you to, Ester doesn't want you to. Perhaps you should listen to them.'

233

My pulse beats slow and hard in my chest. 'They are worried about anything new.' I force myself to sound light-hearted.

'Perhaps.' She gives me a rapid smile.

I stop to wait for Axel to catch up with us. We walk the rest of the way in silence.

We reach the eastern tip of the lake. Frida said Anders's hut lies here. Yet we would have missed it, were it not for a glint from the tin roof. I point it out to Lovisa and we approach. The hut leans against a grassy hill that forms one of its walls. The other walls consist of sticks of wood braided with moss. The shed is grey, battered by weather. A kettle and a clean mug stand in the grass beside the cold fire-place.

'Anders?'

Nothing.

'We met the other day, do you remember?' I knock on the wooden door. It rattles, but there is no reaction from inside the shed.

I look at Lovisa and Axel, and shrug.

'Perhaps he's out in the woods,' Axel says.

I gaze out over the still water, back towards the mountain. When I turn, Lovisa has put her finger in the hole in the door and is opening it.

'Wait,' I say.

Inside the tiny shelter, a man lies on the floor on a bear skin, legs curled up towards his stomach. The room smells of piss and overripe apples. Perhaps he's drunk. 'Anders?'

He lies without moving.

I feel the certainty in my knees first; they weaken. I squat down, put my hand on Anders's shoulder and turn him onto his back. His face is bloodied, dried streaks on his cheeks. There is a large patch of blood on his chest. He is dead. It takes a while before my brain registers that where he ought to have eyes, there are black holes.

Axel gasps: 'Evil!'

Lovisa screams.

The settlers have gathered in the church. All of them are there: Jacob and Helena Palm, Matts and Daniel Fjellström. The shadows transform their pale faces with their large eyes to skulls.

Per Eriksson, the night man, speaks first. 'He died from a knife wound to his heart. One stab.'

'His eyes . . .' I say.

'It must have been done afterwards. I can see no signs of him defending himself, or of any struggle, and they hadn't bled much.'

Someone came when he was asleep. Someone decided to do this.

Axel is sitting in one of the pews, leaning with his forehead on the bench in front of him. Beside me, Frida looks pale. I touch her arm and point to one of the seats, and she sinks down onto it. Above her head, I meet her maid's eyes. 'Things like this always happen here,' she had said in the churchyard. I have to speak with her again.

Per Eriksson holds up the knife that we found in the cottage. 'It was done with this.'

'But that's my knife,' Matts Fjellström says.

'Yours, Matts?' the night man says.

'I couldn't find it yesterday. I thought I lost it in the fire,' Matts Fjellström says. 'Someone must have taken it from me.'

'Who?'

Matts looks around him, but everyone keeps their eyes cast down. It's Matts's knife. He has admitted as much.

'I swear I had nothing to do with this,' he says.

'But who amongst us had anything against Anders?' Adelaide's voice trembles. 'He disturbed no one.'

'What do we do now?' Jacob Palm asks.

'The same thing as we did last time,' Per Eriksson says. 'We send a messenger to the county governor.'

The church is silent.

'I'll go this time,' Daniel Fjellström says.

'Seven days,' Per Eriksson says. 'The governor and his men will be here in seven days. Eight at most.'

People leave. As Per walks along the pew, I grab his arm. Beside him, Adelaide stops. Lovisa approaches.

'I met Anders before he died,' I tell the night man. 'He said an "angel of vengeance" killed the other three.'

'Did he say that? Why?'

'I don't know. You must have been a child here at the same time as them. Did something happen?'

'We played together,' he says darkly. 'Nothing ever happened that would merit this.'

'I've already told you this,' Adelaide says.

'You do realise this means you have a killer amongst you?' Neither Per nor Adelaide answers.

I shake my head. 'And that we don't know what happened when the first three died.'

Per turns to Adelaide. 'Do you think Matts . . .?'

'Never,' she says. 'Besides, he wouldn't have used his own knife.'

'What about the fire?' Per is half whispering. 'Is that linked to this?'

Adelaide shakes her head. Her posture becomes erect. She has decided this is a discussion for another time, a time when I am not present.

236

I see Anders's face before me. It will stay with me for a long time, perhaps for ever. 'For God's sake. If you know anything, you must speak. If this relates to an event that took place when you were children, you could both be in danger.'

As they turn to leave, I take Adelaide's hand. It feels thin in mine. 'I told you what Anders said.'

She looks at me.

'And now he is dead.'

'Magnus, you *must* stop,' she says, and squeezes my fingers with a force that surprises me.

'What?'

'Don't ask any more questions, finish mapping the mountain, leave this village.'

I am not stopping. Never. The more they want me to stop, the more I want to continue.

'What are you so afraid of?' I ask.

She doesn't answer.

'You are the one who's in danger,' I say. 'It will be at least a week before the county governor and his men arrive. A lot can happen in seven days.'

I think, God created the world in that time.

Jacob waits for me outside.

'I threw a stone through Adelaide's window.' His eyes are round. There is white in the corners of his lips. 'But I didn't set a fire. I didn't kill. You have to believe me.'

'It's not up to me to believe or not,' I say. 'The county governor will soon be here. He will see to it that justice is done.'

237

L

'Eight days at the most,' Magnus says, 'then the county governor and his people will come.'

It is close to ten o'clock. Magnus and I have lingered in the drawing room. The priest has gone to bed, he seemed a broken man; we had to help him up the stairs. Frida, too, has retired.

I can't decide what is in his voice: regret or relief. Or both.

'What is wrong with you?' I ask.

'Wrong?' He blinks.

'People have died.' My voice has risen. 'All you care about is that mountain!'

Magnus starts away, and raises his hand as if to stop me. 'I have a headache.' He rubs his forehead with his fingers, then walks to the cabinet to pour himself a drink from the bottle he brought from Luleå.

Three wooden crates stand open on the floor. In one of them lies Carl Jonas Love Almqvist's *Det går an*. I've been told this book is an attack on the institution of marriage. In normal circumstances I would have devoured it; my father forbids such books in his house. The next book is called: *Minerology*. More rocks?

Magnus doesn't sit down, but strolls, moves about, trying not to fall asleep, no doubt. He, too, sees the book. 'Told you,' he says. 'Lots of people like stones.'

There are also some puzzles.

When I was little, my father used to bring me jigsaw puzzles. In the good ones, the pieces sat snugly. If I moved one piece, sometimes others stuck to it and I lifted a whole block. You had to take apart the pieces carefully to see where you had erred.

One Christmas, my father brought me a puzzle from London that built horizontally, but also vertically, creating a cube. It startled me. There were many places where I could go wrong.

Four men are dead. First three, then one. All of them belonged here. Or at least they were born here, played together, lived together, and then something happened that tore them apart. Only two are left who were young at the same time: Adelaide and Per. One had a calling. One committed a crime. Then there are the arguments about whether you were born here or not and the rights that come with it.

All at once, I long for my father's home. I yearn for my room, my bed, my books. I want to creep back inside that warm space where nobody kills anybody else, where the fights are vicious, but most things remain unsaid, and where I don't have to think about anybody but myself. 'Your only occupation is yourself,' Magnus said. Of course it was. It never had to be anything else.

Magnus goes to the open window and leans with his elbows on the sill, his drink in one hand. 'The murders are different,' he says. 'The first ones were not planned.

'Say you were to kill three men. Why would you choose to kill all three at the same time? The risk that they would overpower you is too great.'

I go to stand beside him. The night is light and warm. You could sit outside for hours and watch it. I realise I would want to. The land is mostly vast and frightening, and yet, perhaps, a person could creep into it – like into a room – and it would soothe you and hold you as if you were its own. A couple of faint stars twinkle on the light blue sky.

Magnus twirls the glass in his hand. I get a whiff of the strong liquid and frown.

'Perhaps to ensure you got them all,' I say.

'You could have taken them one by one. If you didn't want them to have the time to react, you could have hurried from one house to the other. Perhaps it wasn't planned, after all.'

Magnus takes a sip of his drink.

'The second murder was,' he says. 'Anders was sleeping. And his eyes were missing. Though why would the killer remove his eyes?'

'Perhaps Anders saw something,' I say. 'Or didn't see something.'

A dull sound comes from the first floor, something being moved, or put down.

Beside me, Magnus straightens up. 'Another thing: Anders was asleep. He didn't know he would die. In a way, that makes his murder more humane than the others – if you can say such a thing.'

'Though to gouge out someone's eyes . . . The murderer must have felt a lot of anger.'

Magnus nods and bites his lip.

'But why leave such a gap between the first three murders and Anders?' I ask.

'And what about the Lapp?'

We are so close to the answer. But then, it is gone again. It's like one of my father's puzzles. We have tried to move one piece, but lifted a whole block. We need to separate the bits, go more slowly, look again. The pieces are all there, but they are sticking to each other.

'It is not a coincidence that these four men died,' Magnus says. 'They were paying for something.'

He lifts his face to the evening rays and closes his eyes. His shoulders slump. He could be sleepwalking. That long, straight nose, the narrow cheeks. He is beautiful. A beautiful, scarred sleepwalker.

I notice I am standing with him, the two of us, arms touching. My breath catches, ever so slightly. I know he has opened his eyes. I feel him turn. I hesitate before I look at him. His gaze is on my mouth. Then he bends towards me. Slowly, his lips brush against mine. He looks into my eyes. I daren't move. Then his tongue is against my teeth, my tongue against his. His hand is on my breast.

We both stop simultaneously. He removes his hand, looks at me. I shake my head: don't say anything.

Not everything can be forgiven.

When we are younger, we don't know this. No matter how vile the act, it is unthinkable to us that there wouldn't be redemption: some act of penance; a love, capable of surpassing all; or a God with a charge to forgive sins and make everything new.

Not everything can be forgiven. It is a lesson most people learn the hard way.

B

The day after Nila carved the face in the tree, evening came again. It's not even two full moons ago, but it could as well have taken place in a different life. When I entered the *kåta*, Nila was still lying the way he had fallen the previous night; so mute, so immobile, for a moment I thought he had died. But then he began to snuffle, as if everything was well, as if the world was unchanged. I didn't lie down. Sleep would not come that night.

Around midnight, I heard Dávvet's voice outside: 'Biijá?'

I glanced at Nila's white head. He used to call me: 'Piijá.' 'My Piijá.'

I folded the opening sideways. The sky's fires were out that night. There were just cold stars and a full moon like a white plate in the sky. We walked past the carved tree. I didn't look at it. I felt as bruised as its trunk must have done.

'He is no longer himself,' Dávvet said.

I slipped in the snow and sensed Dávvet's hand by my elbow. He walked the way you do with old people; vigilant, ready to grasp them if they falter.

'I have tried,' I said. 'He won't listen.'

'Then we have to confront him. As a *sita*.'

We arrived at the fire-place, though the flames had long since been doused. The moon cast a pale light onto us and the world around. I was so tired. But then I thought of the carving and Nila. And I knew he wouldn't stop. Something was changed in him.

'If it comes to it, we will have to make the decision for him,' Dávvet said.

A pebble in my chest, lodged deep in the centre; the sensation of betrayal. But Dávvet was right. When individuals fail, the *sita* has to take over. It wouldn't be the first time. It wouldn't be the last.

And so I nodded.

Dávvet nodded too, and walked back towards our lodgings.

I stood there by a dead fire, in the strange night light, black forest all around me, the remaining snow patches pallid on the ground. The pebble in my chest made it hard to swallow. This was not right. I was making a terrible mistake. I looked around for Dávvet.

But then the *sita* came. Someone made a new fire. Innga put a pelt over my shoulders and pulled me close. Her hip bumped against mine. It's not your fault, Biijá. Old age has taken him, sense left him. Lean into us. We are one and the same.

I couldn't see Dávvet, but I knew he was there. This was my decision to make. He was making sure I knew it was.

In time, the murmurs grew quieter. The fire waned. The time had come. I gathered myself up. 'About Nila,' I said.

We decided to wait until Nila woke up. Some, out of respect. Others, for other reasons. The immensity of what we were about to do instilled itself with each hour that passed. I sat in Innga's *kåta*. The cold moon filled it with a bluish light. Innga tried to stay awake, I am sure she did, but she was soon fast asleep. Jesus in the Garden of Gethsemane: 'Even you, Peter.' I listened to the snorts of Innga and her husband, and thought of lying a thousand nights beside my husband, our breaths mingling in the same way. And now, he lay on his own.

Morning came and we went about our chores, all of us keeping an eye on the door to my *kåta*. Nobody said much. Nobody left the camp, or strayed far. Sleep in, I thought to Nila. Be sick. Don't ever come out. And then I reminded myself it was the right thing to speak with him. More: it was the law. As long as he continued the practices of the old faith, we were all sinning.

Finally, the opening was folded aside and we stiffened. Nila came out, blinking against the light. He looked around; perhaps wondering where I had gone. Dávvet approached him.

'We need to speak,' he said.

Nila looked behind Dávvet, stared at all of us, before following Dávvet with the round, slanted walk of an old man.

We sat down on the stones by the fire, Innga beside me. Nila smiled when he saw me. He still didn't understand. Then Innga put her arm around me, and Nila frowned.

'It has gone too far,' Dávvet said.

Nila tilted his head to the side and scratched his cheek.

'The carving. It has to stop.'

Beside me, Innga's mouth was half open, her eyes clear. Her arm hung limply over my shoulders. It was heavy. I twisted and hoped she would remove it.

Nila licked his lips. 'Something is about to happen at Blackåsen. Something bad.'

'And how would you know this?' Dávvet asked.

'This is about an event that took place in the past. But it is also about all our futures.'

For a moment, he was our old Nila. Please don't mention the spirits, I thought. Please, please, talk to the *sita* like this, in a different way. Find new words—

247

'The spirits . . .'

'No,' Dávvet said. 'No more spirits, no more old beliefs.'

'Listen to me.'

'This is sin,' Dávvet continued. 'It is forbidden. God is clear. And anyway, it's not up to us to try and influence events. It is—'

'Devil worship,' someone muttered.

'Nila, you need to stop, or . . .'

Or? I hadn't thought about the 'or'. But of course there was one.

'The spirits—' Nila said.

'Stop it!' Suonjar got to her feet, screaming. 'God will punish all of us.'

'Listen to me!'

The others stood up, too. I could no longer see Nila. I pushed Innga's arm off, struggled to rise. 'Nila?'

But it was beyond me now. They were in between him and me, shoving him out from the camp.

'Devil worshipper!' they shouted after him. 'Foe of the faith!'

I caught a last glimpse of Nila's face. He was looking back, towards the campsite. He might have been looking at his carving.

The next time I saw my husband, he was dead.

ℳ

I am drawn out of my haze, back into reality. My mouth is dry. I swallow. It takes me a moment to realise what the tapping is.

Goddamn. Rain.

The sky is a dark purple. The land needs rainfall. I have desired it. Now, I don't want it. I have begun digging the first trench on the south side of the mountain, at the east margin of the iron band. The topsoil is clay. Rain will make it heavy and slippery. I'll have to pause the digging.

'Goddamn,' I say. Out loud this time.

I walk downstairs and pour myself a cup of coffee. Lovisa is in the kitchen.

'Good morning,' she says.

I nod. 'How is Axel?'

She shakes her head.

I sense a hesitation in her, a stiffness, a reluctance to meet my eye. Perhaps it is natural after what happened. But I know she understands. Yesterday evening, after what took place between us, I noted the way she looked at me. It was a forgiving look, telling me she understood that my exhaustion was leading me astray, and we would make nothing more of it. I only wanted to lean my head against her shoulder.

I nod to her and walk back upstairs. Outside the priest's door, I listen. I hear a mumbling inside; Frida is there with him, then. To think that seeing Anders dead disturbed the priest to this extent. I would have thought he had seen worse things living out here for so long. I would have thought he was used to it. In my mind's eye, I see Anders's face and shudder. Perhaps there are things you will never get accustomed to.

In my room, I take out all my notes and the maps Rune took from *Bergskollegium*, hesitate, but then walk along the hallway to the priest's office.

I sit down at his desk by the window, my papers spread out before me.

It is one of those hard rain showers where water bounces off the earth and the air is grey, heavy with liquid.

I sort my papers into piles and go through the documents first. There were some early mining claims taken out on Blackåsen – I recognise the usual names – but they were all bought by the King, and thus they will all have gone into the *Gällivare-verken* deal. The villagers could have begun to excavate the iron had they wanted to – the small amount they would have managed to dig up, there being so few of them, wouldn't have disturbed anyone. I wonder why the parish council was so vehemently opposed.

'Close it down,' the minister said. And now, instead, we have a fourth murder. I ought to send a message to him, but unless I walk back to town and travel onwards to Luleå, there is no way of doing that. Now the minister will hear it from the county governor, and he'll wonder. Or perhaps, like last time, the county governor won't say anything.

God, I am tired. The fog inside my head is unbearable. I can no longer think straight. My movements are sluggish. I blink and blink, but cannot focus. I don't even yawn any longer.

I look at the large map. Someone, perhaps Rune, has made

small pencil marks on it. Check marks. As if he has walked the mountain and confirmed that the map is indeed correct. He has made no notes: no cross bearings, sketches, recordings of fold axes, faults, joints . . .

It doesn't surprise me. Rune was that kind of a man – sloppy. When he came to see me this summer, he looked exactly the way I remembered him from Falu Mining School: the crumpled suit, the dirty fingernails, the black eyes.

Check marks!

I wonder where Frida has put his things now that I'm sleeping in the room where he stayed. I remember his bag; his items carefully folded. Strange. Perhaps it was Frida who gathered his belongings up after his demise and packed them.

There is a growling now, too. Thunder. Typical.

I watch the storm cloud thicken and lower itself closer to us. I pick up my pen and look at my papers. I put my pen down again and rise.

It is pouring down. I stand for a moment on the porch, and then I walk towards the church, its red walls bleary in the rain. A walk will refresh me, I think, but the rain is beating hard on my head and shoulders, and it's not long before I begin to run. I take the steps that lead up to the church and enter.

The hall is silent. The light inside the church looks grey.

I sit down on one of the hard benches and look up at the cross in front of me. It's a carved, painted image of Jesus, his body lean and white, the red wound in his side. Since coming here, I am displaying traits I didn't know I had. Mapping Blackåsen has become my only concern. An obsession? The image that comes to me is that of Rune in my office in early summer, eyes sunk into their sockets.

'I'll just map it,' I mumble, a reflex. The other maps are . . . old.

I sigh.

I gaze at the cross again. I wonder how they got it here, and an image forms in my mind of the villagers carrying Jesus through the forest.

£

Water on the inside of the window, a thin mist occasionally breaking into a tear. The world beyond it radiates, the grass so vividly green, the trunks of the fir trees a shiny brown.

I walk to stand in front of the mirror. I watch my face, the round nose, the short locks, the narrow eyes, and don't quite recognise myself. Each time I think about the kiss, the memory of it jolts me. My first real kiss. One that was given and returned. I touch my lips. I look at my eyes, and wonder what anyone could see in them. What could he possibly see in them?

My breath fogs the glass. I draw a line through the patch.

Love. With Eva, the flame inside me was consuming. I couldn't eat or think. It is different with Magnus. I don't need to see him every minute. Knowing he is close by is enough.

Magnus hasn't said a word. Some men blame women; say they enticed them. Magnus wouldn't. He is older, more mature. I can trust him. Poor Magnus, unable to sleep. He has begun to look his age and, at times, he stumbles, as if he is drunk. You can see the effort it takes for him to stay alert, to follow a conversation. When the men from the coast come, I am certain we'll leave.

Five more days and then you can sleep.

My darling . . .

I wish I dared to reach out and caress his scarred cheek.

Just where it meets his beard. I want to touch his eyebrows with one finger. Perhaps one day. I want to kiss him again, but feel strange at the thought.

My sister . . .

My heart clenches and the old anger surges inside me. I should be thinking only about Magnus, not about my sister. Though it's not so strange; I am here with her husband. Isabella will never let Magnus go. Never, ever.

I stare at myself in the mirror. My black eyes seem flat, devoid of life.

I don't know what this means. We will soon leave Blackåsen, and I cannot imagine an 'after'. I wish there wasn't an 'after', but there is always one.

In the drawing room, Frida stands with a book in her hand. 'Oh, hello Lovisa.' She puts the book in one of the boxes. 'I can't decide what to take. Perhaps I should leave everything behind.' She looks at the scarf around my shoulders, at my boots. 'Are you going out?'

I shrug. 'Maybe.'

'You'll fall ill if you are not careful,' Frida says. 'These summer rains seem innocent, but I have learned they can give you quite a chill.'

I stare at the wooden chests on the floor. If my sister ever had to leave her home, she would want to take everything with her. She cares about belongings. All things in that house are chosen with care: the pattern of the wallpaper is reflected in the soft carpets; the tint of the china goes with the table-cloths. In the bookshelves, the books stand sorted by colour and height rather than by topic. It's my father who pays for their apartment. If it came to that, I guess it would be Magnus who would have to leave.

My insides squeeze. 'I am sorry,' I say.

'Why?' Frida asks.

'You were married, you had created your life, and now you'll have to start over.'

Ah, yes. 'I didn't think that would happen, either.'

'Do you think you'll ever marry again?'

She shakes her head.

She loved him, so how could she ever imagine anything else.

Frida smiles. 'When you wed, adult life begins with its responsibilities. You and your husband live closely, closer than you have ever lived with anybody. You'll never think of each other in quite the same way again; it's all you can do to keep respecting each other.'

Magnus and my sister standing, side by side. They respect each other, I am certain.

The rain is beating against the windowpane. I can no longer see the forest.

Frida's voice behind me: 'If you ever decide to get married, Lovisa, make sure you manage to retain that first respect for your husband.'

At Frida's request, I bring a bowl of soup to the priest. Arriving on the first floor, I listen for Magnus, but only hear my own footsteps on the wooden boards and the insistent smattering of the rain. I knock and enter, balancing the tray on one hand. Axel is lying in the bed under the grey wool blanket, and his frame seems to have reduced since I last saw him. He is sleeping, his mouth half open. White bristles have sprouted on his chin and cheeks, a sprinkling of salt.

'I brought you some food,' I whisper, uncertain.

He opens his eyes, closes his mouth, and his gaze fixes on

me. His eyes are clear. I feel relief. I put the tray on his bedside table and help him sit up. I am about to leave, but he gestures to the chair beside his bed. I sit down and watch as he slurps the soup, lips smacking, interspersed with small sighs of contentment.

When he is finished, he leans back against his pillows.

'It's raining,' I say.

He nods and licks his lips. 'I know your father, Lovisa,' he says. 'Karl Rosenblad.'

He says the name slowly. I feel cold.

'A man should never speak ill of another man to his offspring, but what if you think it might make a difference to that child?'

Axel sighs.

'Your father has to be the strongest, Lovisa, in every situation, in every relationship. We were students at the same time and became good friends; I'm afraid I was a lot like him at the time. My stay here in Lapland has changed that.'

Axel relaxes his head back onto the pillow and looks up to the ceiling.

'There are things I wish I could undo; wrongs I'd want to right . . . Wrongs I *will* right.'

He clears his throat and fixes his gaze on me. 'I don't know anything about you. Nothing at all. But I can imagine your life has not been easy. Your father and I used to debate the nature of man. We had opposing views. I believed a person was born with certain qualities – that his life would be largely driven by his innate instincts. Your father thought any human a blank slate that could be tailored to whatever he wanted it to be.'

I swallow.

'I wanted to say that it is likely that whatever has happened between you and your father is not your fault.'

Once I saw a man kill another man. It was at the market, at Christmas time. The winter was cold, the snow blue. Biijá and I were looking at knives on one of the stands. There were different kinds, different sizes, with handles of wood, or bone. The steel gleamed in the light of torches. There was another man there, too: blond, corpulent, standing beside me dressed in a long fur coat. He looked up and stiffened – I swear I felt it, despite our thick winter clothes, despite him being a settler and me a Lapp, and us not rubbing against each other. I followed his gaze and saw a grey-haired man. The man beside me was already on his way, one of the knives in his hand. He stabbed his victim in the back.

Later, I heard that twenty years earlier, the dead man had stolen the other one's woman. Ah, I thought. This was the first time he'd seen him since. 'No, no,' said the blacksmith, who told me the story. 'They lived in the same village. They had houses next door to each other, for all I know.'

Biijá was stunned when I told her. She couldn't understand why he had waited twenty years before doing anything. But I could see the hatred, a small seed lying dormant inside him, underneath the blond hairs on his chest. I could see it hardening with the years, not growing, just always there, as he harvested, repaired his house, raised his children, said hello to his neighbour. It was always there, grating. Nagging away at him for years. There was nothing more to it than that. One day, he'd had enough.

B

We found Nila lying face down in the river. Dávvet jumped into the water and pulled him up by his hair. Nila's mouth hung slack and his eyes rolled white.

Nila. My dear husband, my love, a man who calmed water, a man who knew where to find prey . . . I am sorry.

I sit under a large spruce, my belongings bundled by my feet. Rain hammers the ground. I imagine the water weighing me down, my clothes becoming heavier and heavier, my feet growing roots. I'll become a tree stump and never leave Blackåsen.

'Ester?'

Two figures are in my glade. In the downpour, they seem mere grey shapes. I blink.

'Ester!'

It's Bear and Raven Baby.

'Here.' I croak and try to rise, but my feet have grown roots after all.

'I'm sorry,' Bear says as he swings me up in his arms. 'I don't know what we were thinking of, leaving you here in this weather.'

This? You should see the autumns, or the winters. This is nothing but a summer drizzle. Things dry easily. I only regret I didn't take the time to build a shelter.

I am hot, or cold. I shiver.

Bear carries me. At first, I protest, but soon my head lolls against his heart. Raven Baby holds my bundle and my stick in her arms. She nods to the holes and fallen branches as if it is she who is guiding us. It's a vision, I think. That's when I understand I must be really ill.

I am in a bed, under a cover. The house has swallowed me whole. I am Jonah in the whale's stomach.

At some point during the night, Bear sat here. He said he could no longer think straight.

Why would you need to? I thought. Think whatever way you like. Besides, it is so often about the feeling.

I close my eyes.

Raven Baby sits by my bedside. At least, I think it is her.

'He carved the killer's face into the tree.' It comes out as a mumble.

I don't know how much time has passed before I manage to say: 'Nila speaks to you.'

'Your dead husband?' She shakes her head. 'No, Ester.'

Ester.

My name is Biijá. When we were close, my husband used to call me 'Piijá'. 'My Piijá.'

Did I speak the words out loud or are they just in my head?

Darkness falls again.

If it wasn't a sin, I would speak to them, the dead that line the walls: my mother, my father, my aunts and uncles. My mother looks well, the same round cheeks and peering eyes. My father seems tired.

'I can't talk.' I try to point to the sky. 'God.'

I notice Nila is not amongst them.

I remember Priest is dead.

'They died for the past,' I say, next time I come to.

My father speaks: 'Not the past. It is about the future. And about what the boy will do.'

'What boy?' I ask.

'We killed Nila,' I tell Raven Baby.

My chest scrunches up so I cannot breathe. I have to die now. I cannot live with this.

'Perhaps he took his own life,' she says.

And that is no better at all.

ℳ

In the morning, the sun forces through the dark clouds. I open the window and so I see him coming on the path.

'Per.' I raise my hand.

'Came to find you,' he says.

We stroll towards the road together. The air is fresh after the rain. It is cooler. I take out my pipe, stuff it and light it.

'You asked me whether anything seemed odd,' he says, 'when I saw the first three bodies . . .'

I wait.

'It's ridiculous . . .' he says.

'Say it anyway.'

'He was barefoot.'

'What?'

'The Lapp. He had taken off his shoes outside the door and placed them neatly by the wall. Yet, on the other side, was all that blood and the corpses. The image of his shoes keeps coming back to me. It didn't seem right.'

'Perhaps that's what they do . . .' I hesitate. 'Hunt barefoot?'

'I know, right?' He sounds apologetic. 'There is something else, too. Blood speaks. The pattern inside that room was unlike anything I have ever seen before. Long, sweeping movements. It almost looked as if he had danced.'

I can see it too easily, a barefoot man, dancing, wielding his knife.

'Something did happen one summer when we were young.' Per's voice is calm, but it is clear by the way his eyes squint and his jaw clenches, it is costing him to tell me this. 'When we were children, we used to play close to the old Lapp maze, but we always kept our distance. We were frightened of it. But one year, the Lapps didn't come as usual. The summer after, we felt bolder. It was Jan-Erik's idea – that we'd have a ceremony and then walk the labyrinth. Some Lapp had told his father that, back in the old days, the maze had been used to enter unsafe waters and fight whatever spiritual battles needed to be fought. I remember it because it was such a peculiar phrase – "enter unsafe waters". We all liked the idea of it. As if we were sailors. There wasn't much to our ceremony: a fire, we shouted, and then we walked the labyrinth all the way to its centre. I remember feeling . . . dread. I felt dread. When we were done, I couldn't see or hear anyone else, but I think we all felt the same – that we were no longer alone. Now, looking back, I think we opened the door to something that day . . . Something evil.'

I look away so that he won't see my expression. I don't believe in sorcery, but I want him to tell me all of it as he sees it.

'That afternoon, it felt all right to kill. That afternoon, I did kill. I encountered my father and . . . I don't know what the others did after leaving the maze, but perhaps something happened involving them.'

'Who else was with you?' I ask.

'Me, the four dead men, and Adelaide.'

'Then perhaps someone is taking their revenge.'

'Well, the alternative would be more awful.'

263

A chill runs down my back and I glance at him. Is this what you live with? The fear of being killed by some unnameable evil?

'If something did happen, how come you don't know about it?' I ask. 'Why wouldn't they have told you?'

'After I killed my father, I ran. I wasn't caught for several weeks. Then I spent a long time in gaol. I returned here after my punishment was over, worried the villagers wouldn't have me back – but they did. Nobody ever speaks about the past – mine or theirs – and I have never asked any questions; no matter how strange things seem. This silence has suited me.'

'Tell me about Rune. Why had he come back?'

'I got the impression that it was for a woman.'

'A woman?'

Per nods. 'Whoever it was, she rejected him. He'd been here a couple of days when I met him up the mountain, and he looked desolate. I asked him about it. He said he had realised some things couldn't be forgiven. I assumed he had let this woman down, perhaps by leaving, and that now she wouldn't take him back.'

'Adelaide?' I ask.

'That's what I thought.'

We have reached the road, and we stop.

'What if Adelaide was never in danger,' I say. 'What if she was a victim? What if this is her revenge?'

Per sighs. 'I don't want to confront her.'

'I know,' I say, 'but we have to.'

Per and I walk side by side towards the east end of the village.

We pass the general store. A sign on the door reads: 'Closed'. I can't see Jacob or Helena.

We take the path that leads to the homestead where Adelaide

264

now lives, after the fire. Mosquitoes swarm together with small flies, post-rain bugs. The cottage window stands open. Per puts out his arm and stops me.

What?

He nods to the window, crouches down and makes his way to the house. I follow him. It strikes me I don't know whose side Per is on. He edges forward. I do the same.

Adelaide is on her knees, her forehead against the floor. Praying? The window edges create a frame. I glance at Per. We shouldn't be looking at her like this.

Then she rolls to her side. Blood trickles from her ear. Her eyes are closed.

I hold my breath.

A woman in a yellow dress enters, a knife in one hand, a tree branch in her other. Sigrid. She drops the branch on the floor. Adelaide opens her eyes. Their globes gleam white.

Opposite me, Per inhales.

'Rune told me what you all did. He asked forgiveness,' Sigrid says. 'But I prayed to God for vengeance. God doesn't forgive. He exacts revenge. And He sent the Lapp to kill them. I saw the Lapp when he arrived. I knew where he was going and I followed.'

'Look at me,' Adelaide says. 'Sigrid, you're not yourself. It's me, Adelaide. Look at me.'

'I waited for God to kill Anders, too. I thought he'd send someone else, but then I realised, He was waiting for me. He is like that, God, don't you think? He shows you what needs to be done, but then you have to do it yourself. Is that your experience?'

'Sigrid, listen to me—'

'You watched,' Sigrid says.

'We tried—'

There is a twist on Sigrid's face, and Per is off past me, up the steps. When I enter the room, Per throws himself onto Sigrid. They fall.

Per scrambles to get up, to grip her, but Sigrid is not moving. The knife sticks out of her chest.

Adelaide turns her face to the floor.

PART THREE

L

'If you weren't there, then you cannot understand,' Adelaide says.

We are in the church. Magnus stands behind Adelaide, ready, perhaps, to catch her if she falls. Ester and Axel sit beside me on the bench. Both of them said they wanted to attend, though they should probably rest. All the other settlers are with us, sitting or standing. I take Ester's hand and she glances at me and mumbles, something that sounds like 'baby'.

Adelaide is by the church window. The orange light makes her features seem peaceful. When you look closer, you see the dried brown streak on her temple and under her ear.

'A child's game.' Adelaide gives a strange laugh. 'That's all it was. None of us believed entering the maze would do anything. I remember Anders, laughing, saying it was a shame we hadn't any weapons. Jan-Erik hushed him. He wanted it to be frightening, of course. We walked the maze in a row. Jan-Erik first, Ulf followed him, then Per, Rune, Anders . . . The whole time, we were calling, "Come forth!"'

She licks her lips.

'I walked in last. I saw it before I felt it. It was like a . . . tint in the air. Only it was moving. I squinted. But this . . . cloud, thronged with life. And then we were inside it. Ants. I thought it was a thousand ants, ten thousand ants, a hundred thousand. Later, Ulf talked of water, a waterfall strong enough to drown you. Anders said sand. Yet I could have sworn they were insects, everywhere, in my mouth, my ears, in my eyes.' Adelaide's face distorts. 'I was clawing, spitting, tearing at myself. I fell to my knees. I thought: This is it. I am dead, eaten alive. And then, suddenly, they were inside me, and it didn't matter any longer. I was humming. Per stormed off. I remember Anders, crazy, kicking the tree trunks around the glade, as if he was trying to take them down. Ulf, Jan-Erik, and Rune left. I thought they were chasing after you.' Adelaide turns to Per. 'But further down the mountain, they encountered poor Susanna.'

Adelaide's face contorts.

'Susanna's scream woke Anders and me up. I don't know how much time had passed, but I remember the two of us staring at each other, him standing, me on my knees, and then we both ran. We heard her all the time. We found them by the marsh, but we couldn't stop them. Jan-Erik struck Anders with a branch. It was a hard blow and he was knocked unconscious. They took turns holding my arms whilst they had their way with Susanna.'

Tears stream down Adelaide's cheeks from wide open eyes. Behind her, Magnus has bent his head. I can't see his face.

'Then, whatever had gripped us was gone. The boys came to. Susanna lay there, eyes open, but not with us in any real way. Ulf was leaning against a tree trunk. Rune vomited. Jan-Erik paced by Susanna, cursing and spitting. We didn't know what to do. Jan-Erik wanted to leave her there, or worse. Ulf screamed at him. In the end, we carried her back to the village and told our parents. By then, they had already found Per's father dead. Per himself was missing.'

Adelaide inhales, closes her eyes and opens them again.

'They locked us in one of the houses. In the morning, my

270

father told us what they had decided. He and Jan-Erik's father would travel to find Nils, the Lapp, to ask him how to ensure this . . . labyrinth was closed. The rest of us would carry on like nothing had happened, and we would never speak of it again.'

'But the girl.' I speak in a whisper. 'Susanna.'

Adelaide meets my eye. 'Nobody expected there to be a child.'

I shake my head. They sacrificed the girl to save three boys. Boys that she had to see every day. She never stood a chance.

'Anders didn't want anything more to do with any of us – couldn't tolerate seeing people. Ulf, Jan-Erik, Rune, and I – each of us was ruined in our own way. And Susanna . . .'

She shakes her head.

'What about your calling?' Magnus asks.

'This was my calling,' she says. 'I thought that in order to keep this mountain at bay, in order for us to survive here, a strong faith was needed. A strong faith, with strict rules. God would surely save us . . . Ulf felt the same way, though he chose to devote himself to the Church. When Susanna did away with herself, we all took care of her daughter, Sigrid. We never spoke of what had happened. I guess that Rune decided to tell Sigrid and ask her forgiveness. Why now, after all those years, I don't understand. Sigrid thought the Lapp killed the three men to avenge her mother, and then she continued the retribution.'

Sigrid said she had been waiting for me. She didn't think . . . Did she think I had come to avenge her mother?

I can't help but gasp. Beside me, Axel stirs. His face twists as if he's in pain.

'And the murderer, the Lapp?' Magnus asks. 'How did Sigrid find him?'

She shakes her head. 'I don't know.'

'Who knew about this?'

'All of us who were born here, who were my age and older. Apart from Per.'

She looks at Matts and Daniel Fjellström by the wall. Their features are firm. Adelaide's face softens. 'Those younger than us were just taught that nobody must spend time on the mountain.'

On my first day on Blackåsen Mountain, I almost entered the labyrinth. I remember hearing a stone falling, feeling someone was watching. One of these people probably saved me.

I feel sick. I wipe my mouth.

'We did the best we could,' Adelaide says. 'We did the only thing we could.'

'What about children?' Magnus asks. 'Why are there no children?'

'I don't know. None of us could have them. Perhaps this was part of some pact our parents made with Nils; that this village would have to die out.'

Frida's face is immobile. Jacob's eyes are clear, Helena's mouth, open. Further away, stand the constable's widow, the old, blind man. I can't tell what any of these people are thinking.

Ester has closed her eyes. Axel is looking at his hands.

It is Per who speaks: 'You disgust me,' he says, then turns and walks out.

Ester and I walk back towards the vicarage. Ahead of us, Magnus and Frida walk, supporting Axel between them. Footsteps in the grass and on the gravel behind us, all going in different directions. There are no voices tonight. Poor Sigrid.

What an awful village, sacrificing the girl to save the boys. It's always the boys. What Sigrid must have suffered when she found out. She must have watched them go about life, and pondered their deception. She must have lain awake at night and listened to Adelaide breathing.

'So something did happen to the children while we were away,' Ester says.

'Perhaps *because* you were away,' I say.

'I suppose Nila helped them to shut the maze.'

I remember her feverish agony and what she said about their tribe causing Nila's death.

She sighs. 'It explains so many things. Once Nila said something to them that I didn't understand at the time – about their God forgiving everything. It made them so angry. They must have felt he was threatening them.'

This is why they all came back. Their secret screamed at them. They wouldn't have felt safe away from it, never knowing for certain that it would remain buried.

'In some ways, this all began with a sin of ours,' Ester says. 'There was a reason why we didn't come here that year. A woman in our tribe, Livli. She was married, but took another man, Dávvet. She was sent away, and we decided not to come back here.'

Magnus, Frida, and Axel have reached the vicarage stairs. They lead the old man up the steps.

'Where is Dávvet now?' I ask, trying to keep my voice neutral.

'He's still with us. I think I will lie down for a while.'

'Don't leave the vicarage yet,' I say. 'Stay here a few days.' I take her hand again and her fingers are cool and silky in mine.

She smiles, but doesn't respond.

*

273

I find Magnus in the drawing room inside, a glass in one hand, his bottle in the other. His face is grey, the windows closed.

'Per is right, it's disgusting,' he says after a while. 'These boys raped a girl, and the whole village was willing to blame magic. I hope they all burn in hell.'

'I wonder what would happen if you slept,' I say. The idea comes from nowhere.

He opens his eyes and sits up.

'What would happen if you slept?' I ask.

He rises. His steps sound heavy on the stairs.

There is a period in late summer that the settlers call 'the month of rot'.

In summer things change fast, that is true. Things curdle, turn sour, grow mould. It's the unending light. It's the intensity of the heat. Things want to grow. They want out.

And that is just it.

The light doesn't create. The heat doesn't give birth. Nothing emerges that wasn't already there.

June is a good month to purge. It's a time to flush things out, to eliminate, to seek liberation. It's a month of light. The month of the midnight sun.

B

I can't sleep. It is the wall clock in the room where I lie. The pendulum swings back and forth. *Tick. Tock. Tick. Tock.* I think of acts having consequences, just like the certainty of the pendulum's return.

Tick. Tock.

Once Beahkká told me a secret. I didn't ask for it, and knowing it made me feel soiled, but I listened, said nothing, and, later, tried not to judge.

But telling me changed her. She could no longer be natural around me. She snapped, couldn't meet my gaze . . . I felt she hated me for knowing the weakness she herself had revealed.

This is what happened. This is why Constable hated us so. He couldn't bear that Nila knew. What audacity they showed, telling Nila we had to attend church and that the old ways were forbidden. Once, the old ways had helped them. Perhaps they thought it was all forgotten. Perhaps they had managed to forget it themselves. Nila hinted at the past, and they must have worried about what he might do, who he might tell. I still don't understand why they became stern with us two winters ago. We hadn't changed.

Tick. Tock.

I close my eyes. Is what happened in that maze why Nila and I, too, had no children? He should have told me.

In many ways, we did exactly the same thing as the settlers did: we sacrificed Livli for Dávvet.

My mind brushes by one thought after another. I don't have the strength yet to focus on any one of them.

Tick. Tock.

My body reacts to the sound of the pendulum, waits for it, hears it before it happens. A person shouldn't have noises around them that don't stem from nature. There should never be this kind of certainty in what is coming next.

I walk outside. The night is cooler now, the rain took the hot air with it. Finally, the village is asleep. After everything that was unearthed today, getting to sleep took time, but now all the windows are still and there are no more footsteps.

I walk towards the mountain. The body needs it, the daily walk. The day you stop is when it begins to prepare for death.

I wonder what happened to Livli. Where did she go? How did she live? I never asked myself that before. What heartlessness I, too, have shown.

For a while, I stand on the peak and look at the wounds Bear has inflicted upon the mountain's north side – dull, black crevices. I guess we can think of them as the scars of this summer.

I wonder why the Lapp helped Child of Village. I wonder how the two met.

I notice her then, further away on the crest: Holy Woman, on the top of a stone, looking southwards. Her features seem so sharp and old in the faint light; she could be my age.

We sit without speaking, the mountain dark beneath us. The sun is a ball of fire on the horizon. A stream of red pushes at the blue sky.

Holy Woman sighs. 'I wish I had told Sigrid about what

happened that day, so that she didn't have to hear it from Rune. We did love her. We didn't care for her out of guilt.'

She sounds tired. A thousand years old. She has crossed her arms above her chest and sunk down into them.

'You don't feel bad about . . . Susanna?' I ask. I remember long, blonde hair that you wanted to reach out and touch. We used to call her Singing One. She was such a sweet child.

'Of course I do. But I have been living with that for a long time. And Susanna was gone from the day it happened.' She shakes her head. 'We were so young. I didn't even realise she was with child until the priest came to hold the yearly catechetical hearing. "It's like a plague here at Blackåsen," he said. "Falling pregnant without a man."'

What a strange thing to say, I think.

The sun is growing, the blue of the sky gives way and turns red. The sun paints a road of gold across the forest that leads straight to us.

'Perhaps it is possible to tell Sigrid,' I say. 'Our dead speak. Or, at least, they used to.'

Heresy. In my mind's eye, I see Priest.

'Even if they did, I don't think we are supposed to talk to them or listen,' Holy Woman says.

'Why?'

'They can't possibly be the same as they were when they were with us. I would be afraid to seek them out. I'd worry they had somehow become . . . skewed. No, I think whatever has to be said, has to be said when they are still alive.'

Perhaps I agree with her. There are things I wish I'd said, but I, too, won't seek Nila out.

'It's a harsh faith,' I say.

'Oh, I have no faith, Ester,' Adelaide says. 'I wanted to believe. I fought so hard. But I haven't believed in God for a long time.' She sighs. 'A couple of years ago, I made the mistake of telling Ulf about my doubts. I thought he would understand. It all seemed so very long ago. But Ulf panicked. "Nothing must change", that's what he kept saying. Nothing was to change.'

That's what happened, I think. That is why Priest came to insist we had to attend church every Sunday. He was frightened. He was worried he was losing control.

We sit there, Holy Woman and I, until the red of the sky has disappeared and the blue is back and growing and the sun is no longer a raging fire, but white and benign.

'Will you stay with us for much longer, Ester?' Frida asks in a mild voice when I return to the vicarage. Innga does the very same thing when she wants something; she uses mildness to draw attention to it. I smile.

'Not long now,' I say.

She nods: that is good.

'We'll have breakfast soon.'

M

I am sitting in the priest's office, at his desk but looking out over the meadow. In front of me, spread out, lie my notes and my sketches – and a blank sheet of paper. Instead of the act of mapping feeling like a beginning, it feels like an end.

I have a wife. Her name is Isabella and she braids her hair at night.

Four days. The county governor, Gunnar Cronstedt, will be here in four days, no more than five. He will come to find one body, but instead he will find two.

It isn't really strange that no one ever spoke up. They would have had this community in their grip, the constable, the priest, and Adelaide: one who listened to everyone's confessions, one with the power to arrest people, and one who claimed a personal connection with God. What a miserable place.

I look at my papers again and grab the pencil. Perhaps if I begin . . . If I draw one line, inspiration will come. I sketch the bowed outline of the south side of the mountain.

Nothing. A contour.

I don't have to do it now. I'll have all my notes in Stockholm, too. Only then, I won't be able to verify things if I have questions. I won't be able to go and explore any new line of thinking. I remember a teacher at the mining school speaking of uncertainty. He claimed that it aided the creative process.

'You need to approach your topic with the reverence that self-doubt brings,' he said.

This doesn't feel like self-doubt. This feels like . . . aversion.

I light my pipe. The tobacco tastes sour. I let it burn out.

I don't know how I become aware she is in the office. I turn.

'Ester,' I say. 'How are you feeling?'

'I wanted to ask you for help.'

'Of course, anything.'

She looks past me, at my papers.

I close my books, pile them and my papers in a large heap, and turn back to her.

'I have lost something,' she says.

Lovisa's face comes before me. I can't help but sigh out loud.

'My husband used to have a verse for Blackåsen. I can't remember it.'

'Oh. A verse.'

'You showed me your landmarks. This verse contained a few of those . . . I thought I'd ask what a mapmaker would do if their map went missing.'

'Find it.' I think of *Bergskollegium*'s maps of Blackåsen.

'And if they can't?'

'Then recreate.'

'Recreate?'

'At its core, mapmaking is a creation. In sketching something, you choose what to describe, what to leave be . . . There isn't such a thing as perfect truth.'

She wrinkles her face. 'No,' she says. 'That's not how it is for us. The verse simply *is*. Nila told it, Nila's father told it . . . Maybe someone with their abilities could craft a new one, but I can't.'

'Did you know it at one time?'

'I remember the beginning: "*Beyond The One Who Binds Water. By The One Who Sees. Night turns day, weight turns light . . .*"'

'And you know what that means?'

'It refers to two places on the mountain.'

I feel a prickle of excitement. 'Can you show them to me?'

'Do you have time?'

Four days, my mind says. I shrug it away. 'Plenty,' I say.

We cross the mountain. It is different after the rain – it feels less mountain and more forest. The smells are all earth and greenery.

'How long will you stay here?' I ask.

'Not long now,' she says.

I, too, have a family. I wonder what I will tell them about this journey. I didn't sleep well. There was a lot of work. Lovisa came with me . . .

I can hear my children's eager voices: 'What did she do this time?' 'Did she misbehave?'

My heart beats faster, anger surges in my chest. This is my fault and Isabella's, for that is how we have spoken of Lovisa. I wish others could see the Lovisa I have seen here, but they won't. What am I going to do? Of course, I won't send her to the madhouse, or a convent, but what else can I do with her?

On the north side of the mountain, by the river, Ester stops. 'This is *The One Who Binds Water*.' She points to a knee-high stone. Quartz. I draw it in my book and show it to Ester. We continue alongside the water and arrive at the large pine tree I remember from our mapping. 'This is *The One Who Sees*,' she says.

She points to the ground. '*Night turns day, weight turns*

light. It must mean this, the line between the black and the speckled rock that you showed us.'

She refers to the line between the iron and the iron mixed with quartz. It makes sense.

'Then nothing,' she says and shrugs. 'I have forgotten.'

I bite the end of my pen. 'So if I began with this tree and pointed to the delineation between the types of rock, I might intend for people to follow a route. It could be a map. The things you have mentioned so far are landmarks of sorts, so I suppose that is what we should look for.'

'Delineation?'

'The line, as you call it.'

'Only it didn't begin with the tree, it began with the stone,' she says.

'Whoever wrote the verse, he had to start somewhere. Perhaps that was the first unique feature he came to and he chose it as his starting point.'

I look behind me, at the river. 'I think we should follow the delineation uphill. And as we walk, tell me anything you think of.'

She frowns. 'Anything?'

I shrug, nod.

We have taken four steps when she says. 'My friend Beahkká was born right here.' She points to the earth. 'Her mother didn't make it back to the camp.'

I smile. When Isabella had our children, everything had been planned down to the smallest detail. The bag was packed, the dress she would wear to the hospital laid out, the neighbour instructed how to water the orchids.

'Is there anything here you recognise?' I ask.

She pauses to look around, and then shakes her head.

'Don't worry,' I say. 'Mapping is a long process. Let's continue.'

We walk another twelve yards perhaps, and Ester stops and beams.

'The Twin Trees.' She points to two ordinary spruce trees side by side. 'They were in the verse for certain.'

I take out my book and put the points in it and show her. 'So we began by the river, then we ascended, following the . . . line. The . . . Twin Trees are here.'

Her forehead scrunches up. 'I can't remember the wording.'

'Let's not worry about that now. We could even make that up later.'

Really? Her eyes gleam. I know what she's feeling. The power in mapmaking can be quite enticing.

I nod uphill: Shall we?

I told you everything has a spirit.

Do you remember the spirit of the marsh that my father called forth: the long-haired girl child with greenish skin and claws?

Did you hear what they said about the maze? 'A cloud of fury.' 'Of evil.' 'Ants.' Could you see how Adelaide swallowed, how her lips were dry? The darkness that surfaced in her eyes? Did you understand that it is only her struggle to believe in God that has kept her sane?

The six of them barely slept after that day at the maze. They didn't admit that, not even to each other, but years later Ulf would still sit up night after night, in his armchair turned to face the door, Bible on his lap like a shield. 'I need to study,' he said to his wife, but he never turned a page. Anders worked: set traps, mended nets, whatever had to be done. He never once lifted his head to look beyond the job that was right before him. Jan-Erik went about his routines, too, most often of an evil nature, scheming, plotting. Rune thought that if he never returned, he'd escape, but the memory ate him up. He drank. Didn't help. Per thought about his father. Adelaide prayed.

But they didn't sleep.

I don't feel much for them now: we had an agreement – they broke it by setting the dogs onto our herd. There was a time when I was ready to die defending them – there was a time I wasn't.

But I know how awful their lives were.

287

Have you seen the marsh, how small it is compared to the mountain? Have you seen the maze, a mere clipping on the mountain's base?

'This is nothing compared to Blackåsen,' my father said. 'If you call on something you cannot master, it will master you. Remember this.'

You have to see. Oh, how can I frighten you enough?

This is the time to be afraid. For your breath to turn uneven, your heart to pound in your ears, to look, turn, look around you. Brace yourself.

£

From the window in my room on the first floor, I watch Magnus and Ester leave. Magnus bends his head towards Ester, perhaps listening to something she says. They turn off the path and disappear. I wait. I might glimpse them again. No, they are gone, swallowed by the forest.

They didn't ask me if I'd like to come with them. They probably think I've had enough of the mountain.

And so I have.

I fold up my nightgown and put it under my pillow. The house is so quiet. Somehow, my room feels different, larger. A silence has descended on the vicarage and its garden.

The buzzing of a fly against the window startles me.

Four days. The county governor will be here, and then we'll leave this odious place.

My heart shrinks.

Four days, then Magnus will become the old Magnus. I will be his offensive sister-in-law again. We will travel back to the coast in the county governor's company. The End.

I can see my old self, a hard shell, waiting for me outside Blackåsen. I'll step inside and the door will close.

How I envy my sister for her nearness to him – her ability to go into their drawing room, knowing he will be there, reading a book, or smoking. Sitting down for dinner, with the certainty he will come, too. When we leave, I will no longer see Magnus every day. I might not see him at all. Nor would I want to. I couldn't bear having to mind my manners around him and be careful. 'You wouldn't want to start gossip.' My mother's voice. My eyes fill.

And Ester. Little Ester with her knobbly hands.

Will they remember me as someone special, someone to miss?

It is unlikely. Both Magnus and Ester have something to return to. I don't.

I should give myself to Magnus. At least then he won't forget me. But men don't like loose women. They do at first, but it soon turns to disgust.

There is a knock and I swirl around to face the door as Frida opens it.

'Axel is worse,' she says. 'I want to go and find Adelaide – she knows some things about illness. Could you sit with him?'

'Of course.'

Axel's breath is grating. I sit down on the chair beside his bed and he opens his eyes briefly, mumbles something, before closing them again.

The room feels cold. I stand up and tuck the blanket closer around him.

He coughs. 'Water . . .'

I support his head and give him some from the glass on his bedside table. He swallows with difficulty and sinks down again to the pillow.

'I once did something awful,' he says.

I hush him. 'Don't try and talk. Rest.'

He wheezes and coughs again. 'I was going to make it right, but I am not certain now . . .'

He is quiet for so long, I think he might have fallen asleep. Good. He needs the rest.

'It was this debate with your father . . .'

My father? Why, my father?

'About the nature of man. One of the Lapp women . . . Livli, came to me. She was with child, and the tribe had sent her away. It was winter.'

It's the woman Ester spoke of. Livli and . . . Dávvet?

Axel tries to lick his lips, but his tongue, too, looks cracked. 'She died giving birth. I was going to see the tribe, but they didn't come that year. My wife and I didn't have any children and so the boy . . . the child . . . stayed at the vicarage. And then, a few years later, my wife died. I was alone with this little boy. And I thought of your father . . .'

My hands are clasped in my lap.

'I sent the boy south to him. *Let's see who's right*, I wrote in my letter. *Let's see what you can do with this clean slate.* The boy knew we were sending him away. He didn't want to go. He was petrified. He ran away into the forest and we had to chase him.'

Axel's face crumbles. His hands on top of his blanket twist, fingers clawing.

'When we finally caught him and brought him back to the vicarage, whilst we waited for the carriage, he tried to escape again. I lost my temper and I pushed him. He fell into the fire. The left side of his face was burned off. It was an accident. I had no experience with children . . . I didn't mean to . . .'

I bend my head.

'And I couldn't help wondering . . .' Axel's voice breaks, and he sobs. 'If he had not been a Lapp child, would I have had more patience?'

When I look up again, Axel has closed his eyes. We remain so for ever. Tears drop onto my knuckles.

'I told Nils.' Axel is pushing the words out with difficulty

291

now. 'Much later. Thought we could get the boy back . . . He said to leave it. "Too late," he said.'

There are footsteps on the stairs. Hurrying towards us.

'God forgive you,' I whisper.

'What would happen if you slept?' I asked Magnus last night. If he slept, would he remember?

The immensity of what I have heard strikes me, and my knees buckle. I stop in the middle of the stairway and sink down on one of the steps, put my hand over my mouth and bite my own flesh.

I feel sick.

The house has gone quiet again. Adelaide and Frida are with Axel, but I know it's too late. What he told me was a dying man's confession.

I sit in the drawing room. Twice, someone comes down the stairs, walks into the kitchen, and then goes back up the stairs.

My father. How could he?

This is why he let my sister marry Magnus. It was a punishment for that awful fight they had: marrying a Lapp.

Then what did he plan to do? To throw it in her face at some stage?

I put my head in my hands and rock back and forth. This is so awful. And Axel, a priest – he scarred a child.

Ester said Dávvet is still alive. Magnus has a father. Doesn't he have the right to know?

I kissed him. A Lapp.

No, I kissed Magnus.

It is afternoon when the front door opens and Magnus and Ester arrive back.

'It is a map,' Magnus says to Ester as they walk into the drawing room.

'Yes.'

Neither of them acknowledges me. I search Magnus's face. You could never tell.

'But a map of what?' Magnus asks.

Their cheeks are red. Magnus sits down in an armchair and pushes his legs out straight. Ester lowers herself down onto the edge of the sofa.

Magnus wrinkles his nose. 'A holy site?' he asks Ester.

'I would already know it, if it was.'

'You don't know everything,' I say.

They both look at me as if they haven't seen me before. I didn't mean it like that. A father, I look at Magnus. You have a father. Someone who perhaps would love you.

'Or just a map showing how to best cross the mountain?' Magnus says.

Ester shakes her head. 'No, the verses meant more than that.' She wrinkles her forehead. 'They always gave the . . . essence of a place. The one thing you had to remember.'

'Like the importance of being born here, or not,' I say.

'Born here, or not born here.' Magnus snaps. 'Isn't that over and done with now? Why keep on about it?'

'Because you, too, were born here,' I say.

293

B

Tonight things die in the vicarage.

The old priest goes first. I know the precise moment he leaves to meet his maker. The vicarage walls sigh and slump inwards.

Bear's door is closed. I have passed it several times. Raven Baby's is shut, too. I can feel her inside, tossing and turning, fretting. 'I shouldn't have told him', comes through so strongly, it might as well have been said out loud. By Bear's door, there is nothing.

I just stand outside. You are one of us, I think. This closeness I feel to you has a reason. You are why I didn't leave this mountain.

I get no response.

As Raven Baby spoke, Bear's face reflected so many emotions, I couldn't tell which one, in the end, he was left with. But, like me, he knew the old priest had told Raven Baby the truth. I remember the old priest in the church – asking me if I had 'told him'. Likely he was talking about Magnus. Nila knew about Livli's child, and about him being sent away. Why would he not have told me something like that?

In the wolf hours, Bear's door flings open. Rapid, hard steps down the stairs, then the front door slams. I follow. Down, through the hallway, out into the night.

Cotton grass and yellow dandelion make pale specks in the dark grass. The sky is torn in strips of pink and light blue. Bear doesn't stop until he's at the end of the meadow. There, he throws his bag on the ground. He walks in amongst the trees and returns dragging a fallen sapling. He leaves again, and there is the sound of branches breaking. Bear is building a fire.

The night light turns the skin on my hands a pasty green. Bear builds the heap as high as himself. The recent rain makes it hard to light. The wet wood hisses and spits. Bear stops trying several times to search for more tinder. When it finally catches, he stands back watching it grow. In time, the blaze becomes so hot, even where I sit, that my skin singes. The flames don't grow outwards, languidly, but roar straight upwards, clawing at the sky. Bear opens his bag and he begins to throw things onto the fire. His papers, his books, all his sketches whirl through the air, white birds flapping, and the fire swallows them.

At one point, I glimpse a pale fleck in one of the vicarage windows upstairs. Raven Baby. It's not your fault, I tell her. It was wanting out; it would have found a way, regardless.

When at last Bear leaves and goes back to the vicarage, I stay. In time, I'll douse the fire.

Bear acts normal at breakfast time. 'Pass me the butter, please,' he says to Raven Baby. Raven Baby holds onto the plate a second too long, begs him to look at her. Bear doesn't.

'We've put Axel's body in the church for now,' says Frida.

Neither Bear nor Raven Baby answer. I mumble something non-committal.

After the meal, Bear surprises me by waiting by the door, bag at his feet.

'Are you certain?' I ask.

'Why wouldn't we continue?' he says.

Outside, he lengthens his steps. You are right to walk this off, I want to say. That is how we do it. Walk and walk until the emotion has bled out.

'I saw you,' I say. 'Last night.'

He walks a foot further away from me than usual.

'You have a family,' I say. 'A father, half-brothers, and a sister.'

Bear laughs, but it is not good laughter. He shakes his head. I say no more.

He has burned his maps but kept our notes. I am surprised he took the time to set them aside last night. Perhaps, even if he doesn't see it yet, he feels a connection to this. I am hopeful.

Yesterday, after the Twin Trees, we walked the line of the iron all the way to the top of the mountain, but I couldn't see anything else that felt familiar.

'We'll do the same walk one more time,' Bear says.

We find the Twin Trees, and begin again. Through the spruce forest, on top of thick moss. I try to concentrate. Talk to me, I say to the land. Show me the next landmark. But there is nothing.

I feel a sting of agony and glance at Bear. He'll soon tire.

We reach the peak and I shake my head. 'I can't see anything.' I want to add that I am sorry.

'Let's go back to The Twin Trees,' Bear says.

He won't have a failure. Not today.

'So,' he says, when we stand by them once again.

I look at the two spruce trees: thin, tall ones, of an equal height. They grow so close that the sides facing each other are weaker, whilst the branches on the opposite sides have grown long and furry, protecting the trees from the outside world.

'They stand in a line south-east to north-west,' Bear says. 'It could be that we should walk either in one direction or the other, rather than go past them.'

That sparks something inside me. 'Between,' I say.

'What?'

'It's "*Between The Twin Trees*".'

'Are you certain?'

I nod. Yes, yes. Up there, that's where we should go.

'Direction south-west,' Bear says, and writes in his book.

We walk in silence. I look left and right for the next land-mark. We pass a stump of a tree, and there it is: the well, a trickle of clear water bubbling up through the bright green moss.

'*Life of the Earth*,' I point. 'The well. The verse said *over* the well.'

I can't remember any of the text, but it doesn't matter, for it is not really a verse – it is a map.

'*Beyond The One Who Binds Water. By The One Who Sees. Night turns day, weight turns light . . .*'

And then, something-something, '*between the Twin Trees . . . over the Life of the Earth . . .*'

I am doing it. I chuckle. I am creating the verse. Ha, if Nila could see me now. It's not only him who could do this—

A pheasant shoots up with a clamour. My foot is swept from underneath me. The knowledge of the blow comes before the pain. Then, the agony towers above me and surges down; a tidal wave so immense, it brings me to my knees.

'Ester?' Bear's voice from far, far away.

Oh, God.

It's my ankle.

'Ester. Are you all right? Ester?'

I am on all fours. Breathe, I tell myself. Breathe out through the pain. But the agony is so strong, I could vomit. I need to see it. I hold my breath and heave myself onto my bottom. My eyes well up. But my foot is straight. Oh thank you, Jesus. I am old now. I can't be certain I would survive if I broke a foot and couldn't walk.

Nila. It was he who did this.

What rubbish.

Bear is squatting down, my ankle in his hands. 'A bad sprain,' he says, 'but I don't think it is broken.'

Once I broke my arm; my left, in the middle between elbow and hand. I was sixteen, and the *sita* was walking a hillside that was covered with scree. The rocks slid away under my feet and I fell on my arm. I sat up and noticed the hand was pointing in the wrong direction. Then I screamed. The elder pulled it to set the bones straight. That pain . . . They stabilised it with sticks and leather bands. It healed. But I was young then. And my left arm is still stiffer than the other one. It still hurts if I use it too much.

I look to see what happened . . . what crevasse or cavity I stepped in. After all, something made me twist my foot. But the moss is smooth. Raspberry bushes grow at its edge. Their branches stretch out, long and prickly. Holy Woman said the dead became skewed.

I believe in God, the Father almighty, creator of heaven and earth . . .

Nothing will ever be the same. From now on, I will always be scared. I will always have to watch where I put my feet.

Bear was wrong. You can't just remember the landmarks, you have to have the rhyme too. There was dread in the verse. I used to be scared. A warning.

'Do you think you can carry on?' Bear asks.

I want to say no, but then I look at his face. The glow of forest, of sky. Of mapping. Bear's needs.

'I can do this,' I say.

M

'Are you certain you can carry on?' I ask her again.

Ester is white. She leans on her stick, but limps. We should stop, of course, but selfishly, I can't bear to go back to the vicarage – Lovisa's large eyes following my every move. *Are you all right? Magnus?*

I feel sick. No, I am not all right.

I am a Lapp. I am of a less pure blood. I remember the governor, Gunnar Cronstedt, saying the Lapps were like children; 'less evolved' was the expression he used. As soon as Lovisa told the story, I knew. How? So much suddenly made sense. Why can I not remember anything?

In my head I hear the minister's voice: 'Your life begins here and now.' 'Your life began when you came to live with me.'

I have a sour taste in my mouth.

What am I supposed to say to Isabella?

Isabella won't want to know. But I have to tell her. The minister . . .

How could he do this? I thought I was like a son to him.

And how could he let his daughter marry a Lapp without telling her?

Or . . . does Isabella know, too?

Oh God. What am I supposed to do after this? Who am I supposed to trust?

I am a Lapp.

According to Lovisa, the priest sent me south to the minister almost as a bet. A bet! 'I don't want you on Blackåsen,' the minister said before I left. Why? Did he worry that I'd find out? Did he suddenly care? It doesn't matter. As soon as the county governor arrives, I'll leave. I'll try and forget all about this miserable place. I should never have come.

Whenever I look at Ester, I try to keep my face neutral, but I am certain she sees what's seething inside me. Revulsion. 'A different breed.' Even the old priest said so at the steamboat. Shame on me. But it's what I am feeling. Lesser worth.

I keep my face low.

On the peak of the mountain, Ester shakes her head.

'I want to say right,' she says.

She walks ahead of me along the ridge, her limp worse now.

'Let's go back,' I say.

'Let's find the next landmark,' she says.

We come to a flange in the mountain. A small path slithers on one side of the outcrop. On top of the boulder rests a mound of stones – a cairn? It could easily fall.

I eye the stones. 'Let's turn around,' I say again.

'Not yet,' she says.

She hobbles onto the shelf, her back towards the boulder, taking one step to the side, then another one. I follow her. On the other side of the outcrop, she stops. She is pointing at its base, at a small opening.

This? Her nod is uncertain.

I squat to look inside. The opening is large enough for a man to enter if he crawls. I can't see much, but it could be a tunnel, slanting downhill.

'What is the word?' I ask.

She hesitates. 'It is "in",' she says.

'Are you certain?' I ask.

She nods.

Ester said the verse contains the essence of the mountain. In my mind's eye, I see Adelaide's white face in the church. I remember a map framed with painted angels with devils' horns.

Nonsense.

'We'll need a torch,' I say.

It takes time to make a torch and to light it, and all the while I avoid looking at the hole. I feel strange. Then I get angry with myself. It's a rock formation!

Ester hands me the torch and I shine it into the opening. I can see perhaps six feet ahead, but then the darkness takes over and there is no telling how long it continues or how it evolves. The slope is about fifteen degrees. I find a small stone by my knees and roll it inside. I hear it land. Then there might be a grotto beyond the tunnel. At least, it is not a huge cavity. The thought of falling through the air makes my stomach turn. Ester throws a larger stone into the passageway, hurling it hard.

'To make certain no animal is inside,' she says.

We wait, but nothing comes out.

'Bear?' I ask.

She shakes her head. 'They wouldn't go in there.' I can't read her face.

'I can't climb down there with the torch,' I say to Ester, and hand it to her. 'Once I reach the bottom, please slide it to me.'

There's no question of going in head first. I lie down and stick my feet in the hole, half-expecting something to bite at them or claw my legs. My heart is pounding. The tunnel is tight, and I edge onwards. What if I can't get out? When I am about three feet down, my feet don't touch the ground any longer. There is a cave in there.

I continue on, and first my feet touch rock, then my knees. I pull my head out last. It is pitch black.

'Try sliding the torch down,' I say, speaking up to the light. Nothing. I wait. I try not to think what might be in here with me. The torch comes, and gets stuck halfway. I slide my upper body back into the tunnel and pull it out. My breathing is laboured. But the flame burns well, so there is enough oxygen in here. Breathe, I tell myself. I raise the torch. It is a cave. The rugged roof is dry. The hollow is perhaps seven feet high and long. I stand up. There is a steady downhill slope leading away from me. It's covered in powder – sand, crumbled stone.

'I'll look further in,' I call up to Ester, but there is no reply.

I sweep the torch from side to side as I walk. The tunnel smells of dust. The walls are rough. The slope becomes steeper. I won't venture too far from the opening.

'The essence of a place.' The essence of Blackåsen is a cavern. It doesn't make me feel better.

I have already gone too far. I stretch my torch forward for one last look. Something glimmers a few steps further. 'It can't be.' I say the words aloud.

The shimmering yellow vein is out in the open, one foot wide, like a path leading down into the mountain.

Gold?

My breath hitches. 'It can't be,' I say again.

Gold.

If this is gold, the find is enormous. I stumble down the

slope. I need my pickaxe, I need to sample this. I need to . . . What I have seen so far would make this the biggest gold find in Sweden, in Europe, perhaps the world.

I stop and turn. I realise I can't see the opening any longer. I half run up the slope. The light from the torch flickers.

'Ester?'

No response.

'Ester!' I call.

A moment, and then she is in the opening. Her head in the surrounding light, a pin-head.

'You have to come down here,' I say.

Ester is smaller than me, and soon she is inside the cave. She didn't bring her stick, and I give her my arm for support. Come . . .

We hobble down the tunnel and I point with the torch.

'Gold,' I say.

My face twitches. I try and stop it. Ester sinks down on the ground.

I need to see more. The glimmering streak just continues and continues. When I am a few yards into the mountain, I realise Ester hasn't come with me, and suddenly I am gripped by fear. I scramble back up, but she is still there, and there is still light by the exit.

'Someone has been here recently,' she says. 'Unless you did this.'

She points to the stones by the rock wall. She is right. They have been moved, piled up. They might, once, have covered the metal.

'We need to get out,' I say.

She climbs first. Her shoes with the toes pointing upwards in a tip make it difficult for her to move upwards. She puffs. I put my hands underneath her feet for her to get some grip.

I keep supporting her feet until my whole arm is inside the tunnel. The light floods. She's out. It's my turn. I leave the torch behind and begin my ascent, scuffling forward on my elbows. I try to help with the tip of my toes. It is too tight. I'll never make it. My heart is pounding in my chest. Don't think. One inch at a time. As I reach the surface, I crawl out, fingers trembling. I scrape my lower back and my thighs before I can finally kneel and then stand, blinking against the light. My knees feel weak. I sit down beside Ester and drink some water.

Gold.

I can't be certain until we've done the tests, but I know in every fibre of my body what we have found. Apatite-bearing iron sometimes occurs together with sulfide minerals, which can contain metals such as copper and gold. There are similar stories about Lapps leading us to discoveries. They know the mountains better than any of us.

I'll have to send people here: a proper cartographer, a chemist . . . I'll take samples and anlyse them before putting things into motion. I will go down into the cave one more time, and follow the ore into the mountain to get a rough estimate of its size.

My head is buzzing. There is so much to do. Who could have thought! I want to tell someone . . .

Lovisa. Of all people, I want to tell Lovisa.

Beside me, Ester's face looks cloudy. She sits tight-lipped and gazes at the horizon, eyes thin slits. Surely, she understands the importance of this. Imagine what this could do for Sweden. Imagine what it will do for this region. What it will make possible . . .

I'll make her see that this find will benefit her people, too. Her people. A nick in my heart.

I won't think about that now. I don't know for sure that Lovisa was right. There are thousands of orphans, thousands of scarred ones . . . I look nothing like a Lapp.

The word makes me cringe.

'This changes everything,' Ester says out loud.

Here you are, berating yourself. As if the world was all about you. Your petty worries, your small concerns ... Have you learned nothing? You sicken me.

You say you have no cause — so find one!

You say you are of no worth — so be useful!

Are you in there? For once, care about something larger than yourself.

Rise up, you worm of a human being. Shake the dust off your soul. Act. Or, at least, let yourself be used. Let your life mean something!

L

I am pacing, hands hitting my thighs. How could I have been so stupid as to tell Magnus what I had learned? Did I think I was doing him a favour?

A Lapp! I told him he was a Lapp.

I hit my forehead with the palm of my hand.

I destroy things. I destroy people. How did Eva feel about being kissed? Not once have I thought about that. My parents would have sent her away afterwards, my father ensuring he ruined her reputation. I only ever think of myself.

I am so sorry, Magnus! Oh, please come back. We won't tell anyone.

That hardly matters. Magnus will always know. My father knows.

The front door shuts. Frida walks down the porch and takes the path, a basket on her arm. I run down the stairs and into the drawing room, to the cabinet beside the bookshelf, and pour myself a glass of aquavit from Magnus's bottle. Anything to quell this pain. I take a large gulp. It burns my throat, my chest, and I cough, and it spurts out of my mouth and nose—

The door to the drawing room opens. Frida? No, it's the maid. I wipe my face on my sleeve. *Go away. Go away!*

'I wanted to speak to your friend,' she says. She has a lisp. I didn't notice it before.

'To Magnus?' A bubble of spirits pops in my throat. I cough again and my eyes sprout tears.

'Magnus,' she nods. It sounds like 'Magnuth'. She glances over her shoulder.

Why would she want to speak to him?

'He's not here,' I say. 'He won't be here until later.'

Through the window, I watch the maid leave. Frida is coming along the path from the road. The two women meet and briefly stop. Then the maid pushes her head down and hurries on. Frida stands still, looking after her. I have to hide the glass. Wash it. Too late, Frida has begun walking, long steps.

I put the glass on the floor underneath the sofa and pull one of the wooden crates closer. I breathe in my palm and smell it. Awful. I try to force more saliva into my mouth, to swallow the smell down. I grab a book from the box closest to me, then sit down on the sofa and open it.

Frida enters. She throws a glance around the room. I smile to her, then continue staring into the book. What on earth am I looking at? Rocks? I picked the *Mineralogy* tome. 'I forgot my purse.' Frida places the basket on a table, walks and sits beside me on the sofa. She puts a finger on the page before me and presses down, lowers it.

'So what did Lina want?' she asks.

Who?

'My maid?'

I shrug. 'Nothing.'

But Frida doesn't let go of the book.

It dawns on me what it is about Frida that reminds me of my sister. They have that same look in their eyes: determination. Perhaps even passion. I can't help but gasp.

I've never thought of Isabella as strong. I've thought her

emotionless and mean . . . But she has strength. And she is clever.

Perhaps my sister knows. Yes. Somehow she knows that Magnus is a Lapp. Like me, she wanted to be free of my father and his house, and she would have done anything. She took the way out she was offered. Marrying and breeding to gain freedom. Even if it was a Lapp. As long as nobody knew . . .

In my mind's eye, I see my sister watching Magnus in a crowd. Watching over him.

I think of Frida, widowed, leaving to make a new life. They make up their mind and act on it, these women. Nothing is allowed to stand in their way.

My pulse begins to throb in my ears.

Frida smiles. 'Nothing? I am not certain I believe you.'

B

Bear and I sit at my campsite. He picks at the dirt under his fingernails, spreads his fingers and looks at his hand. I led him to it. I have opened the mountain's secret. Not even when I realised the verse was in fact a map did I understand to let be. Oh, what have I then done?

He is one of us. He must see what this would do. What it would destroy. He has heard what this mountain is capable of . . .

Bear's face is tight. I won't listen to anything you say, it says. I won't hear it. I am not you.

I don't want to know what my face says.

High above us, an eagle climbs.

It would have been so easy to make the mound of stones above collapse and cover the opening, with Bear inside. *Do it*, something inside me screamed. *Do it!*

But I could never . . . Never. Besides, someone else has been there recently. Someone else knows about the gold. The question is, who? How do I stop the madness that will surely follow?

Now, I must take one step at a time. I must think.

I put my hand on Bear's arm. He startles and stares at it. I remove it and decide not to feel hurt.

'Someone was there not long ago,' I say.

He sighs and lets his hands fall in his lap.

'It changes everything,' I say. 'I mean . . . the murders.'

'Could be,' he says.

'We have to think again.' I search for the eagle with my eyes. 'Start with the gold as the reason for them dying, and map the story in reverse.'

'Map in reverse?' He smiles and his face relaxes, as if I am suddenly speaking his language.

'Who would gold benefit?' I ask.

He falls serious. 'But it would benefit everyone, Ester. All of us.' He stresses the word 'us'.

When I don't say anything, he sighs again, 'Right,' he says. 'Rune was a mineralogist like me. Let's say that someone asked him to come here for the sake of the gold . . . Who would have known about it?'

The eagle flies closer now. Its circles are smaller. It has spotted something on the ground.

'Perhaps the Lapp,' I say. It is possible he knew. The verse proves that Nila did.

'Could he have asked Rune to come here?'

I shake my head. It's unlikely they would have known each other. Even if they did, it would have been hard for the Lapp to contact him.

'So perhaps, for some reason, the Lapp told the parish council,' Magnus says, 'and they sent a message to Rune.'

The eagle dives, and there is a frenetic scuttling. Bear startles. I half rise, but the pain in my ankle jolts me back to sitting. The bird caught something. It's a sign. A good sign.

'Do you think all the villagers are aware of it?' Magnus asks.

The eagle rises again, heavy now, prey in its claws. A rat? I try to see where it lands, where it has its nest. 'I can't imagine

313

they do,' I say. 'Gold is gold. If they all knew, someone would be unable to leave it there.'

He nods. 'You are right. Adelaide must know, though. She was part of the parish council. She was at the meeting prior to events.'

'How did she know to leave?'

'Her maid said they fought. Perhaps there was a disagreement and Adelaide was on the Lapp's side. Perhaps he didn't see the need to kill her?'

I think of Holy Woman sitting not far from here, saying she was pondering the death of Sigrid. Perhaps she had come to make sure the gold was untouched. And then, even after all that has happened, she didn't tell anyone; she knew to keep quiet. Unlike me. Oh, why did I ask him about our verse?

Bear frowns and sits silent for a while. 'Anders was probably killed by Child of Village. After what she had heard, in her state of mind . . . She saw the first murders as God's vengeance for her mother.'

'So then, you and Adelaide and I know about the gold,' I say. 'So far, Adelaide has said nothing. You and I, too, must keep quiet.'

Bear nods. 'I want to speak to the maid and ask her if she heard anything of what was said during the fight.'

The eagle is rising again.

M

'You know, finding gold in a mountain doesn't change anything,' I say.

Ester leans heavily on her stick. She doesn't respond. We are walking back towards the village.

'And normal people don't kill for gold,' I continue. 'Likely, what happened here had nothing to do with that.'

We have reached the church, and Ester stops. Her skin looks green. 'I actually don't think I can continue,' she says.

'Do you want me to help you inside?' I ask.

She shakes her head and sinks down on one of the gravestones. 'I want to sit here for a while.'

I hesitate. 'I will go and speak to the maid. Then, I'll come and get you.'

I'll be careful in asking my questions. I know what I said, but, in truth, gold can turn the mind of the most sensible of people. In some form, it was likely the motive behind the first three murders.

I pass the shop.

What would Jacob do if he found out about the discovery? What would the brothers do, Matts and Daniel Fjellström?

I halt. The county governor will be here in three days at the most. The best thing Ester and I can do is pretend that we don't know anything. Otherwise, we might put our lives in danger. I should not speak with the maid. I should not put anything more in motion. I could place us at risk.

But as I turn around, Frida's maid comes out of the shop. She stops. 'I left a message with your lady-friend at the vicarage,' she says.

'Lovisa?'

She nods. I look up and down the road. It's empty. The door to the shop is closed.

'I was remembering that day, like you asked me to, and there is something that doesn't add up.'

'In what way?'

'Adelaide says she had left. Frida says she was in church. One set of feet ran upstairs. Yet they were both in his office, later.'

'What do you mean?'

'After the men's screams, there was only one set of footsteps running in and upstairs.'

I shake my head. 'Yes?' I say again.

She sighs, as if I am daft. 'But don't you see? If Frida was in the church, and Adelaide had left, and yet they were both in the priest's office later . . . How could it be only one person running upstairs? One of them must have been on the first floor already?'

Adelaide didn't leave. She was there when the men were killed.

The maid is still looking at me.

'Are you certain?' I ask.

She nods.

'Don't tell anyone else,' I say. 'No one. You understand?'

Her eyes widen. She's realising why I am telling her this. She throws a glance over her shoulder.

I leave her there and begin to walk back towards the vicarage.

Adelaide . . . It could also have been Frida. Now, I am uncertain.

And Lovisa is alone with Frida in the vicarage.

L

'So what did my maid think she had seen?'

'I swear,' I say, 'she didn't say anything.'

Frida and I are still on her settee. My hands sweat, yet I am shivering as if cold. My body knows it's in danger. Frida's blue eyes look dull. I hear the old man's voice in my ear: 'It got to them. It will get to you too.'

'It's difficult to think of everything,' Frida says, more to herself than to me. 'I wonder what she thinks she knows . . .'

Three paces to that door. Then a hallway, the front door, the path past the church. I'd never make it. I am weak, useless . . . Frida would be stronger, more determined, like my sister. I could never win a fight with my sister. I'd never even try. I'd rather lie down, close my eyes, and get it over with.

Frida leans against the backrest, hands in her lap. 'You see,' she says, 'there is gold on the mountain.'

My mouth feels dry. 'Then how come Magnus hasn't found it?'

'It is well hidden. Unless you actually know where it is, I am certain you'd never find it.'

I glance towards the door again. Frida follows my gaze, then looks up to the ceiling. She doesn't worry about me. She, too, knows she'll win.

'Of all suitors, I had to choose Ulf.' She shakes her head. 'And he never thought to tell me what marriage to him would condemn me to: childlessness, trapped with a man consumed by his fears, on this mountain, for ever. On our first day here, I met Sigrid and I knew; she was a duplicate of Ulf. I confronted him and he told me what had happened when they were young. He should have lied. How could I love him after that? How could I stand him?'

Frida's lips curl. 'Twenty years I put up with him and this village. Twenty long years.'

I look at the door again. I wonder when Magnus and Ester will be back. Not soon enough.

'Here I was, in the deep forests, with a rapist for a husband.' Now, Frida sounds breezy, as if she's telling any amusing story. 'And then the Lapp came to speak with the parish council.

'From what I understood, he had fled his own tribe. They do that, you know, the Lapps, turn on the ones who used to lead them when they come under the influence of the Church. When I first heard about it, I would look at Ulf and laugh at the idea that this was the kind of man the Lapps rejected their leaders for. Anyway, the Lapp wanted them to take him in and let him stay in this village until his death. In return, he promised to show them gold, more gold than they could imagine. I was listening by the door. I could just imagine the expression on their faces: shock, greed, fear . . .

'They didn't want to talk with him still in the room, and so Ulf told him they needed to think about it, and asked him to come back and see them in a few weeks' time.

'As soon as he left, hell broke loose. How they fought. "Remember what happened?" Adelaide screamed.' Frida is distorting her voice. '"We're talking about gold," Jan-Erik retorted. "He's one of their spiritual leaders," Adelaide yelled. "So what," Jan-Erik said. "You and the priest aren't the only ones with claims to holiness." "He wants us for something." And so on. The only thing they could agree upon was to send for Rune. Him being a mineralogist, they thought they might need him.'

Frida pauses. She folds her legs underneath her and straightens her dress. Something she said reverberates in me. 'He wants us for something.'

Power, I think. *What would someone be willing to do, to recover a single grain of it?*

The line sounds like something from a poem. Or a song. I can't remember . . .

'I spent my days searching for the Lapp's camp,' Frida says. 'It took time, but eventually I found it. I was certain that sooner or later he would go to the gold, to make certain it was safe. I watched him as much as I could without Ulf beginning to wonder where I was. After about a week, I think he fell ill. He lay by his fire, arms flailing, as if the bugs were bothering him. He began talking to himself. "I am not listening," he would cry out, or: "You are not stronger than me." Those kinds of things.' Frida shrugs. 'Fever, no doubt.'

No, I think. Not fever. Not talking to himself.

It's hard to think. I feel like I am underwater.

'Rune arrived in the village and they tried to find the gold themselves – well, Rune and Jan-Erik did. I guess they thought that if they could find it, they wouldn't have to give the Lapp anything, and they wouldn't need Ulf and Adelaide to agree. Ulf didn't know what to think about the whole thing, and Adelaide was vehemently opposed. Any time they met, it would end in argument. They couldn't find the gold either, and their next meeting with the Lapp was fast approaching.

'The night of their meeting, the Lapp finally did go and see to his gold. I followed him. I was in such agony of indecision. I wasn't certain what to do or how to go about it. After, I followed him all the way to the village. He was walking very slowly now, struggling. In the graveyard, I caught up with him. When I touched his arm, it was so hot – he was burning up. The way he startled . . . it was like he was expecting someone else. 'Do you realise what they will do?' I asked him. 'These are not good men.' And I told him what they had done to Susanna.

'I could see him turn.' Frida's eyes narrow as she remembers. 'It was as if he got some renewed power from somewhere and surrendered to it. He straightened up and his eyes became clear. He didn't say anything. He simply walked on; a different man. I followed him to the vicarage door, up the stairs, down the hallway towards Ulf's office . . . He stopped to remove his shoes . . .

'I never imagined he would actually kill them.' Frida pauses. 'Never.'

I can't breathe.

'It was remarkably fast,' Frida says. 'He swirled between them and they fell one after the other . . . It felt unreal . . . Then the door downstairs opened and someone came running. I hid in my room. When I heard Adelaide scream, I joined her.'

You watched him kill your husband, I think. And then you played the shocked wife.

'From what I understood later, they had decided to accept the Lapp's offer, three against one.' Frida puts her hand on my arm as if she's telling me any story. 'Adelaide had stormed out, and then the Lapp came.'

'Why did he stay with the bodies?'

'I have been thinking about that. I don't know.' She shakes her head. 'It was over.'

Yes, I think. It was over. Only it wasn't. It isn't. You are still here.

'The only problem was that Adelaide, too, knew about the gold,' Frida says. 'I wondered if she would tell the others.'

'The fire. That was you.'

She nods. 'I thought that if she continued to be scared . . .'

Frida could have killed her. Though Frida saw her own husband die and didn't care. I exhale and find her looking at me.

'Now, Lovisa . . .' Frida's face is serious, 'I have someone who can help assess the discovery and put the right things in motion. There is an opportunity here for you. Imagine a life where you don't have to worry about money, where you can live independently, without being reliant on the goodwill of men . . . All you need to do is keep this to yourself.'

'All right,' I say.

Magnus will be here soon.

Frida looks me in the eye and nods. 'No, I see it in your face. I didn't think you would.'

Listen. Still yourself. Can you hear the drums? They are beating for you. Can you feel their pulse in your veins? Tick, tick, tick.

Tick, tick, tick.

Do you see now what this mountain does to people? It cannot be contained. The woman you see before you used to be normal: selfish, yes, manipulative, yes; but in the eyes of the world, normal. Now she thinks nothing about four dead men. If they open the mountain up, many, many more will die.

She reminds you of someone . . . Your sister? Ah yes, I can see that.

Now, you have to close this down.

You are not on your own. We are behind you – me, my father, and a thousand more like us.

When I let the water take me, as I breathed it into my lungs, I felt terror. But it was soon gone. Do not fear, Raven Baby. It will be quick and I will guide you.

Take off your shoes. Sneak them off, as if to rest your feet. Stretch your toes. Push the shoes back with your heels. Neatly, neatly, there.

Now, slow down. Relax into me. Close your eyes. Can you feel the pulse? Can you feel it?

B

The boneyard lies stark in the sunlight. Bumblebees drone above the grass. Despite the recent rain, the earth looks dry.

I stand up. The pain is unbelievable. My ankle doesn't bear my weight at all. Perhaps it is broken. I hobble towards the vicarage. The path to Priest's house is so short that I have never noticed the distance before, but today, walking it might take me all afternoon.

I hear the bark of a snow owl.

Even Adelaide knew not to tell anyone about the gold, and I didn't. The others will never forgive me. I'll never forgive myself. Bear . . . My heart clenches at the thought of him.

The snow owl *krek-kreks* again, here on Blackåsen?

'Biijá.'

It's Dávvet. There, between the trees. I start walking towards him. He meets me halfway, wraps an arm around my waist and carries me into the shadows.

'You didn't hear me call,' he says. 'Have you then already forgotten everything?'

Tears are seeping from my eyes, I can feel them on my cheeks. He looks away, gives me a moment to gather myself. I wipe my face with the back of my hand.

'Come home,' Dávvet says.

Home. The *sita*, which I left to grieve my husband's death. I take a step away from Dávvet and my ankle collapses under me. He grabs my arm and lowers me onto a stone. I am still angry with him – with us. What we did was unforgivable.

Dávvet nods: he knows. 'Nila killed himself,' he says.

Is that what happened? If so, because of us. We rejected him. We forced him to.

Dávvet's brown eyes are soft, 'We are bound to disagree about Nila, you and I,' he says.

I simply look at him: What do you mean?

He sighs. His hair is grey now, but still as thick. As he bends his head, it falls into his eyes.

I don't let go of his gaze: No, let's have it out, once and for all. You came here to find me. Now, we talk.

'Nila changed.' Dávvet says this using his gentlest tone. 'I know you can't see it, but the rest of us did. I think it happened early.'

'I don't understand?'

'I think his powers got to him, ate him up. I think he yielded. At some point, he decided that he knew best. He stopped listening to the rest of us and that is not how it is supposed to be: the elders lead, but the *sita* has to decide. This might have also been why he didn't want to teach anybody else anything. He didn't want to share it.'

'You're bad.' I say this with heat. 'You have been, ever since your youth.'

'No, Biijá,' Dávvet shakes his head.

'Livli—'

'I was thirteen,' Dávvet interrupts me. 'I was a child.'

Was he only thirteen when it happened? I know he was young, but thirteen—?

'She fell pregnant,' I say.

He nods. 'I know.'

He, too? Why didn't Nila tell me that there was a child?

Why didn't I try and find out what happened to Livli after she left us? The heartlessness we all showed . . .

'I wasn't the only one who had an unlawful relationship with her,' Dávvet says.

'In that case, why didn't you tell?'

'I was thirteen years old. Perhaps I thought I was doing the *sita* a favour. Perhaps I was told that it would be better if I took the blame.'

Who would have told him this?

I look away; I know who.

It wasn't heartlessness that made us not enquire after Livli's whereabouts. It was righteousness. We felt we were right. Her sin would soil us. Nila said . . .

Nila said she would pull the wrath of the spirits down on us.

My eyes fill again, for I know who Bear resembles, and it isn't Dávvet. It is Nila.

My chest heaves.

A squirrel runs up a tree. There is a rasping of tiny claws on bark. Dávvet follows it with his eyes, again giving me space.

'Two years ago, Priest came to find me. He told me about what happened that day at the maze. He told me about living the rest of his life in fear . . .' Dávvet says. 'Do you remember that night, with the dog pack?'

Of course I remember.

'I went to see Nila after our talk at the fire. I wanted to ask him not to fight with the settlers. I wanted to tell him how very frightened they were. Instead, Nila scared me. "We had an agreement. Those dogs," he said, and I knew he wasn't talking about the animals, but about the settlers. "They broke that bond. Now it's us against them.'

'There's gold in Blackåsen,' I whisper.

'So there is,' Dávvet says. 'I think Nila had a vision. I think he knew that the Lapp would reveal the gold, and Nila was ready to do anything not to make that happen. Anything.' Dávvet shakes his head. 'That last night – he yelled at us to worship, remember? I think he thought we could fight this in the spiritual world. When we weren't willing, Nila acted. You see, Biijá, I think that Nila killed himself because he knew he'd be stronger on the other side.'

I feel cold through and through. I don't dare to look at the forest around me.

'They'll break the mountain,' I say.

'But of course they will,' he says. 'It will bring on awful things. And there is absolutely nothing we can or should do about it.'

My head hurts and I rub my forehead with my knuckles.

Dávvet nods. 'I want you to come home, Biijá. We all do. I'll wait for you on the other side of the river. Think about it, but not for too long.'

ℳ

Ester is by the vicarage porch, hand on the railing, foot on the first step. I run past her. No time to explain. I tear the door open.

'Lovisa?'

Where is she? Two steps to the drawing room.

Lovisa is standing in the middle of the room. Frida lies by her feet. Lovisa's hand is bleeding. There is glass on the floor.

I look at Frida. Is she . . .?

'I don't know,' Lovisa says, wide eyes holding mine.

Ester limps in. She gasps.

'She tried to kill me,' Lovisa says. She chokes, swallows. 'Magnus, she said there was gold on the mountain and that was why they died; her husband and the others. She was there. *She* made it happen. I grabbed the glass from underneath the sofa and . . .'

She raises her hand and then stares at it, noticing the blood dripping onto the floor. Ester undoes the ribbon around her waist and binds Lovisa's palm.

I squat down and turn Frida over. Her body is limp, but she is breathing. I search amongst her hair for the wound and find it on her temple. She moans and her eyelids flutter.

'She'll live,' I say.

★

'We need to tell the others,' I say. 'Adelaide, Per, Jacob . . . We'll have to keep Frida somewhere until they come from the coast. Don't worry,' I tell Lovisa. 'You acted in self-defence. Anyone can see that.'

Frida is sitting on the settee, pressing a cloth to her head. Lovisa is staring at her, eyes dull. It's the shock.

'Don't do this.' Frida attempts a smile. 'It's gold, Magnus. Enough for all of us.'

Ester's face twists in disgust. With her ankle, Ester can't go and get help, and no question of sending Lovisa.

'I'll go and get the others,' I say. I hesitate between Lovisa and Ester, but hand my knife to Lovisa. 'I'll be quick.'

'Don't tell them about the gold,' Lovisa says.

'No,' I nod. 'I won't.'

I hurry towards the road. Frida watched her husband die and said nothing. Is this what it will be like when the gold becomes common knowledge? No. Normal people do not behave like this.

Something is niggling me, but then I have just been told that a woman who I respected and—

I reach the road and stop. No, there is something wrong.

It's to do with the knife . . . the way Lovisa took it from me. She didn't just hold it, aiming it towards Frida, like I had been doing. She held the knife the other way, as if she were about to stab someone.

And there is more; Lovisa was barefoot.

I start to run. My feet crunch the gravel as I pass the church. Oh, please don't.

Slow . . . I am too slow.

I run up the steps and throw open the door, and there they sit, the three women, in heaps on the floor: Ester, Lovisa, and Frida. Frida is hunched over. There is blood all around her, blood on Ester's front, and on Lovisa's . . .

'What have you done?' I yell at them.

'She tried to run,' Ester says.

Lovisa is not looking at me.

'Oh God!'

'I killed her,' Ester says.

'What have you done?' I repeat. But I am looking at Lovisa.

We open Ulf's grave mound and bury Frida next to her husband. It takes most of the night to dig the trench. I have to stop several times as nausea overwhelms me and wait until it subsides. We have wrapped the body in a curtain, and we lower it down, then we close the burial place up. I hope her husband haunts her. I hope she haunts him. I worry about how to hide the signs of digging, and I remove whatever vegetation has had time to grow on the other two graves. That way, at least they'll all look the same. Hopefully, no one will come to mourn these men just yet.

Ester, Lovisa, Adelaide, and I know about the gold. And none of us will ever speak about it. Me, to protect Lovisa. The other three for other reasons.

Lovisa's eyes seek mine; I refuse to meet her gaze.

Before morning, it is time for Ester and Lovisa to leave. We have cleaned up the blood, but sooner or later, someone will look for Frida. Lovisa needs to disappear.

'You are Bear.' Ester puts her hand on my cheek and looks me in the eye. 'I knew you would do the right thing. Don't worry about Lovisa. The *sita* will take care of her. Are you certain you won't come with us?'

A family, brothers, sisters . . . Lapp blood. I shake my head.

Her eyes fill, but she nods and smiles. She claps my cheek

with her hand and begins to walk, supporting herself on her stick.

Lovisa has half closed her eyes, displaying her eyelids, and the perfectly rounded, raised eyebrows. She raises her chin and looks at me: Well, then.

Oh, Lovisa.

I pull her towards me. Her cheek presses against my chest and I kiss her hair and then her forehead, smelling sun and skin. I want to say: *What did you do? Why, oh why?* But we always say too much. And not enough. I hold her away from me and look in her face.

'You'll come back.' My voice sounds thick. 'Later.'

Her eyes are full of tears. She blinks. 'Yes,' she says.

'It would be an honour for any man to be married to you.' I have to clear my throat. 'It is an honour for me to be your friend.'

I watch Lovisa and Ester walk away until neither of the two women can be seen and my heart wrenches in my gut. I will miss her. I have a wife, I think. Though for the life of me, I cannot remember her name.

Then I carry out Frida's boxes and make a big fire.

Mid-morning, Matts Fjellström, and Adelaide come to the vicarage.

'We saw smoke,' Matts says.

'I am burning my notes.' The words stick in my throat. 'You were right, some things are not supposed to be mapped.'

A book with a green cover falls out of one of the boxes on the fire. It is Carl Jonas Love Almqvist's *Det går an*. Its edges begin to glow, the paper turning black.

Matts and Adelaide are both gazing at the book. Likely,

332

they heard us dig at night. In this light, they might have seen us, too.

'Frida has left Blackåsen,' I say, even though the lie is pointless. 'She has gone to be with her family.'

'Good,' Matts says.

'She never did want to live here,' Adelaide says, eyes holding mine.

We nod to each other and they leave.

It is true, some things are not supposed to be recorded. Others must remain buried. I stare up at the grey lump of the mountain. It has taken something from me and I won't forget. I think about the trenches I dug on its surface. I took something from it, too. Neither of us won . . . I wonder what happened to the mapmaker Hermelin on his journey here. Oh, I am so tired.

When all that remains is a glowing heap of cinders, I go back to the vicarage. I open the window, pull an armchair before it, and sit down. I reek of smoke and fire. I lean my head on the backrest and close my eyes—

I am in the forest. Patter of bare feet drumming against the ground. Mine. The priest's. He's after me. I have to run. He's going to send me away . . .

When I wake up, the county governor's hand is on my shoulder. Out in the yard, three men are standing by the dead fire. One is poking in it with his foot.

'What on earth happened here?' Gunnar Cronstedt asks.

I sit up and shake my head to clear it. 'There was a second killer. Her name was Sigrid. Her mother, Susanna, did away with herself when she was young. Sigrid blamed the villagers. She killed Anders and tried to kill Adelaide, too. In the ensuing fight, Sigrid died.'

'That's precisely what Adelaide Gustavsdotter and Matts Fjellström said when we asked them questions,' he says. 'Well then, both killers are dead now. The Lapp was hanged a few days ago.'

So they did hang him. I remember the Lapp on the bench in Luleå prison: the old face, the long straggly hair and the bony body. I feel the same hesitation rise inside me. 'Barefoot,' Per had said. Lovisa, too, had been barefoot.

Nonsense. It's the solitude and the sleeplessness. You can begin to see things that don't exist.

'Where is Frida?' The county governor looks around.

'She travelled south. She has gone to live with her parents,' I say.

He frowns. 'Oh.'

As we begin to walk back towards the coast, I think of the minister and what I will tell him. As little as possible, I decide. At some point, I will take my revenge on him. I am not certain what to think about Isabella . . .

Oh God, Harriet. Oh, what will I tell my daughter?

'So, did you go up on the mountain?' the county governor asks.

I shake my head.

'No,' he says. 'There's nothing to see.'

The mountain hovers above us as if trying to tell me something, but I am not looking up.

'I am surprised about Frida,' the county governor says. 'She didn't leave a note or anything?'

For him?

And why does he call her 'Frida'? Not 'the priest's wife', or 'Mrs Liljeblad' . . .

Something strikes me then, something Frida said. We were

334

having dinner. 'It's the county governor's favourite,' she said about the red wine. 'When we first travelled here from Uppsala, we stayed at his residence . . . he brought us a bottle . . .'

The county governor came here to fetch the killer . . . Would Frida have had the time to speak with him about the gold? I remember how surprised he was, when I first arrived. As if he hadn't planned on telling us in Stockholm what had happened.

Gunnar Cronstedt squints up at Blackåsen Mountain, eyes gleaming.

And I wonder . . . I wonder . . .

My father taught me that everything was connected: humans, animals, and nature; the living and the dead. 'In the underworld, the dead live lives matching ours. If you walk barefoot, you can sometimes feel the soles of their feet against yours.'

I took off my shoes, but felt only the rasping of blueberry sprigs. 'It's a skill,' he said. 'I will teach you.'

Now I am dead. My hands are tied. I need someone to see and hear me. My woman has gone home, taking Raven Baby with her. There is nobody else.

You are open like a mountain rift. Many would step straight in, but I won't. I will talk and hope you listen.

I watch you walking south, your long hair in its twist, your drawn face, and that scar . . . I can't help but sigh. I fear you won't understand any of what I am about to tell you and we don't have much time. I don't even know if you'll hear.

My name is Nila.

You shrug as if to shake off a fly.

My name is Nila and I need you to hear my story. Can you hear me?

ACKNOWLEDGEMENTS

I am deeply indebted to a number of travel accounts from the period, mainly: *Travels through Norway and Lapland by Leopold Von Buch*, 1813; *Try Lapland: A Fresh Field for Summer Tourists* by Alexander Hutchinson, 1870 (the wonderful piece of information about skulls and bones drifting in Luleå graveyard comes from him, and I have also let Magnus's and Lovisa's steamboat journey follow his route via the hamlet of Ratan); the missionary Peter Fjellstedt's travel account from Lapland, 1857 (published by Karin Snellman, URKUNDEN nr. 13/1990); the notes made by missionary Ludvig Bergström, summer 1880 (published by Karin Snellman, URKUNDEN nr, 7/1988); the extracts from the diary kept on a journey to Lapland by the missionary Walter Gustafsson, summer 1880 (published by Karin Snellman, URKUNDEN nr. 9/1989); and two books: *From Nasafjäll to SSAB–Three Hundred Years of Iron Handling and Mining in Norrbotten* by Staffan Hansson, (Centek Förlag, 1987) (my translation of title), and *Gällivare-verken 1855–1882* by Alf W. Axelson, (Norrbottens-kurirens tryckeri, 1964).

The experience and time of three men were invaluable in writing this book: Dr Michael Daly, Dr Jonathan Evans, and Professor Laurence Robb – all experts in earth sciences. I so loved our conversations and found them fascinating to the extent I almost wished the book would never finish so we could keep talking. All faults and sidesteps in the text are mine and mine alone.

This book would not have happened without Janelle Andrews at Peters, Fraser & Dunlop, and Kate Parkin – at the time – Hodder & Stoughton, and Nick Sayers – Hodder & Stoughton. Your encouragement and advice, leeway and pressure just at the right times – you championed me through this. Thank you also to Rachel Mills and her team at PFD for your immense professionalism and fabulous advice.

Dear, dear writing friends. Thank you for all your time and love: for the listening and reading; for the encouragement and the critique; for the editing . . . Theanna Bischoff, and my fellow students at the Alexandra Writers' Centre in Calgary, Mary Chamberlain, Viv Graveson, Haroon Hassan, Fergal Keane, Laura McClelland, Elaine Morin, Alex Ruczaj, Saskia Sarginson, Lauren Trimble.

A special thank you to three people: my beloved father-in-law Dr John Taylor for reading the first drafts many times and sending me notes with brilliant ideas, and my dear friends Lorna Read, for reviewing the original text, and Brigitte Mierau, for sending countless emails and articles to encourage me and tell me that whatever I was feeling 'was part of the process'.

And, of course, David, Anna, and Maja. Without you, always and for ever, nothing.

Q&A

WITH CECILIA EKBÄCK

◈ **Does Blackåsen Mountain exist in reality?**

Not as a physical place, but its nature is something I remember from my childhood: a combination of the places and memories I have from Hudiksvall, where I grew up; Knaften and Vormsele, the two small villages in Lapland where my grandparents lived; and Sånfjället, a mountain close to the Norwegian border, where our family had a cabin.

Blackåsen is the embodiment of what I felt like growing up in the north of Sweden. It represents the fear, the doubts, the religious fervour, the loneliness, and the need to fit in and to belong.

In this book, Blackåsen was given coordinates, which caused me great anxiety as these were in effect superimposed onto existing land. I can only hope the current inhabitants don't mind . . .

◈ **What was the inspiration for *In the Month of the Midnight Sun*?**

When I finished my first book, *Wolf Winter*, I knew that Blackåsen wasn't yet done with me. I wasn't done thinking about it, and, as I am fascinated about the impact a place, physical or imaginary, has on people, I was also interested in what this mountain would be like some 140 years later. What would be different? What would be the constant thread of what it was like to live near this mystical place?

The inspiration for *In the Month of the Midnight Sun* then came mainly from a true story told in passing. At a party at my parents-in-law's house, a man was telling me how, as a young medical doctor, he had escorted a mass murderer from a distant northern village to the closest town for medical evaluation and sentencing. While he was talking, I was feeding my twins who were then a year and a half old, and I didn't listen closely. I regretted it. In my mind, I kept coming back to that voyage and what it would have been like for him and the perpetrator. I wanted to know.

◈ **What are the benefits or difficulties of using the same mountain as the setting in a novel?**

The benefit is that you know it inside out – its physical presence and its mystical bearing over the inhabitants. The difficulty is that you know it too well. Blackåsen is almost a character in its own right, and its nature is such a big component of what it is. I struggled with how to describe it a second time without repeating myself. I knew I needed to get access to it in a different way. This is why I let Magnus be a mineralogist – or, as we call them today, a geologist. I knew he would look upon it differently from the way the settlers in *Wolf Winter* had. As a scientist, he would dissect it objectively. And in a way, he was after its power. The valuable minerals that lay deep in its bowels.

It was also a conscious choice to let *In the Month of the Midnight Sun* take place during one month, in summer, whereas the action of *Wolf Winter* was spread over most of a year. The summer in the north of Sweden is a fascinating time of year. So much energy and life, and so much action compared to the relative sombreness and darkness of winter.

◈ **Are you using multiple points of view in this new book, too?**

Yes. After *Wolf Winter*, I swore I would stick to one point of view the next time I wrote something – it can be quite exhausting to be in the heads of several people. But I just love the confrontations and the meetings you can get when you use several viewpoints. I love the fact that you get to see that 'truth' is really quite arbitrary. A bit like mapmaking. It really depends on where you stand and what you see when you look.

At first, I wrote the book with just Magnus and Lovisa as point-of-view characters, but it didn't feel right. I felt I was missing something vital. Then Biijá came along. And later, Nila.

◈ Why are you using first person and present tense this time?

I have an aversion to books in the first person and the present tense. I have an aversion to books that use several timelines, but in this book I challenged all my aversions. This wasn't easy. But because these three people are lost – each in their own way – this is just how it had to be. When you are lost, you are 'me', 'here', 'now'.

◈ Will you keep writing historical novels?

I still struggle with the fact that I am seen as a writer of 'historical fiction'. As for the 'historical', I have a bad memory and little patience for details. But I knew when I returned to Blackåsen that I wanted enough time to have passed from the first book for it to be completely different, but not so much that we couldn't recognise certain things. A hundred and thirty years seemed just right. And again, it is such a fascinating time, on the verge of industrialisation, knowing the extent of change, but not knowing what the new world will look like. I will say what I have said before: even though I have had great help from many knowledgeable people, the writing is mine, and ultimately I will always prefer a fascinating tale to the truth.

And as for 'writer', I still don't feel comfortable calling myself that. No – more – I actually don't want to be a writer. I love what comes with it: the writing (naturally), the thinking, the meetings with people you otherwise wouldn't have met, the freedom of how you use your time. But the rest of what comes with the label, I'd rather be without.

And no! I won't always write stories set this far back in the past. The idea I have in my head currently is a story that takes place in our time.

◇ Is it more difficult or different to write That Second Book?

It is much harder, yet also much easier. It is harder because the pressure is on; you know it will become a book, you feel the weight of your responsibility to your eventual readers. It is easier because you have learned so much from writing the first one.

◇ Has your writing process changed?

There are some big changes: I am now writing full-time, whereas before, I wasn't. Then there are all the new demands that come with publication.

When I actually started writing *In the Month of the Midnight Sun*, I reverted back to what I had previously done: writing between four and seven in the morning, editing once my daughters were at day care. Early morning is when I am most efficient and creative – my head is clear, and there are no distractions.

As for the process itself, I think it has become easier for me to create 'characterisations'. I still find 'plot' very challenging. I am somewhat more disciplined now, and keep a writer's diary, which helps me to articulate thoughts from muddled impulses to something clearer. That is where I discuss with myself the book I am currently writing. It also helps me be more disciplined in continuing to learn 'the art of fiction'.

What was fascinating in this book is that I felt the process of mapmaking, the work of a geologist, really resembles in some ways the process of writing. Mapmaking is much more *creating* than I had realised. I loved writing Magnus's sections where he is drawing; it was an opportunity for me to look at my own process.

◇ What are the goals of the characters in your book?

I think the three of them are really lost and are searching for something solid in their lives. Biijá suspects she is lost – she is torn between two landscapes. Lovisa knows she is lost – she doesn't know where she's going. Magnus doesn't remember his past, but thinks it doesn't matter, so in some ways he is the most lost of the three of them.

 Is Magnus an unreliable narrator?

All three of them are, to some extent – I think that is inherent when you write in the first person. Magnus doesn't lie to us. I think he is too righteous to lie. He just doesn't remember the truth.

 Who is your favourite character in the book?

It is probably Lovisa. I find her very frustrating, but also very endearing.

 Who was the hardest to write?

Also Lovisa. She swings from despair to defiance with such rapidity.

 What about that ending?

Yes . . . I so want to leave the reader with an ending that keeps reverberating within them. I hope I can make them think about what a next chapter might look like . . .

 Which other writers do you like?

I love Hilary Mantel's books about Cromwell. I love the Norwegian writer Alex Sandemose, Philip Roth, Graham Greene, Ali Smith, Siri Hustvedt.

I still keep Saul Bellow's *Herzog* on my bookshelf unread. Every time I start reading it, I think to myself that surely this is the most brilliant book ever written, and then I can't continue reading, because I think, 'what if I will never find anything better?' And thus I put it back on the shelf.

 Do you have a favourite Scandinavian writer?

I read the writings of a number of Swedish thinkers: Ylva Eggehorn, Olof Wikström, Tomas Sjödin.

As for novels, amongst the translated ones, I really like Finnish Sofi Oksanen, Swedish Torgny Lindgren, and Icelandic Yrsa Sigurðardóttir. I love the crime writers Åsa Larsson, Henning Mankell, and Jo Nesbø.

 What language do you find it easier to write in, Swedish or English?

I left Sweden when I was twenty years old, so my Swedish is still that of a young adult in the 1990s. It has taken me a long time to be able to write in English, but now it is easier for me to write in English than Swedish. I still make a lot of grammatical errors, and find that some Swedish expressions do not translate well. Nevertheless, sometimes I use them even if they are poorly translated, because they demonstrate a way of thinking, or they impart a wisdom.

I fixate on words and use them to death – but this is me being obsessive and isn't linked to writing in a second language. In my first version of *Wolf Winter*, I had several hundred 'doors' and several hundred 'eyes'. This time, for some reason, it was 'hair'.

I write slowly. I need to use both dictionary and thesaurus. I need other people to help me proofread.

 Do you write about what you know?

Less this time. For *Wolf Winter*, a lot of the facts of daily life were things I knew, or had been told about since childhood. For *In the Month of the Midnight Sun*, there was more research, more interviewing. Learning new things was fascinating and also very frightening. You don't know what you don't know, and I continually worried about what I hadn't known to ask about.

 Will your next book be set on Blackåsen?

I don't think so. I have one more book for Blackåsen, but just not yet. At this point, I have some other ideas I am really keen to explore further . . .

AUTHOR'S NOTE

I have always been fascinated by journeying and exploring new territory, both in the actual and metaphorical sense. Maps especially intrigue me: how can something 'factual' also be subjective, so that two people draw two different plans of the same territory? How to draw a new map when you find the old one has become obsolete. What to portray, what to leave out, how to organise your thoughts? Or, even to some extent, what comes first: the map or the terrain? To my great delight, *In the Month of the Midnight Sun* enabled me to explore some of these musings further.

The industrialisation in Sweden began relatively late, in the middle of the 1800s, and almost in response to the needs (for timber, mainly) of other, already industrialised countries. The development happened rather hesitantly. It was clear that modernisation had to take place, would take place, but there was much debate as to the pace, and by what means. Some welcomed the changes. Some longed for the uncomplicated past. Many felt an increasing alienation, and people began to ponder concepts such as nation, class, and gender. Others speculated and took advantage of changes when the nation removed trade barriers. In this new world, pedigree came to mean less than who you knew and the money you had.

The Swedish Parliament under King Oscar I was still composed of the same four social classes: the nobility, the priests, the bourgeois, and the farmers – as it had been since the fifteenth century. This construct poorly reflected the changing society. The representations of the nobles and the priests were disproportionately large; some groups were not represented: for example, those who lived rurally but did not own land, industry workers, and the growing middle class – teachers, doctors, men of industry. As from around 1830, there were demands for more freedom and democracy, but 'democracy' was still equated to mob rule, and thus feared.

The revolutions of 1848 – political upheavals across Europe – also impacted Sweden. During the first half of the nineteenth century, political demonstrations become customary, and in 1848 there was such an outbreak of violence that the military had to be called in. In 1856 there were new demands for reforms which led to the abolishment of the existing form of parliament, and the adaptation of a two-chamber system – the first chamber elected by the county councils in the largest counties, and the second chamber elected in single-member constituencies, though only men with a certain income had the right to vote.

The double moral standard in society was staggering. There was a 'war on sexuality'. The true woman was described as unknowing, innocent, and asexual. The woman was considered responsible for the man's sexuality. As from the middle of the 1800s, the women's movement grew in Sweden, with demands on economic justice and the right to vote. In 1858, an unmarried woman – if she requested it – could be declared of 'lawful age' at twenty-five. In 1874, a new law gave a married woman the right to decide about her income, but she remained 'a minor' until 1921, which is also when the full right to vote was granted for women.

The general view of the Sami was derogatory; their nomadic life was regarded as a lower stage of development that would eventually die out on its own. The Sami religion used to comprise animism (all natural objects have a soul), polytheism (a multitude of spirits and gods), and shamanism (altered states of consciousness), but the systematic campaign of forced Christianisation of the Sami people that had taken place since the 1300s had worked, and by the middle of the nineteenth century, the Sami were Christianised.

Ever since the seventeenth century, Sweden had been a major exporter of bar iron to Europe from central Sweden. During the seventeenth and eighteenth centuries, attention turned to the north, where the trees to make charcoal to fuel the blast furnaces were in abundant supply. Iron works were set up in several places in the middle of the 1700s, but the distances involved were enormous and the climate unforgiving. According to Alf W. Axelson in his book, *Gällivare-verken*, it was cheaper to transport iron from the mines in central Sweden, work it in the northern furnaces, than it was to use iron from the region itself. The regional ironworks and connected land were acquired by the monarch during the early 1800s, and jointly termed '*Gällivare-verken*', but the losses continued to surpass the gains. Already in 1840, the works focused more on the sawmill industry than the iron, and in 1855 the Crown managed to find an acquirer for the assets in a Swedish–Norweigan consortium, which later metamorphosed into The Gellivara Company Limited, set up in 1860 in London. But it wasn't until the railway was constructed and processes invented to develop phosphorous iron that mining finally started on a large scale in 1888.

So much for reality. Now, back to mapmaking, to our Blackåsen, and the tale. I wanted one of our characters to be a man of science, someone 'without pedigree', but successful. I wanted him to represent what is 'new' about society, and contrast him with someone who looked upon the world in a very different manner (this later became our Sami character Biijá/Ester). And I wanted to write about maps. I had worked Blackåsen as 'place' so much in my first book, *Wolf Winter*, I felt I needed a different way of accessing the mountain and its nature – a deeper level. And so our Magnus became a mineralogist – a geologist as we call them today – and Blackåsen was given a large deposit of iron.

In October 2014, I was having breakfast with my dear friend, geologist Mike Daly at Piccadilly in London. The earlier Sami cult was strongly linked to holy places: stones, wood, an unusual stone or rock, or a whole mountain, and we were discussing what it might have felt like to a Sami person if a geologist arrived, wanting to dig these up. We also talked about how to draw a geological map from scratch, and what someone like Magnus would have known at the time. On an impulse, Mike took me to the Geological Society in Burlington House. It was so early, they had not yet opened, and we waited outside on the pavement – me, worried about missing a flight, Mike, who has certainly travelled more than me, unconcerned. The wait was well worth it. At the Geological Society, 'The Map that Changed the World' (as it is described in Simon Winchester's book) is available for viewing. It is the first true geological map of anywhere in the world, depicting England and Wales, engraved and coloured, and quite breathtaking. The map is marked 1815, and it was made by William Smith, a canal digger, who discovered that one could follow layers of rocks across a nation, then further, making it possible to draw the underside of the earth. To think that this was how our geological understanding began, by the work of one man, is amazing.

I have let the iron block inside Blackåsen take the same shape and quality as Kiirunavaara in Kiruna County – a mountain that holds one of the world's largest continuous bodies of iron ore: big enough to matter, far enough away to be troublesome, and phosphorous. There is no gold in Kiirunavaara to the extent I have described existing in Blackåsen; to be honest, gold hardly ever comes in veins large enough to be visible to the naked eye. Though it does happen.

The location of a fictitious Blackåsen Mountain caused me some anxiety. But, as maps were a large part of the narrative, I felt its exact position had to be stated. I hope current inhabitants of that land don't mind suddenly having a mountain appearing amongst them. A *cursed* mountain, moreover

The Sami people are referred to as 'Lapps' in this book too, as that was still the name used at the time. The Sami were, as mentioned, Christianised at this time. The turning against their own religious leaders, their *noiades*, likely happened earlier, but I wondered . . . or, to use something my character Frederika thought in *Wolf Winter*: 'If you once thought you had the truth, could you ever leave it behind even if you rejected it, or would you carry it with you, that option of a different life?' I wanted to explore this further: this experience of being torn between two religious landscapes. And as labyrinths in stone were deemed to have been built as late as 1850, I let this struggle take place in this book.

The Kautokeino Uprising really did take place in 1852, when a group of Sami attacked and killed leading figures in their village in Norway. The event was most likely a reaction to the low status the Sami had in Norwegian society, and was closely linked to a revival movement that took place under the priest Lars Levi Laestadius that encouraged the Sami to find equality.

The Sami have been reported to have a negative attitude to the mining of Lapland – not strangely. In 1634, silver was discovered on Swedish Nasafjäll, close to the border with Norway. Sweden tried to encourage colonisation, with little success. Sami people were conscripted for three-year periods to transport the ore with their reindeer, which prevented them from conducting their usual way of life.

The last execution in Luleå took place in 1828. The last execution in Sweden, in 1910.

Falu Mining School did exist but, as far as I know, no pin was given to students.

The main characters in this book are fictional, even when their official roles exist.

Discover Cecilia Ekbäck's acclaimed debut novel

Wolf Winter

Winner of the 2016 HWA Goldsboro Debut Crown Award.

'Exquisitely suspenseful, beautifully written,
and highly recommended.' Lee Child

There are six homesteads on Blackåsen Mountain.

A day's journey away lies the empty town. It comes to life just
once, in winter, when the Church summons her people through
the snows. Then, even the oldest enemies will gather.

But now it is summer, and new settlers are come.

It is their two young daughters who find the dead man,
not half an hour's walk from their cottage.

The father is away. And whether stubborn, or stupid, or scared
for her girls, the mother will not let it rest.

To the wife who is not concerned when her husband does not
come home for three days; to the man who laughs when he
hears his brother is dead; to the priest who doesn't care; she asks
and asks her questions, digging at the secrets of the mountain.

They say a wolf made those wounds. But what
wild animal cuts a body so clean?

Out now in paperback and ebook.

HODDER

In the best books, the ending often comes as a shock.
Not just because of that one last twist in the tale,
but because you have been so absorbed in their world,
that coming back to the harsh light of reality is a jolt.

If that describes you now, then perhaps you should track down
some new leads, and find new suspense in other worlds.

Join us at www.hodder.co.uk, or follow us on
Twitter @hodderbooks, and you can tap in to a
community of fellow thrill-seekers.

Whether you want to find out more about this book,
or a particular author, watch trailers and interviews, have
the chance to win early limited editions, or simply browse
our expert readers' selection of the very best books,
we think you'll find what you're looking for.

And if you don't, that's the place to tell us what's missing.

We love what we do, and we'd love you to be part of it.

www.hodder.co.uk

 @hodderbooks

HodderBooks

HodderBooks